Praise for Robert Thorogood

"A fantastic whodunit with laugh-out-loud moments."

—The Sun

"The perfect cozy crime to curl up with."

—Heat

"I love Robert Thorogood's writing."

—Peter James

"I really enjoyed it. A great escapist yarn from start to finish and a real tonic."

—Simon Kernick

Also by Robert Thorogood

THE QUEEN OF POISONS

A NOVEL

ROBERT THOROGOOD

Poisoned Pen
PRESS

Published by Poisoned Pen Press, an imprint of Sourcebooks
P.O. Box 4410, Naperville, Illinois 60567-4410
(630) 961-3900
sourcebooks.com

Cataloging-in-Publication Data is on file with the Library of Congress.

Printed and bound in Canada.
MPB 10 9 8 7 6 5 4 3 2 1

For Penny Thomas

Chapter 1

SUZIE HARRIS WAS ON A mission.

She wasn't sure she'd be able to see it through. In fact, she knew the chance of failure was high, but she was going to give it her best shot. She was going to try to sit through a Marlow town council planning meeting.

Suzie hated meetings, and the idea of a planning meeting seemed even more impossibly boring, but she'd recently come up with a ruse to make a financial killing, and she figured she'd need allies on the planning committee. So she'd decided to attend one of their meetings to discover who the key personalities were, how they made their decisions, and—most importantly—if any of them could be bullied into looking favorably on any application she later submitted.

The meeting was being held in the town council, a pretty Georgian house that overlooked the River Thames by Higginson Park. The entrance was a highly polished black door that wouldn't have looked out of place on Downing Street, and while most of the two-story building was set aside as office space, it also contained an old debating chamber that was still used for formal meetings. Entering it, any visitor found themselves standing on a viewing gallery for spectators with a few steps that led down to a large room that contained half a dozen desks, filing cabinets along the walls, and a serving hatch that opened onto a little kitchenette. On the far wall, the town's coat of arms of a swan captured in chains was carved into a wooden shield that looked down on proceedings. Like the town of Marlow itself, the debating chamber managed to be both grand and pocket-sized at the same time.

On this occasion, a screen and projector had been set up beneath the coat of arms so the committee could better inspect the planning applications as they worked through the agenda. Suzie, having arrived nice and early, was sitting in the little gallery with a notebook and pen ready to write thumbnail sketches of the council members, detailing their strengths and—more importantly—any potential weaknesses she could exploit.

The first person to arrive was a man in his fifties who was wearing a pin-striped suit, a blue shirt, and a sky-blue silk tie with pink dots on it. He was broad shouldered and had plenty of swagger about him, and his smile was so natural and effortless that Suzie found her heart give a little skip.

"You here for the planning meeting?" he asked.

"That's right," Suzie said, before reminding herself that she wasn't in fact a schoolgirl who found men attractive just because they had a sharp jawline. As he squeezed past her and trotted down the stairs to the chamber below, he lifted his elbows to show how very fit he was, before striding over to a desk where there was a pile of printouts already waiting.

"Are you here for a particular application?" he asked.

It was only at that moment that Suzie realized she hadn't worked out a cover story for her presence.

"Yup," she said, if only to buy herself time.

"Which one?"

"I'm sorry?"

"If you've got interest in a particular case, it's important we hear what you have to say. What application are you connected to?"

"You know," Suzie said, desperately extemporizing, "the one…on the… the main road. The big house—I mean, it's not all that big at the moment, but the owners want it to be…you know, bigger."

Even ever-optimistic Suzie could see that her cack-handed explanation had confused the man, but before he could ask any follow-up questions, the door opened and a woman entered. She was about sixty years old, and whereas the man seemed to radiate goodwill, this new arrival, Suzie thought, seemed to suck the joy out of the air as she looked about herself. Her manner reminded Suzie of all the many dry-as-dust teachers who'd been disappointed with her at school.

"'But soft,'" the man called up from the chamber below, "'what light from yonder window breaks?'"

"Don't be facetious," the woman snapped, before wrinkling her nose as she squeezed past Suzie. "Sorry, do you mind?" she said.

"Not at all," Suzie said, already deciding that she didn't like the woman. She struck her as the sort of person who knew the cost of everything and the value of nothing—and the cost would always be "too much."

"Good evening, Marcus," the woman said as she sat down at the desk. "Have you any conflicts of interest you need to declare this time?"

"That's for the chairman to know," Marcus said with a wink as he headed over to the serving hatch at the side of the room.

Suzie could see that there was a man in the kitchenette, bringing cups and saucers to the counter of the hatch. He was wearing blue polyethylene catering gloves as he put down a wooden caddy of tea bags, and she found herself thinking that it really was health and safety gone mad that catering staff had to wear protective gloves to serve tea.

"Cup of tea, Debbie?" Marcus asked the woman as he took a cup and saucer over to a metal samovar that was sitting on the counter in the hatch by a Nespresso coffee machine.

"No, thank you," Debbie replied.

"Suit yourself."

Marcus returned to the table with his cup of tea.

The main door opened again and a man entered, although he stopped when he saw Suzie blocking his way.

"Well hello," he said with a nasal voice that managed to be amused, patronizing, and superior all at once. Looking at him, Suzie saw that he had thinning hair that he combed over his otherwise balding pate, and a long, pallid face that made Suzie think of a soap-on-a-rope that was nearing the end of its life. The man had about the same amount of charisma as well, she thought.

"Do you want to get past?" she asked.

"Don't mind if I do," the man said, believing himself to be quite the wit, and then he pushed past Suzie and headed down the steps to the main chamber.

"Hail fellow, well met," he said by way of greeting to Marcus. "Debbie," he added, and Suzie once again noted the superior tone to the man's voice.

"Tea, Jeremy?" Marcus asked.

"None for me, thank you," Jeremy said as he sat at the table. "Not unless and until the council supply us with the biscuits they promised at the last main committee council meeting. In their absence, I won't be taking any caffeinated libations," he added, and then reached for a copy of the briefing notes.

Suzie saw the man in the catering gloves turn away from the hatch and head toward a fire door at the back of the kitchenette. As Jeremy called from the main chamber, "Unless there are some biscuits this time?" the man opened the door and left, letting the fire door close behind him with a heavy clunk. Suzie smiled to herself. It almost certainly wasn't a coincidence that the man had left just as Jeremy had started making demands.

"Oh," Jeremy said as he realized there was no longer anyone in the kitchen to serve him.

"Well, if it isn't Suzie Harris!" a mellifluous voice announced from the doorway as Geoffrey Lushington, the mayor of Marlow, entered the chamber. He was about seventy years old and he was quite short and plump, with a thick shock of unkempt white hair that surrounded a perfectly circular bald patch on the very top of his head. Suzie always thought he looked a bit like a gnome. A jolly gnome with an impish sense of humor. Everyone in the town liked him.

After the first time Suzie and her friends Judith and Becks had helped the police solve a series of murders in the town, Geoffrey had insisted on throwing a drinks reception in honor of the women. He'd said at the time that all local success should be championed, and no one had been more successful than Suzie, Judith, and Becks. Suzie had liked him instantly.

"So what's your interest in the planning committee tonight?" he asked as he passed Suzie and trotted down the stairs.

"Oh, nothing much, Geoffrey," Suzie said, realizing she had to modify her cover story since her calamity with Marcus.

"Is that so?" Geoffrey said, heading over to the window to the kitchenette, picking up a little coffee capsule, and slipping it into the Nespresso machine.

"Just exercising my democratic right to witness the committee in action," Suzie said, playing what she hoped was an ace card.

"Quite so, quite so," Geoffrey agreed, as the machine poured coffee into a cup he'd put under the spout. "Although you've not attended a council meeting before."

"Haven't wanted to before now."

"Fair enough," he said, taking his coffee over to the table.

"Actually," Debbie said, standing up, "I think I will have a coffee after all."

As she went over to the Nespresso machine, Marcus offered a glass jar of sugar cubes to Geoffrey.

"Sugar?" he asked.

"Thank you," Geoffrey said as he plucked out a cube. He plopped it into his coffee, gave it a stir, and said to Suzie, "Although, I can't help noticing that the last time I passed your house, you'd finished your building work."

It was true. After having been left in the lurch by a cowboy builder some years before, Suzie had finally managed to get the extension to her house finished by signing up to a reality TV program. As part of the show, the TV company completed the building work that had been left unfinished, but they also tried to confront the original builder who'd done a runner. In Suzie's case, all they'd been able to discover was that he'd wound up his company and retired to Spain. When the episode finally aired, Suzie had been a little disappointed when it didn't make more of a splash, but she'd perhaps overestimated how much the general public cared about daytime home makeover television shows.

Nonetheless, the whole experience had had a happy epilogue. It was because of the conversations she'd had with the TV show's architect that she was currently attending the planning meeting. Not that she was going to tell anyone on the committee this fact.

"You're not wrong there," Suzie said to Geoffrey. "The building work's finished."

"Wasn't there a TV program or something?"

Suzie tried not to be offended by Geoffrey's lack of engagement with her television career.

"Anyway," Geoffrey continued, turning to face the other members of the committee, "anyone know where Sophia is?"

"She didn't say anything to me about being late," Debbie said.

Geoffrey looked up at the clock on the wall. It was a few minutes past seven thirty.

"Well, I'm sure she'll turn up in due course. How about we get started?"

"Point of order," Jeremy said, raising a hand.

"You're not doing this again," Debbie said.

"We can't start the meeting without Sophia. We're not quorate."

"Then you can't raise a point of order," Marcus said as he stirred his tea.

"What's that?"

"If we're not quorate, the meeting hasn't been convened, so there can't be any points of order just yet."

Marcus tapped his teaspoon on the side of his cup and placed it in his saucer with a smile.

"No, good point," Jeremy agreed, trying to save face, "Good point."

"So how about we convene the meeting," Geoffrey said, "rattle through the applications as speedily as possible, and I'll get the first round in at the George and Dragon."

"Not until Sophia arrives," Jeremy said.

"I'm sure we can be quorate as long as more than fifty percent of us are present," Marcus said.

"That's not what the standing orders say. Debbie, you're secretary, are you minuting this?"

Debbie seemed to wake up from a reverie.

"What's that?"

"I said, are you minuting this?"

"Of course not," she said. "The meeting's not started."

"So I call the meeting to order," Geoffrey said. "Item 1, the proposed addition of dormer windows to the first floor of 13 Henley Road."

Debbie opened a notebook and picked up her pen, ready to start taking notes.

"This meeting isn't legal," Jeremy whined.

"Of course it is," Marcus said.

"Jeremy, don't you remember what happened last time?" Geoffrey said.

"And there it is!" Jeremy said. "Always patronizing me."

"I'm not," Geoffrey said.

"He's really not," Debbie added.

"And there you go, taking sides!"

"I'm not," Debbie said, irritated. "Chairman, please can you speak to Jeremy."

"He's not the chairman!" Jeremy said.

"I think you'll find he is," Marcus said, enjoying the bust-up tremendously.

"He isn't."

"No, really, he is."

"He isn't," Jeremy said, banging his fist hard on the table. "Authority is only invested in the chair once the meeting's convened, and *we're not quorate!*" he added with a fury that startled everyone in the room, including himself.

No one wanted to break the silence that followed.

"Sorry," Jeremy eventually said. "I've been under a bit of pressure. Don't know where that came from," he added, hoping it could mend the fences he'd just smashed.

"I'm so sorry I'm late," a breathy voice announced from the door.

Suzie looked over and saw a tall woman in her fifties standing in the doorway. She had rosy cheeks, straight blond hair down to her shoulders, and dark eyeliner that accentuated her eyes dramatically. The woman radiated good health, and perhaps, even more so, wealth. Her hooped silver earrings, exquisitely cut summer dress, and polished brown brogues made Suzie tug at the blue shirt she was wearing under her dog-walking coat.

"Hello," the woman said to Suzie with the interest of someone inspecting an exotic animal in a zoo.

Suzie realized she didn't know what to say to someone so radiant, and the woman sashayed past her, leaving the fragrant notes of what Suzie guessed was a very expensive perfume.

"Sorry I'm late," the woman said to the others as she headed down the stairs to the chamber below.

"*Now* we're quorate," Jeremy said in a voice that suggested he finally felt vindicated.

"Ah," Sophia said, "has there been a procedural issue in my absence?"

"Nothing we couldn't handle," Marcus said. "Now, can we start the meeting?"

"How are you, Sophia?" Geoffrey asked.

Suzie couldn't be sure, but did Sophia's smile falter before she answered?

"I'm well, thank you, Geoffrey," Sophia said as she sat down at the table.

"A cup of tea?"

"No, thank you."

"Or coffee?"

"I think we should just get this meeting over and done with, don't you?" Sophia said with a smile, but once again, Suzie picked up what she thought was an odd vibe. In her notebook, she wrote "Tension between Sophia and Geoffrey?"

As the meeting got underway, Suzie settled into her chair. This was her chance to discover who she should approach about her own planning application.

Sophia, she guessed, was far too posh and self-regarding to be someone she could ever influence. In Suzie's experience, people like Sophia didn't pay much attention to people like Suzie.

Marcus seemed perhaps a better prospect. She'd certainly enjoy getting to know him, she knew. But, again, there was a patrician air to him that put Suzie slightly on guard. He was perhaps too well-dressed, too pleased with himself—too much of a peacock. And she was pretty sure she'd have been far more capable of influencing him if she were a man rather than a woman. Or younger and prettier.

As for Debbie, she seemed such a negative person that Suzie knew she'd never be able to convince her to do anything as daring as her suggested planning proposal.

This left only Jeremy and Geoffrey. From Jeremy's outburst about correct procedure, Suzie guessed she'd never manage to influence him, so what about Geoffrey? The more she considered him, the more she thought he could be just what she was looking for. After all, he'd thrown a drinks reception for her, so he was already predisposed to like her. And he was also so obviously a positive soul. It also helped that he was chair of the committee. If she could get him onside, she was sure he'd be able to convince the others to go along with her plans. Yes, she thought to herself, things were looking up for her, they were looking up indeed.

As Suzie allowed herself to start thinking about a future of untold riches, she saw Geoffrey take a sip of his coffee, cough once, then choke quite badly—and then cough much more violently—and then he fell off his chair and dropped to the floor, where he lay entirely motionless.

Sophia was the first to react, crying out "Geoffrey!" as she dropped to his side. Marcus, Debbie, and Jeremy rose from their chairs in horror.

Sophia called out to the room, "Someone phone for an ambulance!"

Debbie was finally stung into action, and she pulled out her phone, jabbing at the screen in panic. As she did so, Suzie started to head down the stairs to help, but Jeremy stepped across to block her path.

"You can't come down here, it's for council officers only."

Suzie had the briefest impulse to push Jeremy to the side, but she could see that Debbie was already talking to the emergency services, and she realized her time could be used more profitably elsewhere. She headed back up the steps, pulling out her mobile and pressing speed dial as she went. It started ringing as she pushed through the door that led into the little corridor outside the debating chamber.

"Judith," she said as the call was answered, "it's me, Suzie."

"Hello," Judith said from the other end of the line. "How are you?"

"Oh, good, thanks for asking. Much better than the mayor of Marlow."

"What makes you say that?"

"Well, there's no easy way to say this, but he's just died. I think it's possible he's been murdered."

Chapter 2

TANIKA MALIK WAS READING HER daughter Shanti a bedtime story when her mobile started ringing from elsewhere in the house.

"Shamil," she called out, "can you get that?"

Tanika turned back to her daughter, who was sitting on her lap. She smelled of biscuits, soap, and fresh laundry, and Tanika knew that these moments were the happiest of her life, even if the story her daughter insisted they read—about a forgetful fireman called Sam—was one that she'd read a hundred times before. No, a thousand times before. Knowing the words by heart at least allowed Tanika to concentrate on Shanti rather than having to look down at the page.

Shamil appeared at the door, Tanika's phone in his hand. She could tell from the look on his face that it was work. Tanika's stomach clenched. She'd recently started a new role at the police station, which meant she was "on call" twenty-four hours a day, even when she was technically off shift.

Hoping her smile didn't falter, she turned back to Shanti.

"Daddy wants to finish the story with you," she said.

"Daddy!" Shanti said, only now noticing Shamil in the doorway.

"What are we reading?" Shamil said as he came over, handing his wife's phone to her as she got up and left the room—although Tanika stole a last moment in the doorway. Her husband was by all accounts pretty useless. He didn't have a regular job, instead believing he'd one day be a hotshot DJ, and he wasn't the most punctual and reliable partner with whom to raise a daughter. And there was no point expecting him to do the laundry, or remember to get the car to the garage for its annual tune-up, but Tanika knew that his love for her was eclipsed only by his love for their daughter. And although it broke her heart to be wrenched away from Shanti's bedtime routine—once again—she knew that it didn't break Shanti's, and that's what mattered. It was all that mattered. And bringing murderers to justice—that was the other thing that mattered.

Tanika slipped along the corridor to answer the call.

Just under twenty minutes later, she drove up to the Marlow town council building and pulled up next to an ambulance and two police cars that had already arrived. As she got out of her car, she noted that Suzie Harris's dog-walking van was also parked nearby.

Tanika's eyes narrowed as a young detective constable called Antonia approached her.

"Thanks for getting here so quickly, boss," she said.

"Tell me Suzie Harris isn't here," Tanika said.

"Suzie Harris?"

"Looks like a small mountain, and dresses like she's about to climb one."

"Oh, Suzie Harris! You mean, one of the key witnesses."

"She witnessed the death?"

"She did, although you need to know, the other witnesses are saying the victim was poisoned. It's why I called for you. We could well be dealing with a murder."

"Is she on her own?"

"Who?"

"Suzie Harris?"

"Of course. Or she was when Mr. Lushington died. She's got two friends with her at the moment. For support."

"'For support,'" Tanika grumbled to herself as she headed over to the main door.

As she passed the ambulance, Tanika caught a glimpse of Suzie off to one side talking nineteen to the dozen with Judith Potts and Becks Starling.

"I'm not talking to you," Tanika called out to the women as she swept onward to the building.

"I'm a witness!" Suzie said to the police officer's retreating back, but Tanika didn't break step as she vanished inside.

"Pleased to see you, too," Judith said, folding her arms.

Judith Potts was in her late seventies and her eyes sparkled with intelligence—although, this evening, they also sparkled from the quick snifter of whisky she'd had earlier that evening.

"I can see why she's cross," Becks offered.

Becks Starling was the wife of the vicar of All Saints Church, and was, by some distance, the most timid of the three friends.

"You can?" Judith asked.

"We're like bad pennies," Becks explained. "Always turning up when there's a murder."

"Speak for yourself," Suzie said. "I'm not a bad penny. And I didn't just 'turn up,' I was there when he died. No one's had a worse evening than me."

"I think," Judith said as diplomatically as possible, "Geoffrey would say he'd had a worse evening."

"But how am I going to get my building plans approved now? I bet the committee won't be able to sit for months. Not without a chairman."

"Come on," Judith said as she headed over to the building.

"Where are we going?" Becks asked.

"If Tanika won't tell us what's going on, we'll do the next best thing," she said as she cupped her hands against the glass of a window that looked into the main debating chamber.

"She won't be happy," Becks said.

"She's never happy," Suzie remarked and joined Judith at the window. "Or she isn't with us, anyway."

"I don't think we should be spying on her," Becks offered, continuing to hang back.

"Suit yourself," Suzie said as she cupped her hands to the glass.

Inside, Judith and Suzie could see that Tanika was talking to a police photographer while two paramedics were zipping the mayor's corpse into a black body bag.

"And you're *sure* Geoffrey was poisoned?" Judith asked her friend.

"He took a sip of his coffee and keeled over, stone-cold dead."

"The poison was in his coffee? Did you see who made it?"

"I think he made it himself," Suzie said as she tried to remember. "You see that hatch over there?" She indicated the serving hatch on the opposite side of the room. "He put one of those coffee capsules into that Nespresso machine. Not that I was watching all that closely. I didn't expect him to die."

"Did the others also make coffees from the same machine?" Judith asked.

"I don't think so. Marcus was the first person to arrive, and he made himself a cup of tea from that silver urn. He then moved away. As for Jeremy, he didn't go anywhere near the coffee machine—but Debbie did!" Suzie said excitedly as she remembered. "She turned down a cup of tea when she first got there, but after Geoffrey had made himself his cup, she went over to the Nespresso machine and made herself a coffee. Uh-oh, we've been rumbled," Suzie added, and stepped away from the window.

Through the glass, Judith saw Tanika stride up the stairs to the little gallery and head out of the room. A few seconds later, the door to the council building opened and Tanika strode out.

"What are you doing?" she asked sharply.

"Us?" Judith asked in mock innocence.

"Yes, you."

"We weren't doing anything."

"You were looking through the window."

From her position a little way away, Becks held up her hand to get Tanika's attention.

"I wasn't," she said.

"It's important we inspect the scene of the crime," Judith said imperiously.

"You think so?" Tanika said, shifting her weight onto her hip.

"In case you miss something, as I'm afraid you have."

"I'm sorry?"

"You've missed something."

"Now this I'd like to see. You stand outside the building and think you can tell me I've missed something?"

"Like the sugar bowl."

"What sugar bowl?"

"Exactly!" Judith said, now really very pleased with herself. "Where is it?"

"What on earth are you talking about?"

"Do you agree that Geoffrey was poisoned?"

"It's how the scene's so far presenting."

"Well, that's good to hear—you believe it's murder for once. But just because the victim drank from his coffee cup and then died, it doesn't mean the poison was in his coffee. What if it was in the milk? Although that seems unlikely, seeing as Suzie says Marcus made himself a cup of tea, which no doubt had milk from the same source in it. So if the milk wasn't poisoned, what else might have been? And that's when I noticed two sugar lumps on the saucer to one of the cups that's still on the table. Which is odd, to say the least. Because as far as I can tell, there's no bowl of sugar cubes on the table. And I can't see one on the floor where it might have been knocked over, either."

Tanika took a moment to remind herself that Judith's manner could be infuriating, but she was rarely—if ever—wrong. She sighed, and then said with a weary smile, "You can't help yourself, can you?"

"If by that you mean what I think you mean, then thank you."

"So, here we are again, ladies. You're planning to investigate, aren't you? All three of you. Just to get it out there in the open."

"Oh, no," Becks said. "It was pure coincidence we could help with the murders last time. And the time before. This murder's none of our business."

"None of our business?" Suzie said, outraged.

"Well, you know what I mean," Becks said, not wanting to start a fight. "We all got pulled into those first murders very much against our will, didn't we?"

"And I can't help noticing that here, once again, you are," Tanika said.

"I didn't know Geoffrey was about to die, did I?" Suzie said. "I was here to try and bribe him into looking on my planning application favorably." Suzie only belatedly remembered she was talking to a police officer. "I mean, not 'bribe'—that would be illegal," she added in a rush. "I wanted to see how he operated, that's all. Get a sense of what made him tick."

"But I know how this goes," Tanika said. "Now that the three of you are here, you'll be wanting to investigate whether I agree to it or not. So here's what

I think we should do. Tomorrow morning, I want you to come to Maidenhead Police Station, where I'll officially hire you as civilian advisers for the case."

The three friends were stunned.

"You won't try to stop us?" Judith asked.

"I've brought you in before, I can do it again."

"But that was against your detective inspector's wishes."

"I wouldn't worry about that. This time I know the detective inspector will approve."

"Has he forgiven us for last time?" Becks asked hopefully.

"Hardly. If anything, DI Hoskins dislikes you even more. But it doesn't much matter what he thinks," Tanika said with a sly grin.

"Why?" Suzie asked. "Has he been moved on? Or—I know!—did a sting operation catch him with his hands in the till?"

"Oh no, he still works at the station. But he's no longer superior to me."

"How can that be?" Becks asked.

"I agreed to be fast-tracked, I took my exams—I'm now a detective inspector."

Judith and her friends were briefly speechless, and then Becks came over and gave Tanika a big hug as Judith and Suzie started to call out their congratulations.

"But this is simply the most marvelous news!" Judith said, summing up the feelings of them all.

"It is," Tanika agreed with a bashful smile that also managed to radiate deep pride.

"Your father must be so proud of you."

"He now wants to know when I'm going to be a superintendent, but you're right, he's proud."

"Of course he is."

"Well, this is a turn-up for the books," Suzie said with a chuckle. "The old gang back together again."

"Indeed," Tanika agreed. "Although you promise you'll do as I say? It's still pretty unorthodox, hiring civilian advisers, even if I know it's the right thing to do."

"Don't worry, you can trust us," Judith said as she rootled in her handbag for her little tin of boiled sweets. Pulling it out, she popped the lid and offered it to her friends. "I think this is cause for a celebration. Travel sweet?"

As the four women reached into the tin to choose their sweet, Judith found herself thinking of the four musketeers touching swords before embarking on a mission.

"One for all?" she asked.

"And all for one," her three friends said.

They all popped sweets into their mouths, and Judith bit down on hers with a satisfying crunch.

Chapter 3

THE NEXT DAY IT WAS a cold and fresh spring morning, and the town was abuzz with the news that Geoffrey had been murdered. In all the coffee shops, and from the Methodist Hall to the rowing club, it was the only topic anyone could talk about. For many, their shock was accompanied by a sharp sense of loss. Geoffrey had been a Marlow man since birth, and his years of service and unflappable good cheer had meant he'd touched the lives of thousands. Within hours, piles of fresh flowers and messages of thanks were being left by the door of the council building, and there was a steady stream of people going into All Saints Church to light a candle in his memory.

Judith, Becks, and Suzie presented themselves at the reception of Maidenhead Police Station at 9 a.m. The somewhat bemused desk sergeant agreed that there were indeed three lanyards waiting for them, although it was hard to tell who was more surprised by this fact—him, or Judith and her friends. Having issued them with their passes, he pressed a button and a door beyond the desk opened.

Going through, the women found themselves in a stairwell that led upstairs. They'd been in the police station before—they'd even once been allowed to help Tanika semiofficially—but they'd always known they were outsiders who'd been brought in as a last resort. They had no idea how their arrival at the beginning of the case would be greeted. Or rather, having gotten to know some of Tanika's colleagues, they had a very good idea how they would be greeted, and they weren't looking forward to it one bit.

Once they arrived at the second floor, the three friends paused by a set of double doors. Judith straightened her hair, and then she pointed to a bit of green that was stuck in between Suzie's teeth.

"Thanks," Suzie said as she used a dirty fingernail to scrape at her tooth.

"Gosh," Becks said but didn't finish the thought. She didn't need to. Her friends were thinking similarly.

"You know what I do when I feel out of my depth?" Judith said to no one in particular. "I just keep swimming. Come on, ladies. Chin up, shoulders back."

Judith pushed the double doors open and led her friends into the incident room. There were half a dozen plainclothes officers working at desks, a large whiteboard on a side wall with information stuck to it, and glass walls at the end that led to other offices, one of which Tanika occupied. She saw Judith and her friends arrive and came into the main room.

"OK, everyone," she called out to get her team's attention. "Listen up. These are our civilian advisers for the case. Some of you may recognize them from the Dunwoody case a few years ago, when I'd like to remind you they were able to make key contributions. And as you also know, I used them in an informal basis following the murder of Sir Peter Bailey last year. Again, their help proved invaluable, so this time I'm getting them in from the start. Let me introduce them. First, we've got Suzie Harris. She was present when Mr. Lushington died. She's a dog walker, so she knows everyone in Marlow."

"And radio presenter," Suzie added.

"What's that?"

"I've also got a Sunday evening radio show on Marlow FM. It's called *Pets' Corner with Suzie Harris*."

"OK—"

"And some of you may recognize me from *Paul Merchant versus the Cowboys*."

Tanika's team were looking at Suzie blankly.

"It was on ITV2 a few months ago—just before *Catchphrase: Catchiest Moments*."

"But if Suzie knows everyone in Marlow," Tanika said, trying to wrest back control, "so does Becks Starling here."

"I don't, you know," Becks said before wincing as Judith dug an elbow into her ribs to stay quiet.

"She's the wife of the vicar of All Saints Church, and there's nothing about the internal workings of Marlow she doesn't understand."

"I wouldn't say that, either," Becks said. "Really, I know nothing."

"Which leaves only Judith Potts," Tanika said, trying not to sound exasperated as she bulldozed on. "She's a professional crossword setter, never takes no for an answer—in fact, she quite often doesn't take yes for an answer—and has one of the sharpest minds I've ever encountered."

Judith glowed from the compliment.

Tanika introduced her team to Judith and her friends, and the women picked up on a range of emotions from the police officers. Most were skeptical, amused even—which didn't bother the women one jot, that's exactly how most police officers had always treated them—but there was one man who looked particularly sour. His name was Detective Sergeant Brendan Perry. He was in his fifties and he had the manner of someone who wanted to be somewhere else.

"They're officially working on the case?" he asked Tanika.

"In an advisory capacity."

"But they'll get full access to the files?"

"They've had full access before."

"They can interview witnesses?"

"We'll see about that," Tanika said, not wanting to back down in front of her team, but also agreeing that having the women out and about interviewing witnesses was perhaps a step too far.

During the introductions, Judith had drifted over to the whiteboard and was looking at the crime scene photos.

"Anyone find the bowl of sugar?" she asked.

"What's that?" DS Perry asked.

"At the scene. A sugar bowl?"

Tanika could already feel the tentative coalition of support among her team start to fracture.

"I'll take that as a no," Judith said. "Then what about the postmortem? Has it been carried out yet?"

"It has," Tanika said, relieved to get onto safer ground. "It says Mr. Lushington died after ingesting aconite. And the labs say aconite was also found in the residue of coffee they found in his cup."

"And what's aconite when it's at home?" Suzie asked.

"It's a plant," Judith said, "sometimes referred to as the Queen of Poisons. It also goes by the name of monkshood, wolfsbane, and leopard's bane. In Greek mythology, it's what grew out of the ground when Hercules dragged the three-headed Cerberus out of Hades. And it's what Romeo drinks to kill himself at the end of *Romeo and Juliet*, now I'm thinking about it. And what the witches brew in *Macbeth* as well—where it's called 'tooth of wolf'— Shakespeare really had a thing for aconite."

"How do you know all that?" DS Perry asked.

"When you've set crosswords for as long as I have, you pick up all sorts of arcane information. Like the fact that leopard's bane is an anagram of 'adorable pens,' which I've always found rather charming."

"But why is it called the Queen of Poisons?" Suzie asked.

"Because it's just about the most poisonous plant there is," Judith replied.

"OK," Tanika said, realizing that, far from getting the conversation back on track, she'd allowed Judith once again to derail it. "We've got an interview room we've set aside for the three of you. Let's set you up there."

"But what about sugar?" Judith said, not moving from her spot. "You said the postmortem found Geoffrey had ingested aconite. Was there any sugar in his system?"

"As it happens," Tanika said, "there was. And before you ask, sugar was also found in the dregs of the coffee in his cup."

"Which makes it a bit of a mystery, doesn't it?" Judith said triumphantly. "Since no bowls of sugar were found at the murder scene, where did the sugar in his coffee come from?"

"Antonia," Tanika said, turning to the young officer whom the women had met the night before. "Could you go back to the murder scene and have another look? See if you can find a sugar bowl, or sachets of sugar—or any traces of the stuff anywhere."

"Yes, boss," Antonia said as she started to get her things together to leave.

"Happy now?" Tanika asked Judith as a peace offering.

"Oh, no," Judith said with a smile. "I won't be happy until we've got Geoffrey's killer behind bars. Come on, ladies," she added before heading to the main door.

"Where are you going?" Tanika asked.

"Yes, where are we going?" Becks asked as she and Suzie caught up with their friend.

"To my house," Judith said. "That's where we'll be working."

"But I've got a spare office for you here," Tanika said.

"Oh, no, that won't do at all. The three of us live in Marlow; we're not coming all this way every day when we've got a perfectly good base in my house. Don't worry, we'll be in touch when we need you," she said before heading off—Suzie and Becks trotting to keep up with her.

Tanika looked at her team and could see how skeptical they all were.

"Get back to work," she said before heading back to her office.

Once there, she sat down at her desk and put her head in her hands. She'd worked so hard to become a detective inspector. It had involved the most incredible sacrifices. By hiring Judith, Suzie, and Becks, had she just put her career in jeopardy?

Chapter 4

JUDITH'S HOUSE WAS A GORGEOUS Arts and Crafts mansion that sat on the River Thames on the outskirts of Marlow. She shared her home with a barely tame Bengal cat called Daniel, floor-to-ceiling bookcases jammed full of reference books, and an old Blüthner grand piano that she only played late at night if she'd had a few too many drinks. A layer of dust covered every surface, the fireplace was almost never swept out, and discarded clothes and old crockery lay in piles.

Living on her own was bliss for Judith. On the whole. At a surface level, it was certainly true: she set crosswords for the national newspapers, she swam most days in the Thames that flowed past the bottom of her garden, and she broadly did what she wanted when she wanted, without reference to anyone else, least of all, any man. But at a deeper level, there was a tragedy she always carried with her. Her abusive husband had died many decades ago, and she'd found herself starting to hoard all of the local and national newspapers soon afterward. Before too long, she'd found that *all* publications, from parish magazines to council-issued newsletters, had to be saved. And when the piles of paper had threatened to overwhelm her, she'd decided to convert a couple of rooms on the side of her house into an archive, and then hid the whole thing behind lock and key. She'd been forced to reveal her secret archive to Becks and Suzie when they'd started investigating the murder of her neighbor, and she'd even half-cleared one of the rooms since then so they could use it as a makeshift incident room. However, there was no way she was getting rid of the rest of her archive. It meant too much to her, even if she couldn't quite articulate what that meaning was. But she'd no more get rid of it than she'd get rid of a limb. It was part of who she was.

On this particular morning, as Judith led her two friends to the locked door in the corner of her sitting room, the sun shone brightly through the mullioned windows, and golden daffodils could be seen outside poking through the thick grass of the lawn.

"I think if Tanika wants to work at the police station, we should work at the police station," Becks said for the hundredth time.

Her friends ignored her for the hundredth time as Judith took the key from around her neck and opened the padlock.

"I don't suppose you've had a clear-out?" Suzie asked as Judith pushed the door open and entered the first of her two archive rooms.

In the further half of the room, there were still towers of ancient newspapers that reached up to the ceiling, and other mounds of papers where some of the towers had long ago toppled.

"I see the answer's no," Becks said, before letting out an almighty sneeze. "Sorry!" she said as she pulled a hankie from her handbag and held it to her nose.

The area of the room nearest to the women had three fold-out garden chairs in front of a large map of Marlow that was pinned to the wall.

"So how do you want to do this?" Suzie asked.

"How about I write the names of everyone who was at the meeting last night on paper and we can stick them up on the wall one by one," Judith said. "We can discuss them as we go."

"Have you got any spare paper?" Suzie asked as she indicated the many thousands of newspapers elsewhere in the room.

"Very funny," Judith said, picking up a pile of unused index cards. "So, the victim was Geoffrey Lushington. How about you make yourself useful, Suzie. Can you give us a quick rundown of how he was last night?"

Judith wrote "Geoffrey Lushington—victim" on an index card and pinned it to the wall next to the map. She then stuck a pin in the map where the town council had their office, picked up a nearby ball of red wool, and strung the wool between the two pins.

"Sure," Suzie said. "He was basically how he always is. Upbeat, you know? I dog-sat for him, back in the day. He had this gorgeous spaniel called Monty. Wouldn't do what he was told, completely untrainable, I loved him. But Geoffrey was always friendly, nothing was too much bother. He didn't even mind when I failed to turn up to look after Monty, which happened a few times. In fact, now I'm thinking about it, he ended up dog-sitting for me a few times."

This didn't surprise Judith or Becks. Suzie had always been a bit of an engine of chaos, and they could well imagine how her clients might end up doing her work for her, while also no doubt still paying her.

"That chimes with my dealings with him," Becks said. "He always made an effort to talk to me at all those awful events I have to attend. Not that they're awful!" Becks added, fearful she'd let the side down. "But they can be a bit 'samey,' and most dignitaries only want to talk to Colin, seeing as he's the vicar. I'm just his 'plus-one.'"

"You're *nobody's* 'plus-one,'" Judith said.

"Thank you. But Geoffrey wasn't like that with me at all. He always wanted to know how I was. And ever since he threw that reception for us, he's been more interested in me than Colin."

"Yes, that's my memory of him as well," Judith said. "It's rare to meet a man who's prepared to treat you like you're actually a useful member of society. He wasn't threatened by women at all, was he?"

"Which makes it all the more peculiar that he was killed," Becks said. "Whoever would want to kill a man that lovely?"

"Good point," Judith said. "It makes me think we should really focus on the 'why' of it." Judith wrote "WHY?" in big letters on Geoffrey's index card. "Seeing as he was such a good man, why did he have to die? Do either of you know what he did for a living?"

"He was a publisher of some sort," Suzie said. "His house was covered in books, anyway. They were everywhere."

"What about family?"

"I don't think there were any kids," Suzie said. "But he was married. Back in the day."

"What happened to his wife?"

"She died, I think. Some time ago."

"Just to ask the question," Judith said, "his death couldn't have been suicide, could it?"

"I don't think so," Becks said. "He was far too kind to do something so horrendous in public. He'd have worried how it would have affected everyone else who was there. Which reminds me, Suzie, what were you doing at the meeting last night?"

"Me? Oh, not much," Suzie said as though it wasn't worth mentioning.

"But you said something to Tanika about how you were trying to bribe Geoffrey," Judith said. "What was that about?"

"I did, didn't I," Suzie said as she realized she'd have to come clean. "OK, so if you must know, I wanted to see how planning applications are treated. Maybe even get an idea of how I should apply to make sure my request got through."

"What planning application?" Judith asked, surprised.

"Just a small thing."

"But you've finished your building work," Becks said. "The front of your house looks wonderful."

"Thanks. But when we had one of those breaks in filming, the TV show's architect and me got talking. He was saying about this craze in Japan, and he reckoned someone should start emulating it here."

"What craze?"

"You promise you won't tell anyone? I'm not having someone else get wind of the idea and set it up before me."

"Of course not," Judith said.

"OK. Ready? The answer's…a pod hotel."

"A pod what?" Judith asked.

"You know, those pod hotels you get in Japan. Where you basically sleep in a cigar tube."

"You can't possibly mean you want to build one in Marlow."

"Marlow's perfect!"

"But where are you going to build it? You don't own any land you could build a hotel on."

"I own a garden," Suzie said a touch defensively. "And it wouldn't be a full hotel at first. You can buy the units stand-alone, so I was looking to put sixteen pods in as a start. And the thing is, it's a bit of a legal gray area. My architect friend said you don't need planning permission if whatever you're building is lower than the height of a standard fence."

"No, I'm sorry, you've lost me," Judith said. "You were going to build a hotel that wasn't going to be as tall as your garden fence?"

"That's right. It would be eight units across but only two units up—to start off with."

Judith and Becks didn't quite know what to say to that.

"But keep it under your hat," Suzie said.

"It sounds like you could keep the whole hotel under your hat," Judith said.

"That's not funny. Everyone knows how popular Marlow is with tourists. And I've got side access to my garden. All I need is for the council to put in a drop curb and I reckon it's easy money."

"Assuming the planning committee allow it in the first place," Becks said.

"Exactly. Which is why it's such bad timing, Geoffrey getting himself killed like this."

"And talking of how he was killed," Judith said, "there's one thing I didn't mention when we were at the police station. Aconite is an extremely fast-acting poison."

"I saw that for myself," Suzie said. "Geoffrey took one sip of coffee and was dead within seconds."

"Which means the poison must have been administered by someone who was there with him."

"Are you saying one of the planning committee's the killer?" Becks asked.

"I think that's exactly what I'm saying. I suggest we work out who it was."

Chapter 5

"SO," JUDITH SAID TO SUZIE, "who else was at the meeting?"

"OK," Suzie said, trying to marshal her thoughts. "To Geoffrey's immediate right was Marcus Percival. I don't know him," she added.

"Then why are you blushing?"

"I'm not blushing, why would I be blushing?"

"I know his wife, Claire," Becks said, always happy to smooth over any awkwardness. "She's very sweet, I like her a lot. She keeps horses, loves her dogs—they've got two children at Holy Trinity. And the few times I've met Marcus, he's always seemed very friendly. I mean, obviously he is, he has to be, he owns Percival's Estates." Percival's was the preeminent estate agents in Marlow. They tended to sell only the most expensive homes. "It also helps that he's drop-dead gorgeous."

"And doesn't he know it," Suzie said, trying to distance herself even further from her recent embarrassed flush.

"He's vain?" Judith asked.

"Perhaps," Becks said. "Or maybe he's just charming."

"Then does he strike you as a murderer?"

"I think that if I listed all of the character traits of someone capable of committing murder, he's basically the opposite of that."

"He still goes up on the board," Judith said, pinning a card to the wall on which she'd written the name Marcus Percival. "But if he's unlikely to have killed Geoffrey, who does that leave?"

"Jeremy Wessel," Suzie said.

"Oh, I know him," Judith said. "Or at least, I've crossed swords with him. He's an architect I nearly hired once."

"What happened?"

"I was getting the roof of the house fixed a number of years ago, and my builder said there was possible water damage in the joists, I should get an architect to design me a new roof. So I got Jeremy over, and I have to say, I didn't like him. He was dismissive of me—even asking at one point if my husband agreed with the plans I was proposing. Can you imagine?"

"What did you say to him?" Becks asked.

"That it was neither here nor there what my husband thought, seeing as he'd been dead for forty-plus years. But he wasn't just patronizing, I also got the impression that he was incredibly stupid."

"Ha!" Suzie said in delight. "That was my impression of him as well."

"There was a real arrogance to him," Judith agreed. "God knows why. He was also somewhat dismissive of the job I was offering him. He made some joke about how he'd hardly gone into architecture to design roofs. But it was one of those jokes that wasn't really a joke. In the end, I decided not to employ him and leave the roof as it is."

"Even though it was water damaged?" Becks asked.

"Who among us isn't a bit water damaged? It's done well enough these last hundred years, it can do a few years more."

As Judith spoke, she pinned an index card with "Jeremy Wessel" written on it on to the wall.

"And there was something else about him as well," Suzie said. "He lost his temper pretty quickly with the others, and when they challenged him about it, he said he'd been under a lot of pressure lately."

"He did, did he?" Judith said, and wrote "under pressure?" on Jeremy's index card. "I wonder what that's about? So who's next?"

"Next we have Debbie Bell. And I can tell you, I didn't like her one bit. She looked like one of those people who thinks nothing's ever good enough for her."

"She was superior like Jeremy?" Becks asked.

"No, not at all. It was much more negative than that. Like she was disappointed in everything."

"Could she be our murderer?" Judith asked.

"Maybe. But if she killed you, she wouldn't do anything that required any oomph like taking a hammer to you. Or strangling you. It'd be a quick push when you were standing next to a cliff. Or cutting the brakes on your car."

"What about poison?"

"I reckon for someone like Debbie, poison would be her number one choice."

"Well, that's good to know," Judith said, looking at the index cards on the wall. "So, we've got Geoffrey Lushington the victim, and then the three other people on the committee—Marcus Percival, Jeremy Wessel, and Debbie Bell. Was that it?"

"Not quite," Suzie said. "There was one last person on the committee. Sophia De Castro."

"You know her?" Judith said, picking up on Suzie's tone.

"Not in person, but I *know* her, if you know what I mean. You only have to look at her to know she's one of those wealthy people who goes through life thinking they're brilliant. You know, kinder than you, better dressed than you—it's all a competition to her, and she reckons she's winning. And there was something about her relationship with Geoffrey that seemed a bit 'off' to me."

"How do you mean?"

"I'm not sure. They only talked for a few seconds before he died—it was about whether Sophia wanted a cup of tea or a coffee. It was just chitchat, but there was very definitely a weird vibe between them. I made a note of it at the time."

"How interesting," Judith said as she approached the board and wrote "weird vibe with Geoffrey?" on Sophia's index card. "I wonder what that was about?"

Judith could see that Becks's brow was furrowed.

"What is it?" she asked her friend.

"Sophia De Castro?" Becks said. "The name rings a bell. I think Colin once mentioned her to me. Something to do with a scandal, involving the church, I think. Hold on," she said as she picked up her phone and opened a search engine.

"A scandal?" Suzie said, pulling out her phone and typing Sophia's name into Google. "This sounds promising. Let me see if I can find it as well."

There was a distant clunk of Judith's letter box as that morning's post was delivered, but Judith decided that she'd stay with her friends. She took her cup of tea over to a camping chair and sat down. As she took a sip, she felt a warm glow of contentment. As far as she was concerned, researching the background of a possible murderer really was living your best life.

"Oh, OK, she has her own website," Suzie said. "She's into 'wellness,' healing and crystals, and all that guff."

"It's not guff," Becks said. "There's more in heaven and earth than is dreamt of—"

"She has a weekly podcast called *Sophia's Home Homeopathy Show*."

"She's into homeopathy?" Judith asked, wrinkling her nose.

"Why does everyone have to have a podcast these days?" Suzie complained.

"Of course!" Judith said, understanding why Suzie was so irked. "Podcasts take listeners away from your radio show."

"Got it in one," Suzie said. "And I know Marlow FM's not strictly professional, but we do everything like we're professionals. Unlike podcasters," she added darkly.

"I'm sorry," Becks said, holding up her phone. "I'm not getting any hits for Sophia's name when I search for it with the word 'scandal.' Maybe I've misremembered. Perhaps it's someone else I'm thinking of."

"I don't think it is," Suzie said, looking up from the phone in her hand. "Because her website kind of proves she's the killer."

"What makes you say that?" Judith asked.

"It's all here in black and white. She's got a whole section on the herbs and plants she grows in her garden, but she says that there's one part of her garden that's her pride and joy. Her 'Poison Garden'—that's what she calls it. It contains, and I can't believe she's boasting about this on a public website, every possible plant it's possible to use to kill a person."

"Including aconite?" Becks asked.

"There's one way to find out. We should ask her, don't you think?"

Chapter 6

AS JUDITH AND HER FRIENDS got their coats to leave, Suzie noticed an envelope sitting on the parquet floor by the front door.

"Oh wow, a letter," she said, as she bent down and picked it up.

"Is that so surprising?" Becks asked.

"But it's a proper, old-fashioned letter. Look, with a handwritten address and everything," she added, handing the envelope to Becks.

Becks could see that the address was written in a neat, flowing hand, in a dark blue ink that looked like it had come from a fountain pen. She also couldn't help noticing—in truth, it was the first thing she noticed—that the envelope was light blue in color and was made from heavy, linen-weave paper. If she were guessing, she'd have said the stationery was from Smythson of Bond Street.

"Gosh, this is rather special," she said.

"We're supposed to be talking to Sophia," Judith said as she took the letter from Becks and put it on a side table.

"Aren't you going to open it?" Suzie asked.

"No, I'm not," Judith said, and then left the house.

Suzie and Becks looked at each other. What was that about?

All thoughts of the letter were forgotten by the time they arrived at Sophia's house. It was a grand, redbrick Victorian villa that was positioned above a slow turn of the River Thames on the way to Bourne End. The garden sloped down to a boathouse made of brick and stone that had a staircase outside that led to an upstairs room.

"Bloody hell," Suzie said as she and her friends climbed out of her van.

"It is rather grand," Becks agreed.

Suzie waved to some walkers on the other side of the river.

"What are you doing?" Becks asked.

"Making those people over there think I live here," Suzie said, and then headed off to the front door. She yanked on the metal bellpull, and a distant tinkle rang in the house.

"So what's our strategy?" Becks asked.

"Strategy?" Suzie said as though it were a dirty word. "I reckon we go in all guns blazing."

"Is that a good idea?"

Sophia De Castro opened the door, radiating good health. Suzie held up the card on the end of her lanyard.

"Police," she said. "Can we have a word?"

"I'm sorry?" Sophia said, not understanding. "You're the police?"

"That's right."

"We're not," Becks added, before Suzie could speak again. "We're helping the police, but we're not officially them. I'm the vicar's wife—for my sins," she added as a joke that never arrived.

"You were at the meeting," Sophia said, recognizing Suzie.

"We can explain all of this inside," Judith said. "May we come in?"

After a short pause, Sophia said, "Of course," and led them into her house.

The three friends followed Sophia down a thickly carpeted corridor into a pretty kitchen that had a cream-colored Aga oven and fresh-cut daffodils in a vase on a dining table.

"Herbal tea?" Sophia asked as she headed over to a little jug of water that contained a thick bunch of fresh mint. "I've got some fresh mint, if that suits?"

"That would be perfect," Judith said. She noticed a postcard that was pinned by a magnet to the fridge. It showed a golden light shining through the cracks of a repaired porcelain cup with text that read "We are all broken. That's how the light gets in."

"In fact," Judith continued, "it's why we wanted to talk to you. You grow your own herbs, don't you?"

"Of course," Sophia said, understanding coming to her. "You're fans of my podcast."

The women didn't quite know what to say to that.

"Why don't you tell us about it?" Becks eventually offered.

"It's just something I started on the side," Sophia said as she tore the mint apart with her bare hands. "A chance for me to share what I've learned about herbal remedies, and about how the natural world can heal us."

"Do you really have a poison garden?" Suzie asked.

Sophia smiled.

"Oh, yes," she said as she put the mint into a glass teapot, took it over to the sink, and poured boiling water into it from her tap, the fresh and tangy smell of mint filling the room.

"That's fascinating," Judith said. "Could we perhaps see it?"

"I'd be more than happy to show you. It's very popular."

Once they had their mint teas, Sophia led the women through the French doors and across a stretch of lawn that ended in a thick holly hedge. There was an entrance in the hedge that had been created from twisted yew branches bent over into an arch. A wooden sign hung from the top of the arch with a skull and crossbones burned into it.

"Is it dangerous?" Suzie asked as they paused on the threshold.

"Everything in the natural world is dangerous if you don't understand it," Sophia said as though she'd unlocked a deep truth. "And very little is if you do, if you see what I mean."

With a smile, Sophia went through the entrance. Suzie turned to her friends and shrugged that she didn't understand what Sophia was talking about, and then she led her friends through the arch where they found themselves surrounded by plants in raised beds. Off to one side there was a little greenhouse that contained further exotic-looking specimens.

"So, what have you got?" Suzie asked, a bit like a bloke down the pub wanting to know what ales were on tap.

"Well, to start off, you walked through a yew arch as you entered."

"Yew trees aren't dangerous," Becks said.

"The branches aren't, but their berries are. Or rather, the stones of the fruit. You can eat the flesh as long as you don't swallow the stone. It's how the tree reproduces. Foxes in particular love to eat yew berries."

"Why would they eat something that's poisonous?" Judith asked.

"It's all rather clever. The foxes eat the berries because they're so tasty. And then they go about their day while the berry's flesh dissolves in their stomach. Then, once that protective covering's dissolved, the stone is finally revealed and poisons the poor creature in such a way that makes them vomit up the stones they've just eaten. Voilà, the stones can start growing a new yew tree a considerable distance away from the mother tree."

"Wow," Suzie said. "That's impressive."

"It's like I said, everything has a purpose in nature. You only get into trouble if you don't know what that purpose is."

Suzie indicated some nearby plants that had plastic grocery bags tied over them.

"What's with the bags?" she asked.

"Spring's a tricky time for some plants. The bags protect them from frost."

"You've got nettles," Judith said, indicating a cluster of tall plants with furry stalks and leaves.

"*Urtica dioica*. You have to be sure to harvest only the very tips of each plant if you want to make tea. If you use the leaves from the stems, you end up with something worse than overcooked cabbage. And, of course, if you touch the hairs on the stalk, you come out in a stinging rash."

"What else have you got?" Becks asked.

"Everything! Crocuses, deadly nightshade, both holly and ivy, foxgloves, bluebells, daffodils—you name it, I've got it."

"What about aconite?" Suzie asked.

"Of course! What garden wouldn't be complete without the deep purples of aconite. Here, let me show you."

Sophia walked past the nettle patch and stopped by a raised bed that had some plants under glass cloches. There also seemed to be matted hair in clumps around the base of the plants.

"Is that hair?" Becks asked, appalled.

"I take it from my hairbrush every morning."

"Why?"

"It keeps the slugs and snails away. They don't like human hair."

Becks pulled a face that made it clear that she was very much on the slugs' side, but Sophia didn't notice as she indicated a bush of tall stems that had bright purple flowers on the top, their leaves forming fat, drooping "bells."

"You can see why aconite's also called monkshood," Judith said appreciatively. "The flowers look like the cowls monks wear."

"Oh, you're into gardening?" Sophia said.

"Not exactly," Judith said, as she remembered that she really must have a go at cutting the jungle of her garden back one of these days. "It's crosswords I'm into. I have a lot of reference books on plants."

"In which case, you'll know that even touching these beauties can kill you," Sophia said, her eyes shining with delight at the thought. "I must confess, aconite's always fascinated me. You see, all of the other plants in this garden have medicinal benefits, or taste wonderful if you prepare them properly. All that is except for monkshood. It really is lethal."

"Then why have it?"

"It's beautiful! Don't you think? And why should it be exiled just because it's so poisonous? Why are you so interested?"

"Geoffrey was poisoned with aconite," Judith said, deciding that honesty was the best policy.

Sophia took half a step back in shock.

"That can't be true."

"I'm afraid it is," Becks said.

"You can't possibly think it was *my* aconite?" she said in a fluster.

"I can't imagine everyone grows aconite."

"Lots of people do. And I've talked about it on the podcast. Anyone who's ever listened to me—and there are thousands around the world who download my show every week—would know I grow aconite in my garden. They could have got in any way they liked and dug up a plant for themselves. I always say how deadly it is. You know it's known as the Queen of Poisons?"

"As it happens, we do," Judith said.

"So that's what you're saying?" Suzie said. "Anyone could have got into your garden and taken it from you?"

"You saw me last night. I arrived after the meeting had started and just went and sat down. I never went anywhere near Geoffrey or his cup of coffee."

"How do you know he was killed by his coffee?" Judith asked.

"But it must have been his coffee," Sophia said, now seriously flustered. "It was the only thing he drank. And aconite's got a bitter taste. You'd have to hide the flavor in something. That's why I presumed that whatever killed him was in his coffee."

"You say you arrived at the meeting late," Judith said. "Why was that?"

"Is this really important?"

Suzie held up her lanyard with her police credentials on it.

"We think it is," she said.

"Very well. When I left here for the meeting, I discovered I had a puncture in one of my car tires. I had to drive it to Platts garage to get the tire changed—it was all rather inconvenient, as it happens. And I rather resent you asking all of these questions. Why on earth would I have wished Geoffrey harm?"

"I couldn't help noticing there was a bit of tension between you and Geoffrey when you arrived," Suzie said.

"I'm sure you're mistaken."

"No, there was definitely a weird vibe between the two of you."

"I was just embarrassed to be late. And you have to believe me, there's no way I could ever harm Geoffrey. Not since he got me out of a spot of bother a while back. In fact, if he hadn't stepped in, I could have been in quite a bit of trouble."

Judith and her friends caught each other's eyes. Was this the scandal that Becks had been trying to remember?

"Can you tell us what happened?" Becks asked.

"It's somewhat embarrassing, but I wouldn't want you thinking I wasn't being helpful. This was about fifteen years ago, and Geoffrey was chair of the works and buildings committee. He gave me the responsibility of looking after the graveyards."

"That was it!" Becks said as she remembered. "You put people in the wrong graves."

"There's no need to put it like that, but you're right, it was very bad. I got the plans for Bisham graveyard muddled with the overflow graveyard here in Marlow. Only for a short time, mind. Barely a few weeks. As soon as I realized what was going on, I confessed everything to Geoffrey, and he was amazing. He refused to blame me. He just said he wanted to sort it out. Which he did by basically convincing the families who'd got the wrong plots not to make a fuss—or sue the council. The point being, he sorted it out without it blowing up in my face, and I'm eternally grateful to him. Which is why I didn't have any kind of problem with him last night. I owe him more than pretty much anyone else on the planet."

"Do you perhaps remember any of the families who were affected?" Judith asked.

"I've kept a lot of the paperwork from that time in our boathouse at the bottom of the garden. It's my recording studio, and there's a storage area in the eaves. But I don't remember any of the details off the top of my head. It was a chapter of my life I couldn't wait to close. I've certainly not made any mistakes like that ever since."

As Sophia spoke, they all saw a sleek black Mercedes car turn into the driveway and glide up to the house. Sophia's brow furrowed.

"Can you tell us if anyone on the planning committee might have wanted to do harm to Geoffrey?" Judith asked.

"Of course not," Sophia said, distracted by the car's arrival. "Everyone who knew Geoffrey liked him. Now I think I've been helpful enough—would you mind showing yourselves out?" Sophia said as she bustled back to her house.

The three friends looked at each other.

"That's interesting," Becks said. "Did you see how she changed when that car arrived? I wonder who's driving it?"

"I suggest we find out," Judith said, and followed Sophia back to the house.

"We can't follow her!" Becks yelped as Suzie immediately tagged onto the heels of their friend.

Becks sighed. As much as she loved the thrill of investigating, she'd had to come to terms with the fact that she was the only law-abiding member of the three friends, and she knew that this meant that sometimes she had to take the rough with the smooth. She trotted after Suzie and Judith. When she reached them, she joined them in peering around the corner of the French windows, and together they saw Sophia in the front hallway, quickly applying some lipstick before checking her hair. She then looked at herself in the mirror for what seemed a very long moment before putting on a bright smile as she turned and opened the front door. As she called out a hello, a dark-haired man in a gray suit entered the house with a scowl and handed Sophia his briefcase without even looking at her—or stopping, for that matter—as he headed straight up the stairs, leaving Sophia on her own in the hallway.

Sophia dropped the briefcase to the floor and kicked it under the side table.

Chapter 7

JUDITH AND HER FRIENDS DECIDED to repair to the Strawberry Grove café on the High Street. As they got out of Suzie's van, Judith looked at the people going about their day, the colorful bunting that crisscrossed the High Street fluttering above them, and smiled. There really wasn't a lovelier sight than the bustle of Marlow High Street.

"So what do we think of Sophia?" she asked.

"I think she's our killer," Suzie said, matter-of-factly. "The murder weapon was aconite, she grows aconite, case closed as far as I'm concerned. And I definitely think there was something going on between her and Geoffrey at the meeting. Remember, this is a woman who puts people in the wrong graves."

"Yes, that was interesting, wasn't it?" Becks said. "I'll ask Colin about it when I get home. See what he knows about it."

"Good thinking," Judith said. "And I'll tell you who I'm interested in. Sophia's husband. Assuming that's who we saw coming home."

"That was her husband," Becks said. "Only a husband would behave like that."

Suzie and Judith knew that Becks had a somewhat scratchy relationship with her husband, and were happy to agree with her assessment.

"So why would someone as earth-mothery as Sophia marry someone cold like that?" Judith asked.

"You saw the house," Suzie said. "Money. That's why someone like Sophia marries someone like that."

"Ladies!" a voice called out, and they all turned and saw a man approaching. He was sporting a suit that Judith felt was a little too blue for her liking, and a broad smile that made her equally suspicious.

It was Marcus Percival.

"Do we know you?" Judith said, as Marcus reached them.

"Sorry if I'm intruding," he said, turning to Suzie, "but if I'm not much mistaken, you were at the meeting when Geoffrey died."

"I was," Suzie said, more pleased with Marcus's attention than Judith felt was entirely appropriate.

"But I don't know you," Judith said to Marcus in her most matronly fashion.

"My apologies. Marcus Percival. I was on the planning committee with Geoffrey. So I was there when he died—and what a horrible experience that was. But tell me, have you any leads?"

"Why on earth are you asking us?"

"I'm guessing the police couldn't wait to ask the three of you to help out again. Like you did with those other cases. Since one of the famous trio was actually there when Geoffrey died," he added, once again smiling at Suzie, who, Judith noted, was now quite openly grinning.

"They have," Suzie said proudly.

"So tell me, have you got a prime suspect yet?"

"What do you think?" Judith asked.

"Me? Since you're asking, I think it has to have been a shocking and terrible accident."

"I understand his wife died some time ago," Judith said.

"Mary? That's a sad story. I think she and Geoffrey were childhood sweethearts. They got married as soon as they could and were together for decades. He was a big-shot publisher—when he wasn't running Marlow—and she was on just about every charity committee in town."

"What's sad about that?" Suzie said.

"Oh, sorry, of course. She got cancer and died. Must be twenty or so years ago, something like that."

"Did he ever remarry?" Becks asked.

"No. Geoffrey always told me he was a 'one girl' guy. He'd been lucky enough to find love once in his life, he didn't see it happening for him again. Look," Marcus said, wanting to make sure he got his point across. "No one killed him—there's no way—I can't overstate what a nice guy he was. Take my sister. She's something of a lost soul. Always has been, sadly. And a drinker. Which is all fun and games when you're younger, but you know how it goes as you get older. Anyway, a few years ago, she got behind in her rent. Put her head in the sand. By the time I found out what was going on, she owed thousands. It was a shock, I can tell you. But Geoffrey stepped in. Lent me the money to give her. Can you imagine? Don't worry, I paid it back over a number of months, before you jump to any conclusions. But the point is, it wasn't just the way he helped out with money. He also made sure he got to know my sister. Wanted her to know he was there for her. It meant so much to her. He really was one in a million."

"Would your sister be happy to talk to the police?"

"Of course. She worshipped Geoffrey."

"And you really think his death was an accident?" Judith asked.

"It's the most likely explanation. Maybe there was rat poison or something in his cup? I don't know."

"Is it possible someone on the committee did this to him?"

Marcus laughed.

"The planning committee have been together for years. You check over the minutes, there's never been a cross word. We're a good team."

"Didn't seem like it to me," Suzie said.

"You mean Jeremy? He's a bit of a stickler, that's all. And he sometimes gets frustrated when he feels he's not getting his way. It's a pain in some circumstances, but it's good to have someone on the committee who cares about rules and regulations."

"Tell us about the other members of the committee," Judith said.

"What is there to say? Sophia pretends to be all la-di-da and away with the fairies, but there's not a house—or plot of land—in the town she doesn't know intimately. She's obsessed with the development of Marlow and is basically a top bird."

"A top bird?" Judith asked, her eyes narrowing.

"You know, like a top bloke, but a woman."

"And you're sure she wasn't behind what happened to Geoffrey?" Suzie asked.

"Yes, I'm sure."

"But didn't you think there was a weird vibe between her and Geoffrey when she arrived?"

"Not at all. Did you?"

"What if I told you she grows the poison that was used to kill him?"

Marcus's interest sharpened.

"He died from a dangerous plant?" he said. "Well, surely that makes it all the more likely it was an accident. Maybe someone left the plant out, or something, and he ate it by mistake."

"Aconite's highly poisonous," Judith said. "You can die from touching it. It's really very unlikely it got into Mr. Lushington's coffee by chance."

"Well, it doesn't matter who grows it," Marcus said. "Sophia won't be involved. She's a good soul, there's no way she'd harm anyone."

Marcus smiled, happy to have answered Judith's question.

"You didn't mention Debbie Bell," Judith said.

"Debbie? Oh, God, that's a bit embarrassing, isn't it?" Marcus said, not embarrassed at all. "Well, if I didn't mention her, it's because, I'm sorry to say, she's not really that interesting. Don't get me wrong, she works hard for the town, but—you know—she's somewhat forgettable. As I've just demonstrated. But tell me, I'm fascinated. If you think this is murder, do the police agree?"

"How do you mean?"

"Are they treating Geoffrey's death as murder, or merely suspicious?"

"We can't share details of the case with anyone," Judith said.

"No, I suppose not. Well, I'd better leave you to it. But if you have any more questions, do pop along to the office. You know where Percival's is?"

Marcus pointed along the High Street, even though he knew the three friends would already know where it was. Everyone knew where his office was.

The women watched Marcus go and Judith had the strongest suspicion that he knew they were still looking at him.

"You see," Becks said, "it's like I said. He's very charming."

"Not you as well," Judith said.

"What?"

"Suzie went all knock-kneed, and now I see you did as well."

"Me?" Suzie said, surprised.

"Yes. You."

"Didn't you like him?"

"I'm not here to like him or not, but I'll tell you this much, he was mighty keen to know how our investigation was progressing, wasn't he?"

"Oh," Becks said. "Now you mention it, he was."

"I wonder why he was so interested."

The women entered the Strawberry Grove café and, once they'd loaded up with the necessary cups of tea and slices of cake, they repaired to a low table where they continued to talk through what they'd learned. After half an hour of a discussion that was mostly dominated by Suzie repeating that Sophia had to be the killer, Becks said that she had to head home to start cooking dinner, and then an alarm on Suzie's phone reminded her that she had to pick up a miniature schnauzer from a client's house in Hurley. Judith found herself on her own and decided to go home as well. Once there, she knew that on a normal day, she'd go for a swim to help her think, but she realized she didn't quite have the energy.

Instead, she went over to her sideboard and poured herself the merest splash of whisky into a cut-glass tumbler. Downing it in one, she found herself briefly lost in memories of her childhood. Clunking the glass back down on the sideboard, she went over to the dying embers of the fire she'd lit that morning and added a fire lighter and a few sticks of kindling. With a couple of puffs from her leather bellows, the fire crackled back to life. Next, she went to the front door where she'd left the handwritten letter that had arrived that morning. She picked it up, returned to the grate, and dropped it into the fire, unopened. The envelope blackened around the edges before bursting into flame, the charred paper peeling away to reveal the neatly handwritten letter inside. Before she could make out any of the words, the charred edges raced to the middle and the whole thing was aflame.

There, she told herself, that was better.

She knew she'd be able to focus on the case now, and as she sat down in her favorite wingback, she thought about how both Sophia and Marcus had told her that Geoffrey had been a perfect human being. But Suzie was right; that couldn't be true, could it? He had to have had some kind of dark secret, or why would someone have needed to kill him?

A loud bell pierced the air, and Judith jumped as she realized her landline was ringing. She went over to her phone and plucked up the cream-colored handset.

"Judith Potts," she announced.

There was silence on the end of the line. No, that wasn't quite right, Judith thought, she could hear the sound of someone breathing.

"Hello?" she said, irritated. Was this a prank call of some sort?

"Follow the money," a muffled voice said on the end of the line. Judith barely managed to make out the words, it was as if the person was speaking through a wad of fabric.

"What's that?"

"You want to know who killed Geoffrey Lushington? Follow the money."

"How did you get my phone number?" Judith asked, but she heard a click on the line.

The caller had hung up.

Chapter 8

THE FOLLOWING MORNING, BECKS WAS trying to make a positive start to her day while also knowing that it was about to be ruined. It wasn't something she could do anything about, and it was hard for her not to feel resentful.

For once, it had nothing to do with her immediate family. In fact, after all her crime-fighting heroics with Judith and Suzie, she'd found that her status within the family had subtly shifted. Her daughter Chloe was now in her first year at university—she was reading Comparative Religion at Exeter, which had been a surprise to her parents, to say the least. But Chloe's new life as a student had come at the same time as a thimbleful of maturity, and she was increasingly, if grudgingly, seeing her mother as a worthy equal in the family dynamic.

As for Sam, he was now eighteen years old and in the depths of A levels. Or rather, he would have been if he'd been doing any work. As he'd announced to his parents after a terrible round of mock exams only the month before, he wasn't going to do any more active revision for his exams—and his parents shouldn't worry because he was "OK with it." Colin had wanted to come down on Sam like a ton of bricks, but Becks had pointed out that Sam had never enjoyed academic work, so maybe this was his way of giving himself space to develop other interests. Colin pointed out, quite reasonably, that it would be all well and good if Sam had any other interests, but he didn't—beyond his PlayStation, going to the pub, and sleeping. Becks privately agreed, but nonetheless held firm. They were to give Sam space.

On this matter, as in many others now, Colin deferred to his wife. Becks liked to think it was because she was a famous crimefighter, but she guessed that it had far more to do with the fact that she'd recently, and inadvertently, made a small fortune for the family with a run of smart investments. Colin knew what a vicar's pension looked like. He was grateful that Becks had done so much to shore up their financial future. On the whole, and taken in the round, Becks had finally got her home life exactly how she wanted it.

And that's when Marian Starling, Colin's mother, had announced that she was coming to stay. Marian was to Becks's eyes the only person she'd ever met who had no redeeming qualities—and, as she often told Colin, she'd met a number of murderers. Marian had the high-handed manner, breathy voice—and sometimes even dressed like—a drunk pope.

Becks didn't like the fact that she disliked her mother-in-law so much, but she'd been forced into this position by Marian's actions over the years. Colin tended to agree with Becks that his mother was a nightmare, but she held an almost-fatal control over her son.

As Becks and Colin were having a morning catch-up in the kitchen, Marian swept in wearing a woolen kaftan she'd picked up from a solo trip to the Andes to "find herself" the year before.

"Don't mind me," she announced as she went over to the kettle. "Just getting myself a cup of tea. You carry on as you are."

Colin half rose out of his chair, but Becks flashed a warning at him. His mother was capable of getting herself a cup of tea without any help.

"So will you look into the graveyards?" Becks said, wanting to continue her conversation with her husband.

Marian clattered in the cupboard, pulling out mug after mug, looking for one that was clean. They were all clean.

"I can't say I know where to look," Colin said, his eyes darting to his mother as she blew into a mug to get the nonexistent dust out of it.

"Won't there be diocesan records somewhere? Or at some archive?"

"I suppose so."

Marian was now mournfully rootling through dozens of different boxes of tea in a separate cupboard. None of them met her satisfaction.

"It's the same selection of tea as you had yesterday," Becks said.

"Are you sure you don't have any Assam? Colin loves Assam, it's his favorite."

"I—er—went off Assam a while back," Colin said. "Can't you get the records from the council?" he said, returning his attention to Becks.

"We've been told Geoffrey tried to cover the scandal up," Becks said. "I want to know the church's side of the story. It could be a bit different to what the council have got in their archives."

Marian had now found a ramekin of sugar and was peering beadily into it as though it might contain mouse droppings, and Becks stood up from her chair, slapping the palms of her hands down on the table.

"Marian!" she said.

Marian pretended to be surprised.

"You still haven't got caster sugar, have you?"

"We have unrefined granulated sugar in this house, but that's OK, because it all dissolves the same in a cup of hot tea."

Marian looked with infinite tolerance at her daughter-in-law.

"I can taste the difference," she said like the martyr she was. "I'm sorry if I'm making too many demands. I know I'm not perfect, but things have been so hard on me since Colin's father passed on."

"Don't worry," Colin said, stepping in to act as peacemaker, "I'll make you a cup of tea."

"That's so kind of you, I'd never want to be any trouble."

"Why don't you go to your room?" Colin continued. "Take the newspaper with you. I'll bring you a nice cup of tea."

"You'd do that for me? How kind," she added, and then left the room so slowly that Becks was put in mind of a prisoner being led to the gallows.

Once she'd finally departed, Colin went over to the tea things as a way of avoiding his wife, but Becks kept up with him.

"How long is she going to be staying with us?" she hissed.

"She's got nowhere to go."

It was true. Marian had until recently been renting a one-bedroom flat in Sevenoaks in Kent. When her rental agreement had come to an end, she'd tipped up at her son's door.

"She could go anywhere!" Becks said. "But she won't, will she, because we both know the truth of why she's here."

"She wanted to spend some time with her grandchildren."

"Yesterday she called Sam 'Simon.'"

"That's why she wants to get to know him more."

"She's had eighteen years."

"Must we always argue about her?"

"Maybe when you stop defending her the whole time."

"I'm her son."

"Don't I bloody know it."

The kettle clicked and husband and wife looked at each other. In truth, they both knew they were in agreement about Marian's awfulness.

"And why does she keep banging on about your dad having 'passed on'?"

"That's not kind," Colin said in a warning tone.

"He's not dead, he's moved to Frinton-on-Sea."

"Some people would say it's the same thing."

"This is no time for jokes, Colin."

"Look, I know she's irritating, but she's processing the fact that he walked out on her in the only way she knows."

"Three years ago," Becks added. "And ever since then, she's burned through the divorce settlement."

"It's not her fault she doesn't know how to look after money."

"Oh, I think it is."

"Don't say it," Colin said, seeing where the conversation was heading.

"She only turned up here after you told her I'd made all that money on the stock market."

"I was proud of you. I wanted her to know."

"And now here she is, complaining that our biscuits aren't Duchy Originals!" Becks took a moment to center herself. "What will it take for her to leave?" she asked.

Colin sighed.

"You know what it will take."

"Money," she said. "And I'm not giving her any of ours. That's for the children. Seeing as they won't inherit anything from their granny."

"We'll get there," Colin said as he poured boiling water into the cup.

"We'd better, because I warn you, after all of the experience I've gained over the last few years, I think I might be tempted to carry out the perfect murder."

Becks's words were so preposterous that she couldn't help but smile at her audacity. Colin also smiled, although a touch more wearily.

On the table, Becks's phone began to ring. She answered it and listened to what the person on the other end of the line had to say.

"OK, Judith," Becks said. "I'll be with you in ten."

Chapter 9

WHEN BECKS ARRIVED AT JUDITH'S house, she found her friend in the makeshift incident room with Suzie and Tanika.

"You did this for the last murder as well?" Tanika asked, looking with appreciation at the incident board that was now covered in index cards all linked to each other and the evidence with red wool.

"We did," Judith said proudly.

Tanika's eyes were drawn to the towers of dusty newspapers and magazines that covered the other half of the room.

"I used to be a bit of a collector," Judith said by way of explanation.

"*Used* to be?" Tanika asked, an eyebrow raised.

"You need to know what happened to me last night," Judith said, trying to move the conversation on. She then told them about the anonymous phone call she'd received.

"'Follow the money'?" Tanika asked, once Judith had finished her story. "We ran checks on Mr. Lushington as a matter of course, and nothing surprising flagged on his financials. I'll get back to my team. See if they can dig deeper. What can you tell me about this person who phoned you?"

"Not much," Judith said as she tried to remember. "His voice sounded metallic and muffled. Like it was distorted."

"He was using software to change his voice?"

"It's possible, I suppose."

"So it could in fact have been a woman?"

"It might have been, but it felt like a man to me, even if it didn't sound entirely human. As soon as the call ended, I dialed 1471 to see who'd rung me, but the number was withheld."

"Don't worry," Tanika said. "The phone company will know the number—even if it's withheld from you. We'll be able to get them to release it."

"I hoped you'd say that," Judith said. "Once you've identified who made the call, we can pay him a visit. Find out why he's making anonymous phone calls."

"Yes, can I talk to you about that?" Tanika said. "Because I'm grateful for all that you've done, but you shouldn't be talking to key witnesses like Mr. Percival and Mrs. De Castro without first clearing it with me."

"How can we help you if we don't talk to people?"

"There's an order to these things. Ultimately, this case has to stand up in court."

"Nonsense!"

"No—really—it does."

"Of course that's what *you* have to do," Judith agreed. "But it's not the best way to use us. We should be able to talk to who we like because we're unofficial."

"And we never pretend we're the police," Suzie said, which surprised both Judith and Becks. "We say we're just helping out. Nothing anyone says to us is going to be official. Which is the point. In a place like Marlow, where everyone knows everyone, you need unofficial channels."

"You make it sound like 1970s Belfast," Tanika said.

"Suzie's right," Judith said. "We should be allowed to do our thing. Think of us as private detectives."

Tanika frowned. She didn't think that agreeing with Judith's plan was a good idea, but there was also the small matter that she and her friends had already been instrumental in solving two cases.

"How about I update you with where we've got to?" she said as a way of changing the subject.

"Good idea!" Judith said, and popped the lid on a felt-tip pen so she could add to the index cards on the wall.

"Starting with the scene of crime, we haven't found anything in the council debating chamber that seemed particularly incriminating."

"Did you find the sugar bowl?"

"As it happens, Antonia reported back to me that she didn't find any sugar bowl anywhere."

"Well that's interesting," Judith said.

"I'm not sure I agree."

"But sugar was found in Geoffrey's stomach, and in the coffee you found in his cup, so where did it come from?"

"Maybe he had a sachet of the stuff with him?"

"Did you find any empty packets of sugar anywhere?"

"I don't think us finding or not finding little wraps of paper proves anything one way or another. But we did find something of note in the corridor outside the debating chamber. There's a security camera that records people coming and going through the front door, and the cable to it has been cut."

"Really?" Becks said. "Did it manage to record who cut it?"

"Sadly, it doesn't quite cover the door. Whoever did this was able to enter the corridor and cut the cable before they'd walked into view of the camera."

"When did this happen?" Judith asked.

"The morning Mr. Lushington died."

"But why would the killer need to do that? With aconite being so fast-acting, the killer must have been one of the people who was in the debating chamber with Geoffrey—meaning we know the full list of suspects. So why would it matter whether or not the security camera saw them walk down the corridor to the debating chamber beforehand? Or afterward? What happened there that the killer didn't want us to see?"

"Good point," Tanika agreed.

"It's a bit of a mystery, isn't it?"

"And there's something else. We went through Mr. Lushington's private life, and found nothing even close to incriminating. All his emails and texts are about his work as mayor of Marlow, and he comes across as being conciliatory, always trying to get the best out of people—I'd say there wasn't a bad bone in his body."

"That's what Marcus and Sophia said as well," Suzie grumbled.

"But we did find one thing. A selfie on his phone. A photo of a woman's breasts in a lacy bra."

"How exciting!" Judith said, clapping her hands together. "Who's it of?"

"That's the thing, it's not possible to say for sure. It's really just a close-up of a woman's breasts in a black bra."

"I see," Judith said as she wrote "photo of breasts" on to a card and pinned it next to Geoffrey's name on the board. "So he's the sort of man who has a photo of a woman's breasts on his phone."

"Not exactly," Tanika. "He's the sort of man who gets sent a photo of a woman's breasts."

"It was *sent* to him?"

"That's how it's looking. The photo's metadata says it was taken in Marlow on the twenty-seventh of January at 8:20 p.m."

"But that doesn't sound right," Becks said. "When we spoke to Marcus Percival, he said Geoffrey was still devoted to his wife, even though she died twenty years ago."

"No man stays loyal to their wife," Suzie said. "Especially after her death. Let's be honest, most men have shacked up with some new woman before the old one's even at the undertakers."

"Can you describe these breasts to us?" Judith asked Tanika.

"Judith!" Becks exclaimed. "We're not going around inspecting women's breasts."

"Of course not, but that doesn't mean there won't be clues. For example, are they particularly large?"

"I am not happy with this," Becks said, rising out of her chair. "Not happy at all."

"A man was killed!" Suzie said.

"But not by a pair of breasts. Really, this whole conversation is inappropriate."

"The woman in question is Caucasian," Tanika said in her most matter-of-fact police officer voice. "I'd estimate she's middle aged—over forty, if I were guessing, if not older—and I'd say that her breasts were of average shape and size. It's hard to say for sure. But there is one thing. The woman has a distinctive birthmark on the skin a little bit below her left breast. It's about the size of a penny and is in the shape of a diamond."

"Now that's *very* interesting," Judith said as she wrote "diamond birthmark" next to "breasts?" on the card.

"Do we know if either Sophia De Castro or Debbie Bell has such a birthmark?" she asked.

"We don't, I'm afraid."

"Now, would you say that either of them has average-sized breasts?" Suzie mulled.

"I'm really not comfortable with this conversation," Becks said.

"Don't be such a prude."

"I'm not being a prude. You know it all depends on the bra you're wearing, and the cut of your clothes. If the breasts in question are average, then it really could be anyone."

"And to be clear," Tanika said to Judith, "you try and lift any woman's top to find this birthmark, and I'll charge you with assault."

"Don't worry, I very definitely won't be doing that," Judith said with a sincerity that Tanika guessed was false.

Tanika's phone rang and she stepped to one side to take the call. After a few hushed questions, she hung up with a frown.

"Problem?" Judith asked.

"That was DS Perry. He's just finished a follow-up interview with Debbie Bell."

"Why?"

"Forensics developed all the fingerprints they found on the two used coffee capsules we recovered from the Nespresso machine. One of them only has Debbie Bell's fingerprints on it."

"As you'd expect," Suzie said. "I remember she made herself a cup of coffee. She'd have used one of those capsules."

"It's not that capsule that's of interest to us. It's the one that contained the poison that killed Mr. Lushington—because it has his fingerprints on."

"Which makes sense," Suzie said. "I also saw him make himself a cup of coffee."

"But the poisoned capsule he used also has Debbie Bell's prints on it. She says there's a rational reason why her prints got on it, but DS Perry says she was so offhand with him, he wasn't sure he was getting the whole story. Not that she acted guilty or anything, it's more that she was so unforthcoming. It happens sometimes. Particularly with people who are—let's say—more timid than others. They freeze when they see a police officer."

Judith remembered that it had been DS Perry who'd been particularly skeptical about her and her friends' ability to help the police.

"His manner leaves a lot to be desired," she said.

"There's that as well," Tanika agreed.

"If only you had some nice friendly civilians you could get to talk to Debbie Bell instead," Judith said.

Tanika looked at Judith, realizing what she was suggesting.

"OK," she said with a sigh. "Perhaps the three of you could have a quick word with her?"

"Maybe we don't have the time," Judith said primly.

"Don't push it."

Judith's face broke into a broad grin.

"Then we'd be delighted to help the police. Wouldn't we, ladies?"

Chapter 10

DEBBIE BELL LIVED IN A modern-build house by the Marlow hockey club, and when Judith and her friends arrived, they discovered an old transit van already parked outside. Debbie was hovering in her doorway as an older man unloaded cardboard boxes into her garage.

"Hello!" Judith called out as they approached.

The man called a cheery greeting, but Debbie frowned as she saw them.

"Who are you?" she asked.

Judith explained that they were helping the police, but it didn't put Debbie in a better mood.

"I've just spoken to that stupid man," she said.

"The police officer?"

"He asked the most insulting questions."

"I'm sorry to hear that," Becks said. "We've come across him as well, and he's somewhat lacking in manners."

"You can say that again."

"We only have a few follow-up questions, that's all. We won't take up more than a minute of your time."

"And we aren't quite as insulting," Judith said with her best smile.

"What's in the boxes?" Suzie said, pointing at the boxes that were being delivered.

"Ducks," Debbie said.

"Ducks?" Suzie said, startled.

"Not live ones, of course."

"Of course not," Suzie said, although her friends suspected that that was exactly what she'd thought.

As the man put one of the boxes down, the lid popped open and a few bright yellow toy ducks spilled onto the drive.

"Be careful, would you?" Debbie said tetchily.

"They're for the Marlow Town Fair, aren't they?" Becks said. "The duck race."

"That's right."

"I love the duck race," Becks said, but she could see that Judith was none the wiser. "You pay a pound to adopt a little plastic duck. And then they release all the ducks onto the river at the same time. Thousands of them. They all float off to the bridge, a great fleet of yellow ducks bobbing along. And then the first one to go over the weir is the winner."

"What's the prize?" Suzie asked.

"It's not about the prize," Debbie said. "It's about raising money for local charities."

"And it's so very public-spirited of you," Becks said. "I don't suppose you get enough credit in the town for all the work you do—sitting on all those committees. As the vicar's wife, I know that my husband's work is often taken for granted. It really is amazing how people like you keep this town going."

"Thank you, that's very kind of you. Look, why don't you come in?" Debbie said, Becks's words having enchanted her.

As Debbie led the way into the house, Suzie gave a big thumbs-up to Becks, and the three women followed. Once inside, Debbie showed them into a little kitchen that, like its owner, was somewhat drab and tired around the edges. A large fridge blocked the one door that led into the garden.

"So how come the ducks get delivered to you?" Suzie asked.

"I'm the only person on the council's community committee who has a properly lockable storage unit. My garage. And I'm an accountant, so they think I like counting stock, which I can categorically tell you I don't. I have to look after the ducks when they're delivered in spring. And the Santa Claus outfits for the Santa Fun Run when they arrive at the beginning of September. They take up even more space."

"You're an accountant?" Becks asked.

"I've been chartered for twenty-three years."

"Where do you work?"

"Marlow Wealth Management on Spittall Street. Do you know it? It's owned by Sophia's husband, Paul."

"Is that so?" Judith said, remembering Paul's ill-tempered arrival when they'd been talking to Sophia. "What's he like?"

"A hard taskmaster. But fair."

"Trustworthy?"

"Of course. We wouldn't be able to look after our clients' money if we weren't."

"If you're an accountant," Judith said, "what would you say to me if I said 'Follow the money'?"

"'Follow the money'? I don't know. That's what I do, I suppose, but it doesn't really mean anything, does it? Money doesn't move. How could you follow it?"

"Is there any chance Geoffrey might have been up to no good financially?"

"Of course not. He was one of the most morally correct people I knew."

"Are you sure?"

"Quite sure. He was meticulously careful to make sure not even a penny was wasted. Our money belonged to the people of Marlow, he'd tell us. Even imagining he'd be up to no good is impossible."

Judith and her friends could see that the question had irritated Debbie, so Becks moved over to a trio of shelves on the wall that contained dozens of little models of pretty porcelain figurines.

"Are these Lladró?" she asked to change the subject.

Debbie brightened visibly.

"They are," she said. "I've been collecting Lladró figures since I was a little girl."

"They're exquisite."

"Thank you."

Seeing Debbie by the shelves, Judith had a devilish idea.

"What's that one up there?" she said, pointing to a porcelain mermaid on the top shelf.

"That's very rare, and really rather valuable. It's late nineteenth century."

"Maybe you could reach up and get it down?"

Judith mimed reaching up, and her two friends realized what she was doing. Debbie was wearing a dark green shirt, and Judith was hoping that if Debbie reached up high enough, she'd expose her midriff for them to see whether she had a diamond-shaped birthmark on her skin.

"You think I can reach up there?" Debbie said, surprised. After all, they could all see that the shelf was out of reach.

"I'm sure you could if you tried."

Once again, Judith put her hands up to encourage Debbie to do the same. Debbie wasn't having any of it.

"It's far too precious for me to get down, it's worth at least a thousand pounds."

"Of course," Becks agreed. "You can't risk smashing it," she added in a message to Judith to drop the subject.

"What exactly was it you wanted to see me about?" Debbie asked. "I'll need to take stock of all of those ducks in a minute."

"We just wanted to hear a bit more about Geoffrey," Becks said.

"I told the officer who was here all I knew."

"But he was a man, wasn't he? I'm sure he didn't listen properly. And I can imagine how upset you've been since the tragic event."

"You're right, he seemed to have no interest in how Geoffrey's death has affected me. If anything, he treated me like I was a suspect."

"I suppose that was because of your fingerprints on the used coffee capsule," Suzie said.

"But I explained how that happened. I made my coffee after Geoffrey had made his. And when I went to put my coffee capsule in the machine, I saw that his hadn't cleared properly. You know what it's like with those machines. It's so easy for them to get jammed. So I opened the front, took Geoffrey's capsule out, and put it in the little bin. I then closed the machine back up again and made my coffee as usual."

"You're so right," Becks agreed. "Those machines can be so fiddly."

"Thank you," Debbie said, glad to have her version of events vindicated. "But can I ask you something in return? The policeman told me Geoffrey's capsule was full of poison. Is that really true?"

"I'm afraid it is," Judith said.

"But how on earth did poison get into it?"

"Rather sadly, the police have to presume someone put it there on purpose."

"But that's not possible. It's like I said, Geoffrey was one of the most moral people I knew. Why would anyone want to harm him?"

"Sophia and Marcus said the same thing," Judith said. "They both told us stories about how kind he was."

The women could see that Judith's statement had appealed to Debbie's competitive streak.

"As it happens, I've a story that proves that point as well," she said. "A couple of years ago, I had a bit of a health scare. Nothing life-threatening—or so it turned out in the end. But it was worrying at the time. I mentioned to Geoffrey that I was having tests at the hospital, and he dropped everything and said whenever I had to go, he'd drive me. There really was no need. I have a car of my own, but he wouldn't take no for an answer. The parking at the hospital is always difficult, he said, I should be spared that. And he always was there. Every appointment. He dropped me off and picked me up. Never let me down."

"That's lovely," Becks said.

"It is, isn't it?"

"He really was a saint."

"Although, would you say Jeremy would agree?" Judith asked.

"What makes you ask?"

"He kind of lost his temper with you all right before Geoffrey died," Suzie said. "I saw it with my own eyes."

"That's just Jeremy being Jeremy. He's a tin-pot Hitler when it comes to rules and regulations."

The women saw Debbie frown.

"What is it?" Becks asked.

"Well, if you're talking about him having a temper, it's made me remember something. I'm sure it's nothing."

Judith rootled in her handbag and pulled out her tin of travel sweets.

"How about you tell us, and then we can decide together. Would you like a sweet?"

Debbie was delighted by the offer.

"Thank you," she said as she popped a sweet into her mouth. "I'm sure it's nothing, but I overheard Geoffrey having a right old set-to with Jeremy a few weeks ago. It was at the end of a Rotary meeting, so I'm sure it was nothing to do with council business. We're all on the Rotary together and, if you ask me, there's been a real atmosphere between Geoffrey and Jeremy ever since."

"What was the argument about?"

"I don't know. I saw them by Geoffrey's car in the car park. Jeremy looked very angry, and I heard Geoffrey say to him something like, 'I'm not giving it back to you.'"

"'I'm not giving it back to you'?" Suzie repeated, to make sure they'd heard correctly.

"That's right. Or words to that effect. I got in my car and drove off. Although, now you mention it, I wonder if that's incriminating? That they argued."

"Do you think Jeremy's capable of committing murder?"

Debbie sucked on her sweet while she considered her answer.

"You know what? I think not only could he commit murder, he's the kind of man who could go on a killing spree. You know the sort, where the neighbors say, 'He was so quiet, he caused us no bother,' but you look at his mug shot and you're thinking you've never seen anyone look more like a killer in your life."

Judith and her friends looked at each other. Was it possible? Was Jeremy Wessel their killer?

Chapter 11

AS JUDITH, SUZIE, AND BECKS left Debbie's house, Becks turned to Judith.

"You promised you wouldn't look for a birthmark!" Becks said.

"But I didn't," Judith said, in faux innocence.

"You did!"

"I wasn't looking for a birthmark, I was just asking Debbie to reach to a top shelf."

"You're incorrigible."

"I do hope so, imagine being corrigible! How boring."

"But what do we think of Debbie Bell?" Suzie asked.

"I don't know," Becks said. "She wasn't as negative as I thought she'd be."

"She was pretty negative," Suzie said.

"But those figures she collects are rather romantic, and very pretty. I think there's more to Debbie Bell than meets the eye."

"And what about her working for Sophia's husband?" Suzie asked. "Is there anything in that?"

"It's possible. Although you know what Marlow's like. Everyone works for everyone else. Anyway, I'd better be getting back to the vicarage."

"What are you talking about?" Judith said. "You're on important police business."

"I really have to get on. I agreed to make the sandwiches for this after-noon's meeting of the U3A in the Liston Hall."

"But Debbie reckons Jeremy could be our killer," Suzie added. "We need to go and talk to him."

"Tanika only gave us permission to talk to Debbie."

"Listen to you! Is this the Becks who made a small fortune from crypto-currency? The Becks who rallied the whole town to move an oak tree in the middle of a storm?"

Becks couldn't stop herself from feeling a little sunburst of joy at Suzie's description of her, but she was distracted by her phone ringing. She saw that it was Colin and guessed he was trying to find out why she wasn't already in the vicarage making sandwiches.

She pressed the red icon that dropped the call.

"You know what?" she said decisively. "I think I'd very much like to go and interview Jeremy."

A quick search on the internet revealed that Jeremy Wessel's architect's practice was based on the Globe industrial park on the eastern side of the town. As Suzie drove them to it, Becks's phone rang again. It was Colin again.

"I'd better tell him what I'm up to," Becks said. "I'm sorry, Colin," she said as she took the call, "but I don't have time to make sandwiches today."

"That's OK," Colin said on the other end of the line. "I figured you must be busy helping the police—but that's why I'm calling. I've done some digging into your graves story, pardon the pun."

"Sorry, you *don't* mind me not helping?"

"But you are helping—just the police rather than me, and I think that's a touch more important. Now let me tell you what I've found out about your Sophia De Castro."

"Oh, hold on," Becks said, "let me put you on speakerphone."

Becks fiddled with her phone.

"Can you hear me OK?" Colin said from the speaker.

"Clear as day," Judith said.

"Well, it's fascinating, this one. It turns out we've got the old records here in Marlow. And your Sophia De Castro made a real mess-up. There were plots that had been prereserved for one family that she allowed to go on the general list, so two different women and a man who'd been waiting their whole life to be buried next to their deceased spouses discovered that complete strangers had been buried in their plots ahead of them. Even though they'd bought them years before."

"That's horrible," Becks said.

"But it's worse than that, because when Sophia tried to sort it out, she only made it worse—getting headstones moved from one grave to another and getting it wrong again. There's even one poor family who lost their dead relative altogether, can you believe it? Not knowing where your uncle or whoever-it-was is buried?"

"Why on earth wasn't she prosecuted?" Judith asked.

"That's where it gets interesting. We've got letters in the archive that Geoffrey Lushington wrote to the bishop of Oxford. We're in his diocese. And you should see them. They're so impassioned, so convincing in begging for forgiveness for Sophia—they're really the most perfect examples of how to butter up a bishop. You know, it's all 'The quality of mercy is not strained,' that sort of thing."

"'It droppeth as the gentle rain from heaven upon the place beneath,'" Judith said, continuing the quotation from *The Merchant of Venice*.

"Exactly. Your Mr. Lushington really was a very impressive man," Colin said, summing up. "He doesn't bully or blackmail, and it's clear his actions are about as altruistic as it's possible to get. He didn't want a young woman to be tarnished by what was an honest mistake."

"Well, that's fascinating," Judith said. "Thank you for helping, Colin."

"Glad to. Oh, and Becks, Mother says you need a night off, so she wants to cook dinner for us all tonight. One of Sam's favorites."

"She can't!" Becks said.

Judith and Suzie were startled by Becks's vehemence.

"She's only offering to help, darling."

"She's not, she's trying to belittle me."

"I know that's how it often looks, but on this occasion—"

Becks leaned forward and hissed into the phone, "I do the cooking in my home. If she wants to help, she can change the sheets on her bed, or clean her room—or maybe just go out for the evening and stop getting in the way!"

There was a pause from the other end of the line.

"I think that's a bit mean—"

"What's Sam's favorite meal?"

"That's easy. Burger and fries."

"Right. And what have I banned from the dining table?"

Colin's silence confirmed that he finally understood what was going on. Becks had decided the family should cut down on meat and empty carbs as much as possible. It was better for the environment and their health. So, beefburgers had been replaced with vegan burgers, and french fries had been replaced with homemade sweet potato wedges. It had been a long and grueling road to enlightenment, but Becks had finally, after many months of cajoling, got the family to agree that pea burger and sweet potato was just as good a meal as beefburger and fries.

"Oh," Colin said. "I see what you mean."

"She's doing this on purpose," Becks said. "You can see that, can't you?"

"She's already told Sam he can have whatever he wants."

"Well, he can't. While she's under my roof, she'll eat what she's offered. Can you tell her?"

"Me? Sure," Colin said, but everyone in the van could tell from his hesitant tone that he wouldn't.

"You better had," Becks said tightly, and then hung up.

Suzie and Judith waited for Becks to explain.

"My mother-in-law's come to stay," Becks admitted.

Suzie guffawed.

"You don't say?"

"I know it's a stereotype—the difficult mother-in-law—but she's so much worse than difficult, she's positively evil."

"That's quite strong," Judith said.

"On my wedding day, she wore her wedding dress."

"What?" Suzie said.

"Can you imagine? Marian not only wore white, which is bad enough, it was her actual wedding dress. She'd had it shortened, of course, to show off her legs—she's got fabulous legs, and didn't we all see them that day. But she wanted all my friends to see that she was the original bride—with a chaser of 'and I can still fit into my wedding dress' on the side."

"Oh," Judith said. "That *is* evil."

"Colin's dad finally left her three years ago after a lifetime of putting up with her. She's like a child, she won't take responsibility. Ever since she's been spending her money on herself—on whatever she wants. Then, when the money ran out, she sold her house and moved into a bungalow. But does she learn her lesson? She keeps on spending—taking taxis everywhere, buying expensive clothes, having her hair done every week—it's all about doing what Marian wants. Then, when the money ran out again, she sold her bungalow and moved into rented accommodation. But guess what? Soon she couldn't even afford that. So she's come to stay with us. And now it feels like her life's work is to undermine me at every opportunity."

"Oh, OK," Suzie said. "Have you thought of killing her?"

"On a daily basis," Becks said. "But what can I do? She's Colin's mother and Sam and Chloe's granny, I can't just boot her out. Can I?"

"You could put her in Suzie's pod hotel," Judith said.

"Ha!" Becks laughed. "I'd be delighted to."

Suzie adjusted the rearview mirror on her van, and Judith got the impression that her friend was pretending she hadn't heard her joke.

"What's up?" Judith asked.

"What?" Suzie said, as if she didn't know what Judith was talking about.

"You've gone quiet."

"Me? No. I'm never quiet."

"Except for now. Something's up, isn't it?"

"It's just…it's funny you should mention the hotel. You see, I've hit a bit of a snag. I was checking over the plans online, and you know how I said a basic unit's eight pods wide and two pods tall?"

"That's how you're going to get it to fit under the height of your fence," Judith said.

"It turns out I read the plans wrong. The basic unit's not eight pods wide and two tall, it's two wide and eight pods tall."

After a moment of surprise, Judith burst out laughing, and Becks put her hand over her mouth to hide her broad smile.

"You were going to build a tower in your back garden eight hotel rooms high but only two wide?"

"It's not funny," Suzie said. "I've put a lot of work into this and it's all gone to waste."

"No, of course," Becks said, instantly sympathetic. "It must be so frustrating for you."

"It's *quite* funny," Judith said.

Suzie frowned as she drove, and then she sniffed as she considered her situation.

"It *is* quite funny," she reluctantly agreed.

"How tall would this structure have been?" Judith asked.

"Twenty-one meters."

The friends couldn't help but laugh at the idea of a structure twenty-one meters tall in Suzie's back garden.

"I'm such an idiot," Suzie said. "Rubbish. Idiots don't catch killers."

"Or raise two kids so brilliantly," Becks added.

"You think I did a good job?"

"Both your daughters have partners, have jobs they like, and are happy."

"No, you're right. They are."

"And you can take a lot of credit for that. I think it's amazing how you've always hustled. With your dog-walking business, or your radio show, or this hotel idea. You're always looking out for opportunities, and when you find one, you pounce on it. Although, don't you find it exhausting hustling for everything?"

"How do you mean?"

"Obviously you had to when the children were small, but they've set up their lives now, and you've got yours just about right as well. A freelance dog-walking job that gives you plenty of time for other interests."

"Other interests like catching killers," Judith said.

"And a radio show on Sunday nights for you to connect with the rest of the town. That sounds like a full and rewarding life, if you ask me."

Suzie realized that maybe Becks was right. A lifetime of scrabbling to have enough cash to keep her afloat had left her always trying to play the angles of any situation for her benefit, but what if she decided to accept that she was happy instead? It was a radical idea as far as she was concerned, but she wasn't able to interrogate it any further as she pulled up outside the address for Jeremy's business.

As the women got out of the van, they couldn't help but notice that they were in one of the oldest parts of the industrial park. Not every unit was occupied, and the paint on the windows of Jeremy's office was peeling.

"Could do with an architect," Suzie said as they approached.

After they knocked on the door, Jeremy answered with a swaggering smile.

"Good day, ladies. Hey, I recognize you," he added, looking at Suzie. "You were in the viewing gallery when Geoffrey died, weren't you?"

"I was," Suzie said.

"Well, isn't that a coincidence. That you'd tip up here a few days later."

"It's not a coincidence—we're working with the police," Suzie said, proffering her lanyard.

"While also still being civilians," Becks added.

"Oh well, that's a turn-up for the books," Jeremy said appreciatively.

"And we've got a few questions we'd like to ask about your relationship with Mr. Lushington," Judith said.

There was the tiniest twitch at the corner of Jeremy's eye.

"You'd better come in," he said with a smile.

The women could see that Jeremy's smile wasn't very confident. In fact, it wasn't really a smile at all. The women followed him inside, scenting blood.

Chapter 12

JEREMY LED THE WOMEN INTO a small office that had an architect's easel by the sole window and a computer on a large desk that was balanced between two filing cabinets. On closer inspection, Judith could see that the desk was actually a cheap door.

"I was just making a cup of tea," he said. "Would anyone care to join me?"

"That's very kind," Judith said. "I'd love a cup."

"Me too," Suzie said. "Two sugars if you've got it."

"Of course. And how about you?" Jeremy asked Becks.

"I'm fine, thank you," Becks said.

Jeremy went over to a little kitchen area and popped the kettle on.

"If I'm honest, I'm glad of the distraction. I've spent the morning on the placement of the sinks in the new toilet block of the rugby club."

"You're doing the development of the rugby club?" Suzie asked.

"I am," Jeremy said.

"And you sit on the council planning committee?" Judith asked.

"Don't worry, I always recuse myself when one of my projects comes up before the committee. You can't mark your own homework. What were you doing at the meeting?" he asked Suzie as he handed out the cups of tea.

Suzie didn't have the heart to lie.

"I was thinking of putting in planning permission for a hotel," she said.

"Big plans!" Jeremy said, impressed.

"Not big as such," Suzie said ruefully. "More, tall and thin."

"Actually, we've met before," Judith said. "I got you out to look at my roof a few years ago. See if it needed a redesign."

"Sorry, I don't remember. I do lots of little jobs."

"In the end I didn't employ you."

Jeremy didn't pick up on the implied criticism.

"That would explain why I don't remember, I suppose," he said. "Now, how can I help you?"

"We've just got a few questions about Geoffrey," Judith asked.

"'Course. Shoot—although that seems in bad taste now," Jeremy added. "What do you want to know?"

"Well, we've spoken to Sophia, Marcus, and Debbie, and they've all said what a good man Geoffrey was."

"He was that, I'd agree with you there."

"Although you argued with him the night he died," Suzie said.

"That wasn't really arguing, that was more me letting myself get wound up. I shouldn't, really. I'm my own worst enemy sometimes."

"You also said you'd been under a lot of pressure," Suzie said.

"I said that, did I? Well, I suppose all I meant was I'm a one-man band here. And I've got a lot of work on at the moment."

"I don't know, it seemed more than that. You accused Geoffrey of patronizing you."

"That's because he does. Typical layman, frankly. They read a couple of books on Frank Gehry and think they know everything about architecture."

"A little knowledge is a dangerous thing," Judith said.

"Got it in a nutshell. Marlow's a heritage town. You can't get away from that. It's why we get the tourists—the fact that we've got seventeenth-, eighteenth-, and nineteenth-century buildings all jostling next to each other. That doesn't mean there's no room for modernism, but it has to be simpatico with what went before. Geoffrey never understood that relationship. Not that things ever got out of hand," Jeremy added hurriedly. "Especially seeing as I always got my way. Sophia and Debbie in particular were opposed to dropping brightly colored buildings made of plastic into the middle of the High Street.

I could always rely on their votes if things ever got contentious. But don't get the wrong idea. Any proper disagreements we had were once-in-a-blue-moon events. Most of what we did was rubber-stamping perfectly good proposals from residents."

Judith could see that Jeremy had recovered his poise, and she decided to shake him up a bit. "Is there anything specific you and Geoffrey argued about recently?"

"I can't say there is."

"Is that so?" Judith said, looking carefully at Jeremy. "Debbie told us you and Geoffrey argued after a recent Rotary meeting."

Jeremy's eye twitched again.

"She did?" he said as he tried to remember, although the women could see that he knew exactly what they were talking about.

"Geoffrey was overheard telling you 'I'm not giving it back to you.'"

Jeremy licked his lips, his mind whirring, and then his face brightened.

"She thought that was an argument?" he said with a laugh. "Really, Debbie is a pain sometimes. Don't tell anyone I told you that, but she's the committee's resident misery guts. She sees the worst in any situation. Seriously."

"Can you tell us what actually happened that night?"

"It wasn't an argument, that's the first thing you should know. Or a disagreement in any way. Geoffrey was taunting me, that's all. As a joke."

"He was?"

"He and I love a tipple of whisky. It's the main thing we bonded over. And we'd often go for a quick drink after our planning meetings and talk about any particularly fine single malts we'd come across since the last time we'd met. Geoffrey loved peaty whiskies, that was his particular interest. So when I came across a bottle of Japanese whisky that I have to confess I couldn't distinguish from a malt distilled on Jura, I knew I had to lend him the bottle. I wasn't wrong in guessing Geoffrey would like it. He liked it so much he didn't want to return the bottle to me. That's all he meant when he said, 'I'm not giving it back to you.' He was saying the whisky was too good to give back to me. It made me laugh, if I'm honest. I could understand his obsession. I like something a bit more floral—with a proper tang of sulfur—so I didn't mind him keeping the bottle."

"What was the brand?" Judith asked, not believing Jeremy's story for a second.

"It was Kyoto Gold. If you like whisky, you really should give it a whirl. It's remarkable."

"So if we looked in Geoffrey's house, we'd find a bottle of Kyoto Gold?"

"Of course. Unless he's drunk it. He did like to quaff."

"You think he'll have got through a bottle in the last—when was the Rotary meeting?"

"Three weeks ago, I'd say. And yes, he was more than capable of getting through a bottle in three weeks. He lived on his own, and there really wasn't anything stopping him from having a decent slug of the amber liquid every night."

Suzie and Becks shared a look, both of them knowing that it would never take Judith as long as three weeks to get through a bottle of whisky.

"So," Jeremy said, feeling he'd successfully navigated the interview, "I'd discount Debbie's catastrophizing about arguments, and instead focus on the fact that Geoffrey and I were always on good enough terms to go drinking together, and for me to give him bottles of whisky. Seriously. Any disagreements we ever had were just local squalls, entirely professional, and they never amounted to a hill of beans."

"Then can I ask," Judith said, "if Geoffrey had any money troubles?"

"None that I can think of. He never mentioned any money worries to me."

"I see. So if I were to say 'follow the money' to you, what would you say?"

Jeremy shrugged.

"Doesn't mean anything to me. Oh, God, your sugar!" Jeremy suddenly said, interrupting himself. "I forgot to offer you any," he said to Suzie as he turned his back on the women and returned to the kitchen area.

"It's no bother," Suzie said. "I'm supposed to be cutting down anyway."

"Don't worry, here you go," he said, bringing over a little bowl full of sugar.

Seeing the sugar prompted a thought for Judith.

"You didn't have a cup of tea at the planning meeting, did you?" she asked.

"As it happens, no. And nor did I have any coffee, before you ask. But Geoffrey did, if that's what you're getting at. A cup of coffee with two lumps of sugar."

"You saw him put sugar in his coffee?"

"Sure. So?"

"Could you tell us what sort of receptacle the sugar was kept in?" Judith asked eagerly.

Jeremy was nonplussed by the question.

"It was in one of those glass jars. You know, with a lid on a metal hinge and an orange seal."

"You mean a Kilner jar?" Becks said.

"That's the one—the sugar cubes were in a little Kilner jar."

"And did you see the jar after Geoffrey died?" Judith.

"You really do ask the oddest questions," Jeremy said with a chuckle, having now entirely regathered his poise. "As it happens, I did. It was still on the table, by Geoffrey's cup. I remember noticing how it hadn't been knocked over, even though Geoffrey had tipped off his chair."

"The glass jar of sugar cubes was definitely still on the table?"

"Oh, yes."

Judith thanked Jeremy for his time and ushered her friends outside.

"What is it?" Becks asked.

"We work for the police," Judith said.

"Sure do," Suzie said, lifting her lanyard.

"In an advisory role," Becks added.

"Then I think Tanika has to let the three of us inspect the murder scene. Because we've just found out the sugar was kept in a glass jar that night. Ladies, I think we need to find that jar."

Chapter 13

TANIKA WASN'T SURE IT WAS a good idea letting her civilian advisers loose on the murder scene. In fact, she was pretty sure it was a terrible idea. But forensics had finished with the debating chamber, and she had to admit that she was intrigued by Jeremy's revelation that he'd seen a Kilner jar of sugar on the table after Geoffrey died.

As Tanika unlocked the main door to the building and entered, Judith looked up at a little security camera that was mounted on the wall above the door.

"Is that the camera that had its cable cut?" she asked.

"It is," Tanika agreed. "You can see the cable was cut here," she said, indicating a gray cable that ran down the wall. It had been severed at knee height.

"It's really odd that it had to be disabled," Judith said, looking at the corridor. The setting was so unremarkable, really. The door to the debating chamber was on the right-hand side and was covered in POLICE DO NOT CROSS tape. There were three other doors that opened on to council offices on the left, and a staircase at the end that led upstairs. To its side there was a gray public pay phone under a scratched plastic hood, and on the wall there were various council-related posters and a single oil painting of a man in breeches and a tricorn hat from hundreds of years ago.

"It must have been the killer who nobbled it," Suzie said.

"I agree," Judith said. "But why? We know Geoffrey was murdered by one of the people in the same room as him, so why didn't they want to be seen arriving along this corridor? What are we missing?"

"Come on," Tanika said, as she peeled off the police tape and unlocked the door to the debating chamber. "We've got a jar of sugar to find."

As the women entered, Judith asked Suzie, "Where were you sitting?"

"Up here," Suzie said, indicating the viewing gallery they were already standing on.

"And you're sure you don't recall anyone offering Geoffrey any sugar?"

"To be honest, I wasn't paying that close attention."

"I suppose the most likely place to look is the kitchen," Judith said as she went down the little steps to the main floor, crossed the room, and went through the door that led to the kitchenette.

"So have there been any developments since we last spoke?" Tanika asked.

"Hardly," Suzie said. "Debbie explained that her fingerprints were on Geoffrey's coffee capsule because it had got jammed in the Nespresso machine and she had to clear it before she could use the machine. Although she did tell us about an argument between Geoffrey and Jeremy Wessel. When we spoke to him just now, he claimed it was about a bottle of whisky, but it didn't ring true, if you ask me."

Tanika's desire to hear about the women's conversation with Jeremy narrowly outweighed her desire to tick them off for talking to him without clearing it with her first.

"Why's that?" she asked.

"Jeremy acted pretty dodge about it."

"He might have been nervous talking to us," Becks offered.

"No, it was more than that. He's hiding something," Suzie said.

"Could he be our killer?" Tanika asked.

"Could be," Suzie said. "Debbie Bell said she reckoned he was capable of murder. But my money's still on Sophia De Castro. All that positivity is enough to make anyone look suspicious, if you ask me. And what sort of person grows a load of poison in their garden in the first place? That tells me all I need to know."

Tanika smiled. Like the others, she'd got used to Suzie's snap judgments long ago.

"How about you?" Becks asked Tanika. "Have you been able to make any progress?"

"We have," Tanika said. "We've identified the phone number of the anonymous call Judith received."

"Really?" Judith said, her head briefly appearing at the kitchen hatch.

"The call was placed from the public telephone box outside the hockey club. But before you get too excited, I sent one of my officers to check it over and he reported that the surfaces of the phone had been wiped clean of fingerprints. Whoever it was who rang you really doesn't want to be identified.

"And I'm sorry to report, 'follow the money' hasn't led to any breakthroughs, either. I've had our team of forensic accountants go through Geoffrey's bank accounts a second time, and they say he wasn't a big spender, he lived well within his means, and he only had the one bank account. There's no financial irregularities going on with him. So it makes me wonder, what else could 'follow the money' refer to?"

"Could it be council money our anonymous caller is talking about?" Becks asked. "I sit on enough committees to know there's always the possibility to embezzle."

"The town council's archive of historical documents are stored upstairs in the main office. I'll get a warrant to take them to the police station."

"I think that's a good idea. But it can't be only the planning meeting documents. It should be all the committees that Geoffrey sits on. And not just him, you should take anything that's connected to the other members of the planning committee as well. The phrase 'follow the money' is as likely to refer to one of them as it is to Geoffrey. In fact, it's more likely to refer to one of them, considering what people are telling us about Geoffrey."

"I agree," said Tanika. "And you're right about Mr. Lushington. We've not found anyone with a bad word to say about him. He really was loved by everyone. Oh, and we spoke to Marcus Percival's sister—like you suggested. She backed up everything Mr. Percival told you. About how Mr. Lushington helped her financially, but how it was more than that for him. He couldn't bear to think of her being unhappy, and he did everything he could to get her on the straight and narrow. He got a friend to give her a job and encouraged her to go to church. She told me the church and the job gave her the support she needed to kick the booze. She's been clean for these last three years."

"I don't believe it!" Suzie said, royally fed up. "Everyone says how great Geoffrey is—but someone's lying, aren't they? Because someone had reason to murder him. Who was it, and why did he have to die?"

"There's no Kilner jar of sugar cubes in the kitchenette," Judith said, returning to the debating chamber. "So let's think," she said, heading over to the main table. "Jeremy said he saw the jar on the table immediately after Geoffrey died. Let's say it was removed by one of the four people who were at the meeting," she said, moving to the large table in the middle of the room. "Suzie, did you stay up there afterward?"

"Not exactly," Suzie said. "I came down to the floor, but I was told I wasn't needed."

"Is that so?" Tanika asked.

"It was Jeremy. He said they could handle it, and I could see Debbie was calling for an ambulance, so I went back out to the corridor and phoned Judith and Becks."

"Did anyone leave the debating chamber during that time?" Judith asked.

"No."

"So no one could have smuggled the jar past you," Judith said as if this proved her point. "Although I suppose it's possible one of the four other members of the committee might have briefly slipped out through the fire door in the kitchenette."

"I think one of the others would have noticed if someone had gone through that fire door," Tanika said. "In their statements, all four witnesses said they stayed with the body—together—until the ambulance and police arrived. And then they all left together and gave their formal statements next door in the Marlow Museum."

"So, let's think," Judith said, turning on the spot to take in the room. "If I had to get rid of the sugar—and quickly—and there were witnesses everywhere, and no way in or out, what would I do?"

Judith took a step toward some nearby filing cabinets. Opening the drawers one by one, she looked inside and then called back to the others in triumph, "Now what have we here?"

"You've got it?" Suzie said in disbelief, as she and the others went over to join their friend.

Judith had pulled some hanging files forward and was peering into the back of the filing cabinet.

"Has anyone got a flashlight?" she asked.

Becks, Tanika, and Suzie all got out their phones, turned on their flashlight functions, and shone their lights into the back of the drawer where they all saw a small glass Kilner jar lying on its side. It was full of sugar cubes.

"Well, that really is very gratifying," Judith said.

"OK, everyone, let's step away from the filing cabinet," Tanika said, before going over to some evidence bags that had been left by her team. She fished out a clear cellophane bag, briefly putting it down so she could get out a pair of light blue evidence gloves.

"Blue gloves!" Suzie exclaimed as she saw them.

"Yes, blue gloves," Tanika said, her focus on turning the evidence bag inside out. She picked up the Kilner jar with the bag, turned the bag the right way around so the jar was now held inside, and then she carefully ripped the gummed seal and sealed it tight.

Judith and Becks could see that Suzie was looking at the kitchenette hatch as though she'd just seen a ghost.

"Problem?" Judith asked.

"Did the other witnesses mention the guy in the kitchen?" Suzie asked.

"What's that?" Tanika said.

"I only remembered when you put on those blue gloves. The guy that night was wearing the same sort—you know, see-through catering gloves. It seemed like overkill to me."

"What are you talking about?"

"There was someone in the kitchenette before the meeting."

Tanika's mouth opened in surprise.

"*What?*" she said.

"He was gone before the meeting started—that's why I didn't think to mention him. I suppose he was the person who got all the tea things ready for the meeting."

"And the coffee?" Judith asked.

"I don't know. The coffee machine and urn—and all the cups and saucers—were already on the counter when I got here."

Suzie realized how bad it sounded, and Tanika looked suitably exasperated.

"You didn't happen to catch this person's name, did you?"

"I'm sorry," Suzie said sheepishly. "I'd not seen him before. And he was gone before I really clocked him."

"Then, in answer to your question, none of the witnesses mentioned anyone serving in the kitchen that night."

"They didn't?" Judith asked.

"So I'm going to get this Kilner jar back to the station," Tanika said tightly. "And then I'm going to go back to everyone on the planning committee to ask if they know who the person in the kitchen was. And why none of them have mentioned this person before now."

Chapter 14

ONCE TANIKA HAD DRIVEN OFF with the glass jar, Judith and her friends were left standing in the car park, although Judith could see that Becks was deep in thought.

"I feel like such a lemon," Suzie said.

"I wouldn't worry," Judith said. "I'm sure Tanika will be able to work out who our mystery server is. What is it, Becks?" she added.

"What's that?" Becks asked.

"You looked a hundred miles away."

"Oh, it's nothing."

"It's clearly not nothing."

"It's just, we *aren't* the police, are we?"

"We've never said we were," Suzie said in what they all knew was a blatant lie.

"But if I tell you both what I know, then you're going to go off and start acting like the police."

"We won't," Suzie said.

"What is it that you know?" Judith asked.

Becks bit her lip, trying to work out the right thing to do.

"Here's an idea," Judith said. "How about I promise that, whatever you say, we'll tell Tanika and won't do anything unless she agrees to it first."

"OK," Becks said, Judith's words finally convincing her. "The thing is, I know the person who serves tea for all of the council meetings."

"You do?" Suzie asked, delighted.

"His name's Alec Miller. He's been doing it for years."

"How do you know this?" Judith asked.

"He does the functions in the church hall as well. It's a bit of a sideline for him since he retired."

"Do you by any chance know where he lives?"

"He's got a cottage up by Wiley's Field. I sometimes help him get his sandwiches and drinks into his van and drive down with him."

"Then what are we waiting for?" Judith said, leading to Suzie's van, Suzie bustling after her friend.

"Where are you going?" Becks asked.

"We've got to talk to Alec Miller!"

"You promised we'd talk to Tanika!"

"And so we shall—but she's busy with the Kilner jar, it makes sense we make a start, and *then* we report to her."

Becks sighed, perhaps having known in her heart of hearts that this was how Judith and Suzie would react. As she climbed into the passenger side of the van, she said, "Is there nothing you wouldn't say to make sure you get your own way?"

"I've not found it yet," Judith said with a broad smile.

Alec Miller lived in a small cottage that abutted an undeveloped field at the top of Marlow. As the women got out of Suzie's van, Suzie stopped to look over the old gate that led into the field.

"What is it?" Becks asked.

"This is one of the last bits of Marlow that's not been developed," Suzie said. "But it's all going to change," she added, indicating a planning notice that was cable tied to the gate. "They're going to concrete it over and build a load of houses."

Becks could see that the notice announced the field was about to be developed into a housing estate. Any objections were to be lodged with Marlow town council.

"The town desperately needs new houses," Becks said.

"Not by bulldozing fields, they don't," Suzie said.

"Come on," Judith said, and led her friends up to Alec's house, a pair of muddy boots by the porch, a peeling "Neighborhood Watch" sticker in the window.

"So what do we reckon?" Suzie asked. "Are we about to talk to the killer?"

"I don't think Alec's a likely killer," Becks said. "He's just a lovely old boy. You know the sort."

"'Lovely old boys' can still commit murder," Judith said.

"Of course. But I can't imagine what would drive Alec to such extremes. You'll see."

Becks knocked on the door.

A man called out "hold on" from inside, and then they heard feet shuffling toward them.

The door opened, and a tall, thin man in his seventies stood before them in a bottle-green cardigan and brown cords, holding an old pair of binoculars. His dark hair was thinning, but neatly combed, and his lined face broke into a warm smile at the sight of Becks.

"Hello, Mrs. Starling. I was just watching the swifts in the field," he said, holding up his binoculars. "You get the most tremendous view from my top window."

"But you're not him," Suzie blurted.

"What's that?"

"You're not Alec Miller."

"I am," he said. "Who else would I be?" he added with a chuckle. "I've lived in this house man and boy, and I've been Alec Miller since the day I was born."

"But I saw the guy serving at the town planning meeting, and he wasn't you. He wasn't as tall as you, for starters."

"What are you talking about?"

Judith stepped in to clear up the confusion.

"I'm sorry, Mr. Miller, but are you the person who runs the kitchen during meetings at the town council building?"

"I am," Alec said, happy to be back on firmer ground. "It's only part-time, but I prepare the sandwiches and refreshments whenever they have special meetings or receptions. Like I do with the church. Isn't that right, Mrs. Starling?"

"It is," Becks agreed.

"I enjoy the work and it gets me out of the house."

"But you weren't serving on the night that Geoffrey Lushington died, were you?" Suzie asked.

"Ah, got it," Alec said. "I see where you're coming from. No, you're right, I wasn't there that night."

"Why not?" Judith said.

"Well, it's a strange one," Alec said as he cast his mind back. "I was supposed to do the teas and whatnots for the planning meeting as usual, but I got a phone call that morning telling me I wouldn't be needed."

"Who was it from?"

"No idea. A woman."

"Are you sure it was a woman?"

"Oh, yes."

"Can you describe her voice at all?"

"I'm not sure. It was quite breathy."

Judith knew there was only one female suspect with a breathy voice.

"Is it possible it was Sophia De Castro?" she asked.

"I don't know—I don't know the name."

"Hold on," Becks said, getting out her phone. She swiped and jabbed at its screen until she'd opened her podcasts app. "I've started subscribing to Sophia's podcast. It's fascinating, actually. She really got me thinking about homeopathy. There's so much about the world we don't know."

"We know homeopathy's a nonsense," Judith said.

"You say that, but do we ever really know anything for sure?"

"Yes. We know homeopathy's a nonsense."

"Look," Suzie said, trying to get her friends back on track. "This isn't the time."

"No, of course," Becks agreed, and pressed the play icon on her screen.

Out of her phone's speaker, it was possible to hear Sophia intone, "'To keep the body in good health is a duty.'"

"That's her!" Alec said, amazed.

Sophia's voice continued speaking, "'Otherwise we shall not be able to keep our mind strong and clear.' Those aren't my words, although they sound a lot like the sort of thing I'd say. No, they were spoken many years ago by a man called Buddha."

"'A man called Buddha'!" Judith snorted.

"Not now, Judith," Suzie said.

"You're right," Alec said, pointing at Beck's phone. "I'd recognize that voice anywhere. That's the person who phoned me that morning and told me I wasn't needed that evening."

"Did she give a reason?"

"She said the meeting had been canceled, so they wouldn't need me. I'll be honest, I didn't think any more of it after that. Although I can tell you, she was pretty rude about it. Abrupt. And when I tried to ask her why it had all been called off, she hung up. High-handed, that's how I'd describe her. But she'd been clear enough. The meeting wasn't going ahead. So I didn't turn up. And I didn't think any more of it."

"Not even when Mr. Lushington died?"

Alec had the good grace to look uncomfortable.

"I didn't think it was relevant."

"A man is poisoned with coffee—which you normally prepare—at a meeting that you'd been told wasn't going ahead, and you don't think it's relevant?"

"I live up here on my own. I just want an easy life," he said almost plaintively.

"Then I'm sorry to say that that's ended," Judith said. "You'll have to speak to the police."

"Couldn't you do it for me?"

"Absolutely not. The police will have to take a formal statement from you."

Alec looked worried.

"Don't worry," Becks said. "We know the woman running the case. We'll get her to send you a nice officer."

"Thanks, Mrs. Starling. It's much appreciated."

"Please, it's Becks."

"No, you treat the vicar's wife with the respect she deserves. It's the proper way of doing things."

Judith thanked Alec for his help and said there wasn't any reason to detain him any longer. As they left, Suzie was quiet.

"What is it?" Becks asked.

"It's great we know it was Sophia who stopped Alec from going in that evening, but if it wasn't him I saw in the kitchenette—and it wasn't, I know that much—who was it?"

"Do you really not remember what he looked like?" Judith asked.

"I don't know. He had blue catering gloves on his hands, that's all I really noticed. And he was definitely much shorter than Alec Miller."

"I know!" Becks said. "How about we play a game of Guess Who?"

"That's what I'm trying to do."

"No, the game, Guess Who."

"I wouldn't call this a game," Judith said. "A man's been murdered."

"No, I mean the kids' game, Guess Who. Chloe loved it when she was small. You have a number of tiles with faces on them, and you flip them over as you eliminate facial features. So, think really hard, Suzie. Really imagine yourself back in the debating chamber. There's someone serving in the kitchenette. Can you see him?"

Suzie closed her eyes as she tried to remember.

"Yes."

"Dark hair or light?"

"Light."

"Blond or another color?"

"Blond."

"Long hair or short?"

"Short."

"Curly or straight?"

"Straight."

"Glasses?"

"Yes."

"Thick frames or thin?"

"Normal, I guess. Dark colored."

"Any facial hair?"

"No. Oh, God yes, yes there was. He had a little goatee beard."

"Also blond?"

"God, you're good at this."

"Just answer the question."

"Blond. His goatee was blond."

"Was he tall?"

"No—I've already said."

"Then was he short?"

"No. He wasn't that, either."

"Of medium height?"

"I reckon so."

"What about his build? Was he thin or fat?"

"I don't know. I don't remember him looking fat."

"Then was he slim?"

"No, he wasn't slim, he was average."

"OK, so he was average in size. Any earrings?"

"I…I don't think so."

"Or any other markings you noticed? Like a scar on his face? Or one of those rings in the nose?"

"No, he was just this guy who was average height and build, had short blond hair, dark glasses, and a blond goatee—wow!" Suzie said, opening her eyes in amazement. "That's right. That's *exactly* how he looked."

"Brilliant work, Becks," Judith said. "So is this our killer? An averagely built man with short blond hair, a blond goatee beard, and wearing a pair of spectacles?"

"Is there anyone close to the case who looks like that?" Becks asked.

"I don't think so," Judith said. "So who was he?"

"I'll tell you who it couldn't have been," Suzie said. "Any of Marcus, Jeremy, Debbie, or Sophia. They were all in the main chamber at the same time as the blond-haired guy was in the kitchenette. And Debbie and Sophia are women as well, so it doubly couldn't have been them."

"Although was Sophia there at the same time?" Judith asked.

"Of course. I just said."

"But I remember you saying Sophia arrived late. She told us she had a flat tire on her car she needed to fix. Which is suddenly feeling a bit convenient, if you ask me. But did she arrive before or after our blond friend left the kitchenette?"

"Let me think," Suzie said. "Jeremy had just arrived and was grumbling about how there weren't any biscuits—he really was very irritating. That's when the guy in the kitchen left by the fire door."

"Then what happened? Was Sophia the next person to arrive?"

"No, it was Geoffrey next. We had a bit of a chat, he got himself his coffee, he sat down at the table, and then Debbie got herself a coffee, so that took a bit of time, and it was only then that Sophia arrived."

"So she arrived a few minutes after our blond-haired server had left?"

"I suppose when you put it like that, yes."

"Now that's *very* interesting."

"Are we really saying a woman as pretty as Sophia was passing herself off as some bloke in a kitchen only moments beforehand?"

"It doesn't sound very likely, does it?"

"It occurs to me," Becks said. "The blond-haired man could have been just that—a blond-haired man. Someone we've not yet met."

"That's true," Suzie agreed.

"Or maybe we've met him already," Judith added. "But for the murder, he put on a blond wig and fake beard as a disguise."

"Do you have someone in mind?"

"I think I do. Because the only thing we know for sure is that it was Sophia who phoned Alec and told him not to come in that night. And I can't help noticing that her husband, who we saw come home that time we talked to her, was a man who was average in height and size. What if it was him in the kitchen that night?"

"You think it was Sophia's husband who put the poison in Geoffrey's coffee pod?" Suzie said, testing the idea.

"It's a possibility," Judith said.

"Although, we saw how he treated his wife," Becks said. "I'm not sure he'd do anything in cooperation with his wife."

"But I'm sure you can agree we need to talk to her," Judith said innocently. "Seeing as it was her who stood Alec down."

"Oh, God yes," Becks said, not realizing she'd fallen into Judith's trap.

"Oh, I see, so now you're saying we *should* race off to interview suspects?"

"That's not fair, of course we need to talk to Sophia!"

"Good, then I'm glad we can agree on that. And let's not forget, she's the only person here who grows aconite—the Queen of Poisons."

"You don't have to keep telling us that," Suzie said. "You've said."

"That's not what I mean. It's just, it occurs to me, considering what she grows in her garden, that rather makes Sophia the Queen of Poisons."

The three friends looked at each other as they realized the chilling truth of the statement.

Chapter 15

THE WOMEN DECIDED NOT TO phone ahead so they could surprise Sophia—a strategy that backfired when they arrived at her house and discovered that she wasn't in.

"Maybe she's not answering the door to us," Becks suggested.

As they returned to Suzie's van, Suzie pointed down the slope of the garden to the boathouse. At the top of the stairs that led to the upstairs room, a red lightbulb was shining.

"She's in there," Suzie said.

"How do you know?" Judith asked.

"She told us her recording studio's in her boathouse, and that red light means she's in there right now, recording. We have the same red light at Marlow FM."

"How very clever!" Judith said, and started picking her way down the steep slope. Once at the boathouse, she felt a stab of envy. Although she wouldn't change anything about her own boathouse, it was somewhat crumbling and the doors on it were rotting, whereas Sophia's was a gleaming construction in stone with smartly varnished wooden doors.

She and her friends headed up the outside staircase and knocked loudly on the door.

"Paul!" Sophia called from inside. "How many times do I have to tell you?"

Judith pushed the door open and said, "Sorry, Sophia. Not interrupting, are we?"

Inside, Sophia was sitting at a desk with a microphone hanging from a gimballed arm that was screwed into the wall, a laptop in front of her. She was wearing a heavy pair of black headphones that she peeled from her head. Behind her there was a ladder that led up to a mezzanine floor that was stuffed with cardboard boxes and piles of old paperwork. Judith smiled to herself. It didn't matter how polished a person's life was; there were always heaps of old paperwork that had to be stored somewhere.

"What on earth are you doing?" Sophia asked.

"Nice setup you've got here," Suzie said, picking up a spare microphone from a nearby shelf.

"Would you put that down, it's expensive."

"Sorry to arrive unannounced," Judith said without any hint of apology, "but we've got a few questions we'd like to ask you."

"For example, what made you go into podcasting?" Becks said, knowing that they had to take some of the aggravation out of the air.

"Me?" Sophia said, her desire to talk about herself fighting the briefest of battles with her irritation at being interrupted. "I never wanted to," she confessed. "But people kept telling me I had so much to offer. And I realized—I've been very lucky in life, I should share that good fortune with those less fortunate than me."

"So, do you have many listeners?" Suzie asked like a rancher asking how many head of cattle a neighbor had.

"A fair few."

"Only, anyone can set up a podcast these days."

"I quite agree."

"You just need the money for the equipment."

"It's so wonderfully democratic."

"But it's no substitute for the expertise in a proper radio station."

"I have over fifty thousand listeners."

Suzie didn't say anything to that, but Judith and Becks knew that the population of Marlow was about fifteen thousand people; there was no way Suzie's Sunday pet show was reaching even a fifth as many people as Sophia.

"That's how many have listened to you in total?" Suzie asked, trying to find a crumb of comfort.

"No, that's how many listen to each episode. Sometimes it's more."

Suzie coughed, cleared her throat, and then nodded in acceptance.

"That's good," she said.

"What's your latest podcast on?" Becks asked.

"The relationship between the phases of the moon and our biorhythms."

"Biorhythms?" Judith asked before she could stop herself.

"Well, we all know about our monthly cycle, don't we? And how it affects our emotions? Well, the science of biorhythms has also identified that we have a physical well-being cycle that repeats every twenty-three days, and an intellectual cycle that repeats every thirty-three days."

Judith's eyes narrowed.

"I've got an 'intellectual cycle' that repeats every thirty-three days?" she asked.

"It's been proven that the biofeedback chemical and hormonal secretion functions in the body show sinusoidal behavioral characteristics."

"Sinu-whatall?" Suzie asked.

"It means relating to the sine wave, and there's nothing more scientific than a sine wave," Sophia said to Judith, believing she'd proved her point. "It's pure maths."

Becks and Suzie could see that Judith's smile was deadly, but Judith also knew that she shouldn't antagonize Sophia. Not needlessly, anyway.

"You know what, you're right," Judith said, at some personal cost.

"So how can I help you?" Sophia asked.

"We wanted to know about a phone call you made to Alec Miller on the morning Geoffrey died."

"Who?"

"You know him," Suzie said.

"No, I don't think I do," Sophia said.

"He does the tea and biscuits for all of your meetings."

"Oh, him? I've never learned his name. He's Alec, is he?"

"You've never asked his name?"

"I'm sorry, Geoffrey always runs such a tight ship. Sorry, *ran* a tight ship.

We didn't do much sitting around before the meetings. We just cracked on with it."

"But he's been doing that job for years," Becks said.

"And I've been working hard on the planning committee for years. I'm sorry, I never found out his name. And anyway," Sophia added as an after-thought, "I didn't see him on the night Geoffrey died. Are you sure he was even there?"

"As it happens, he wasn't," Judith said. "But *someone* was in the kitchen getting the tea and coffee ready."

"Then I'm sorry, I can't help you. There was no one in the kitchen when I arrived."

"Are you really saying you didn't phone Alec Miller that morning?" Suzie asked.

"I've never heard that name before, and I can tell you, I didn't phone him."

"But we played him one of your podcasts," Becks said. "He recognized your voice immediately. He said it was you who'd rung him and told him not to come in that evening."

Sophia shrugged, seemingly unfussed by this revelation. "Then he's lying," she said. "Or someone was impersonating my voice. You go through my phone records. I didn't ring anyone on the day Geoffrey died—least of all a man whose name I didn't even know until two seconds ago."

"Then can you tell us what you were doing on the morning that Geoffrey died?" Judith asked.

"I don't remember," Sophia said, pretending that the question was barely of interest to her. "Oh, yes, I do know, I was in the house. Doing yoga."

"All morning?"

"And meditation. Yes."

"Can anyone alibi you?"

"Of course not," Sophia snapped. "It's only me and Paul here—he's my husband. And he was at work that morning. He's at work every morning."

Judith was pleased to have provoked Sophia, if only because she felt that it made her seem more human.

"Talking of your husband," Judith said, "do you know where he was on the night Geoffrey died?"

"I've no idea. You'll have to ask him for yourself."

"He runs Marlow Wealth Management, doesn't he?" Judith asked.

"So?"

"And how would you say you get on with him?" Suzie asked.

"What sort of a question is that?" Sophia said.

"Only we couldn't help noticing he didn't say hello to you when he came home the last time we were here."

"He's often tired when he gets home."

"No, it was more than that. And we saw you kick his case under the table."

"You were spying on me?" Sophia said, now openly aggravated.

"We were in your garden," Suzie said, squaring up to Sophia. "It's not our fault we saw what we saw."

"Paul and I have a wonderful relationship, a perfect relationship—he's the best of husbands—now could you very kindly leave my studio?"

The women looked at each other. If Sophia was saying she had a perfect husband, then they *knew* she was lying.

Chapter 16

JUDITH COULDN'T WAIT TO TELL Tanika about Sophia's phone call to Alec Miller, and their theory that Paul De Castro could have been her partner in crime, disguising himself as the blond-haired man serving in the kitchenette. Tanika shared Judith's enthusiasm at the possible lead and sent an officer to interview him.

A few hours later, Tanika read Paul's witness statement and rang Judith to update her.

"It's bad news, I'm afraid," she said. "Paul De Castro has an alibi for the time of the murder. He was at a cinema in Maidenhead."

"Have you checked his story?" Judith asked.

"After speaking to Mr. De Castro, my officers went to the cinema, and three different members of staff remember Mr. De Castro very distinctly that night because he spilled a tub of popcorn as he was going into his screening at 6:30 p.m. In fact, he caused a bit of a scene, insisting they give him a free refill—which they did in the end, if only to keep him quiet. So I'm sorry, but whoever was in the kitchen that night, it wasn't Paul De Castro."

"Then what have the other members of the planning committee said about the man in the kitchen?"

"It's somewhat frustrating. We went back to Debbie Bell, Marcus Percival, and Jeremy Wessel, and they all now admit that there was someone in the kitchen when they arrived, but they didn't think to mention it."

"What, *none* of them thought he was worth mentioning?"

"I know, it doesn't reflect too well on them, does it—thinking that staff who serve them aren't worth noticing. Marcus Percival was the only one who said he'd even spotted that it wasn't Alec Miller in the kitchen as usual, but he only had the vaguest memory of the person who was there. All he could remember was the man was of average height, average build, and had straight blond hair, glasses, and a little blond beard."

"Like Suzie said."

"Indeed."

"It really is strange that they didn't say anything about this man before now. Unless of course they're all in on this together and are pretending they didn't see a blond-haired killer in the kitchen."

"You think that's possible?"

"I don't know, it doesn't feel very likely, does it? After all, if they were all in on this together, why would they need a fourth person in the kitchen to commit the murder? The three of them could just kill Geoffrey themselves. Have you made any progress with who phoned Alec Miller in the morning and told him to stand down?"

"That's an interesting one. We've been able to confirm that Mr. Miller did indeed receive a phone call on his landline that morning—it lasted thirty-seven seconds."

"But was it Sophia De Castro who phoned him?"

"That's harder to prove. All we know for definite is that the call came in from the downstairs phone box in the town council building."

"Does that finally explain why the cable to the security camera was cut?"

"Very possibly. The person who phoned Alec wanted to make sure that there was no video evidence of them making the call."

"Yes, that would make sense. Have you been able to lift any fingerprints from the phone?"

"The whole thing is covered in fingerprints, most of them smeared, but none of them match any of our witnesses."

"Nonetheless, if Sophia was wearing gloves, it could have been her who phoned Alec from the council building that morning?"

"It could. Or it could have been anyone else on the planning committee for that matter. All they had to do was impersonate her voice. But, seeing as Mr. Miller says it was Sophie De Castro who rang him, and we know the call took place, I think we should presume it was Sophia who made the call."

"So is that everything? Paul De Castro can't be our killer as he was at the cinema," Judith said, summing up what she'd learned. "The rest of the planning committee don't notice serving staff, and we don't know for sure it was Sophia who phoned Alec—although it seems the most likely explanation."

"There's one last thing, I'm afraid. I don't think you'll like it. Forensics were able to lift two separate sets of fingerprints from the Kilner jar you found in that filing cabinet. They belonged to Geoffrey—unsurprisingly—and Marcus Percival."

"But why wouldn't I like that? That's wonderful news!"

"I'm afraid it isn't. I spoke to Marcus Percival myself, and he said that of course his fingerprints were on the jar, he'd taken a couple of lumps of sugar for his cup of tea. As he put it, 'Where's the crime in that?' What's more, I had the jar and the sugar tested, and the toxicology results said there was no trace of aconite anywhere—either on the glass or inside any of the sugar lumps still present. The jar of sugar is all a bit of a dead end, I'm afraid."

Judith wasn't happy with this particular development, although she tried not to think about it too much. She then continued trying not to think about it as she sat down to finish setting a crossword for *The Times* newspaper. Once that was done, she then found herself not thinking about it all through her afternoon swim. And she very definitely didn't think about it as she got on her bike and cycled over to Percival's estate agents and waited for Marcus to appear. The moment he left his office, she swept across the road and pretended to bump into him.

"So how did your fingerprints get onto the sugar jar?" she asked by way of an opening.

Marcus smiled tolerantly, entirely unbothered by the question.

"I put some sugar in my cup of tea," he said. "That's how it happened. I picked the glass jar up, took some sugar, and then passed it to Geoffrey. None of this is remotely incriminating."

"It's incriminating, considering where the jar was later found."

"Yes, the police told me it was in a filing cabinet."

"With only your and Geoffrey's fingerprints on it."

"I've already explained how my fingerprints got onto it. And think about it. If I really was involved in his death in any way, and I'd used the sugar to poison him, do you really think I'd hide the jar where it could so easily be found? Or leave my fingerprints on it? No, my fingerprints all over that jar prove that I must be innocent."

"Then how did it get into the filing cabinet?"

"I have no idea. Someone must have moved it."

"Without getting their fingerprints on it?"

"That wouldn't have been hard. In all of the confusion, they could have picked it up with a hankie—or used one of the paper napkins that were on the table. Which just shows that it was this person who acted suspiciously, not me. Or maybe the jar was hidden by a police officer who couldn't be bothered to process the scene properly afterward?"

"That doesn't sound very likely."

"Likely or not, I can assure you I had nothing to do with that jar of sugar after I'd taken my two lumps of sugar and passed it to Geoffrey. Now, I really must get on. I've a viewing I can't be late for."

With an easy smile, Marcus headed off down the High Street, and Judith stood on the pavement watching him go. She felt deeply frustrated, if only because she'd got the distinct impression that Marcus's answers had been too fluent. It was almost as if he'd prepared what he was going to say in advance. Although, she had to admit, he'd already been interviewed by the police once, perhaps it wasn't a surprise that his answers felt well rehearsed.

"What are we missing?" Judith asked Becks and Suzie later that evening as they stood at the incident board in her house.

"A killer?" Suzie asked.

"It's the man serving in the kitchenette," Becks said, indicating the index card with "blond man with goatee and glasses" written on it. "He killed Geoffrey."

"Even though the only person he could have been, Paul De Castro, was at the cinema at the time," Suzie said.

"But that just means it's someone else," Becks said, trying to follow the logic of her statement through. "All we have to do is work out who."

"Fair enough," Suzie agreed. "So how are we getting on with following the money?"

Becks sighed. "I've been going in to the police station in the afternoons to help Tanika's team go through the boxes of council paperwork. I'll be honest, I'm mostly doing it to get out of the house and away from Marian."

"Is she still bad?"

"I'll put it this way—trawling through dusty boxes of old receipts is preferable to spending time with her."

"It's not right you're being driven out of your own home," Judith said.

"I'd agree with you there. But you should know, we've still not found anything in the council records that looks anything like financial wrongdoing."

"Hold on," Suzie said, not quite believing. "You're saying there's no embezzlement anywhere in the council? Every ballpoint pen is accounted for?"

"As far as we can tell. Whenever we check balance sheets, they always add up."

"Ha!" Suzie scoffed. "That's a problem?"

"Just because the numbers add up doesn't mean dodgy activity's not going on."

"How do you work that out?" Judith asked.

"There's more than one way to steal," Suzie chuckled as she picked up a slice of carrot cake and spooned on a bit of extra cream cheese icing. Becks had learned long ago that when she brought one of her homemade cakes to one of their murder meetings, she needed to furnish Suzie with an extra pot of icing.

"But if you can't prove any financial wrongdoing," Judith said, "what have you been able to find?"

"Not much," Becks said, trying to ignore Suzie as she spooned a huge dollop of icing onto her piece of cake. "The town council's well run, all procedures are correctly followed, and there's no hint of any kind of grievances."

"Not even between Jeremy and Geoffrey?" Judith asked.

"Whatever arguments they have in meetings are obviously resolved and don't need to be minuted. Honestly, we've found nothing. The nearest we've come to anything of note is a file of what I'm told are called 'green inkers.'"

"Green inkers?" Suzie asked, spattering cake crumbs.

"It's what the police call them—angry letters written by the public—and I'd say the council get one or two letters, or emails, like that a week."

"Do any of them target Geoffrey?" Judith asked.

"I wouldn't say so, although his name comes up from time to time. If I'm honest, for every critical letter, there are at least ten pieces of fan mail saying what an asset he is to the town. Although there was one thing. I wouldn't have noticed if we hadn't been up there the other day, but I'd say the biggest number of recent complaints have been over the development of Wiley's Field."

"That's the field next to Alec Miller's house," Judith said.

"That's the one. According to the letters, and there are dozens of them, the developer, a man called Ian Maloney, can't be trusted to do a good job."

"Ian Maloney is doing the development?" Suzie asked sharply.

"You've got a bit of cake on your chin," Becks said.

"I have? Where?"

Becks indicated the general area of Suzie's mouth and chin.

"Thanks," Suzie said as she picked up a napkin and wiped her face.

"Do you know him?" Judith asked.

"Not personally," she said. "But I'll tell you this much: Ian Maloney is a crook. His specialty is buying up land, or an old property, saying he'll develop it to the highest specification, and then stuffing it with a load of cheap flats with no parking. I remember, a while back, he bought The Craddock—it was a pub down by the station. Perfectly good pub, if a bit tired. You know? Anyway, the town feared he was going to close it down and turn it into flats, even though he didn't have planning permission. So guess what? He had some builders doing some exploration in the car park behind it when a digger swung around and knocked the side of the pub off. All a big mistake, or so he said. But the pub was no longer fit for purpose. He was able to pull it down and replace it with the horrible flats he'd always wanted to build. The ones which always have people on the roof stopping it from leaking."

"I know those flats," Becks said. "You're right. There's always workmen on the roof."

"Well, that's Ian Maloney. What he's like. A snake."

"Which, I suppose, explains everyone's concerns. Not that it mattered in the end. I looked up the planning committee's decision on the Wiley's Field development, and they rejected it."

"Then there's someone with a motive right there!" Suzie said excitedly. "If his application was turned down, Ian Maloney is *exactly* the sort of guy who could resort to murder."

"That's interesting," Judith said. "Although it's a bit tenuous, isn't it? I mean, have we come across any sort of threatening letters, or emails, or texts to Geoffrey from Ian Maloney about the development?"

"Tanika would have told us if there was anything like that," Becks said.

"I still wouldn't rule him out," Suzie said. "If Ian Maloney wanted to put pressure on you, he wouldn't use anything as official as an email. He'd find some other way of doing it. A way that's more effective, and far more deniable."

Judith's handbag started ringing. She scooped her phone out and saw who was calling.

"It's Tanika," she said as she took the call.

"Judith," Tanika said from the other end of the line, "are you with the others?"

"I am."

"Are you safe?"

"Yes—completely. Why?"

"A neighbor's reported they've just seen someone break into the back door of Geoffrey Lushington's house. I'm in a squad car heading over from Maidenhead, I wanted to check you were OK."

"We'll meet you there."

"No, you need to stay away. We've got this."

"What's that?" Judith said before making a hissing noise.

"It's a police matter."

Judith hissed again—and then made a low warbling noise—before saying, "Sorry, you're breaking up there," and then she ended the call.

"What's up?" Suzie asked.

"Someone's broken into Geoffrey's house. Tanika wants us there as fast as we can."

Chapter 17

GEOFFREY LUSHINGTON'S HOME WAS ONLY a five-minute drive from Judith's house. It was a redbrick new build in the style of a nineteenth-century villa with plastic sash windows and concrete pillars holding up a porch. There were already two police cars parked outside when Suzie's van arrived with a screech of wheels, and Tanika came out of the house as the women approached the front door.

"I said I didn't need you here."

"Is *that* what you said?" Judith said. "The line was so bad."

"We're dealing with this."

"When was the break-in?"

"You can see me, can't you?" Tanika asked. "I'm not actually invisible?"

"We're your civilian advisers," Judith said, deciding it was time to push back. "We can't advise if we're not present."

"And who knows what we'll spot that you lot from Maidenhead would miss," Suzie added.

"At the very least," Judith said, as though she were offering a tremendous compromise, "we should be able to see inside Geoffrey's house. Get a sense of the man. Remember, it was only when you let us look at the murder scene that we found the Kilner jar of sugar."

Tanika looked up to the sky for inspiration, found none there, and looked back at Judith.

"Half an hour ago," Tanika said, "Mr. Lushington's house alarm was triggered by an intruder."

"Did this person get away?"

"That's how it's looking," Tanika said as a uniformed police officer appeared from the direction of the road.

"Boss," the police officer said to Tanika as she approached. "I've found a neighbor who says she saw the intruder."

"What did they look like?"

The officer paused, not wanting to give sensitive information out in front of civilians.

"Don't worry, we're with the police," Suzie said, showing her lanyard.

The officer looked for confirmation from Tanika, who smiled milkily.

"OK," she said, "so the gardens on this side of the road back onto an alleyway with houses on the other side. The neighbor I spoke to said she was working in her upstairs study when she heard the alarm go off in Mr. Lushington's house. She looked over and saw someone dressed in black—with a black hat of some sort—come out of the back door and run across the garden. They left by the back gate to the alleyway and disappeared down the alley."

"Did she see their face?" Tanika asked.

"The neighbor said she didn't. She was so surprised to see someone run out of Mr. Lushington's house, she couldn't be sure whether the intruder was a man or a woman. The only thing she was certain of was that the person was about average height and average build."

Judith and her friends exchanged sharp glances at this piece of information.

"Did she see the color of the person's hair?" Judith asked. "Or did this person have a goatee beard?"

"I'm sorry," the officer said, "she said she didn't see their face."

Tanika thanked the officer for her work and led Judith and her friends into Geoffrey's house. Once inside, Judith found herself smiling. The hallway may have been grand, but there were overlapping Persian rugs, a red-and-blue glass pendant in the ceiling that looked like it had also come from somewhere in the Middle East, and a bookcase stuffed with dusty books that ran down a wall. The house felt warm, welcoming, and scholarly.

"So, once again, we meet our average-build, average-height mystery man from the night of the murder?" Suzie asked.

"It's possible," Tanika conceded. "Although the fact that the man in the kitchenette was average in height and build also means there's a lot of people in the population who'll fit the bill. That's what average means. Let me show you where the break-in happened," Tanika said as she led them into a homey kitchen with white-painted floorboards and a bunch of lavender hanging over the window. Tanika showed the women the little back door, and they could see that shiny metal bolts near the top and bottom had been broken through, and the wood of the doorframe was ripped.

Judith noticed that the main mortise lock on the door hadn't ripped through any wood. In fact, its bolt was still inside the locking mechanism.

"The door wasn't locked," she said.

"Yes, I wondered if you'd notice that," Tanika replied. "The bolts at the top and bottom of the door have ripped through their housings, but the main lock isn't engaged. And I know we locked this door when we were last here. So the intruder had a key and was able to open the main lock. They knew Geoffrey well."

Judith stood on her tiptoes to inspect the topmost bolt.

"This bolt looks brand new," she said.

Next, Judith looked at the bolt at the bottom of the door, which was also shiny. She then went over to the sink and studied the wooden frame of the window that overlooked the back garden. She found another security bolt that shone bright silver.

"All the security bolts are new. I wonder why Geoffrey recently felt the need to up his security."

"Last time you were here," Becks said to Tanika, "did you find a bottle of Kyoto Gold whisky?"

"What's that?"

"Debbie Bell told us that Geoffrey and Jeremy argued a few weeks ago, but when we spoke to him, he said it was because Geoffrey didn't want to give him back a bottle of Kyoto Gold whisky."

"I'll be honest," Tanika said, "we've not had time to look."

"Don't reckon it'll take too long," Suzie said, heading over to a sideboard where there were at least a dozen bottles of whisky.

"Oh, OK," she said, "I know you like your whisky, Judith, but Geoffrey took things to the next level."

Suzie picked up the bottles one by one to check the labels.

"Now that's interesting," she said once she'd looked at the last bottle. "There's no whisky here called Kyoto Gold. Nothing Japanese, as far as I can tell."

"Then maybe it's like Jeremy said," Becks said. "Geoffrey drank it."

"I don't know," Suzie said, peering closely at the bottles. "These are all covered in dust, and none of them are even half-empty. They've been here a long time. He liked his whisky, but he didn't drink fast."

"Which makes sense," Judith said. "When it comes to whisky, you only ever have the occasional dram."

Judith's friends didn't point out to her that she tended to attack her bottles of whisky with an élan that was perhaps more than "occasional."

"So what are we saying?" Becks said. "Jeremy was lying to us about what the argument was about?"

"At the very least," Judith said, "when Geoffrey said, 'I won't give it back to you,' he wasn't referring to a bottle of Japanese whisky. Because there isn't one here."

A female officer came in from another room.

"Boss," she said. "We think we've found what the intruder was after."

Tanika, Judith, and her friends followed the officer across the corridor into a room that looked like Geoffrey's study. There was a large desk by the far wall, lots of old black-and-white photos of Geoffrey with various authors and other luminaries on the walls, and shelves that were neatly stacked with box files.

The police officer lifted up a metal filing case onto the desk. The lid had been bent back as though by a crowbar, but the lock had held. Whoever had tried to get into it had failed. Judith noticed a sharp letter opener on the desk. It almost looked like a knife.

"This is recent damage," Tanika said as she inspected the box. "It wasn't like this after the murder. I'd have noticed."

"But it's still locked," Suzie said.

"I think we need to find what's inside," Tanika said.

"I've got something we can use in the squad car," the officer said, and left the room.

While she was gone, Judith tried to take in the study. Like the rest of the house, it was homey, and she found herself looking at the shelves of box files. They were old and dusty, but she could see that Geoffrey had written the name of an author on the front of each one, and the boxes were arranged alphabetically. He was an organized man, and his publishing work was clearly still important to him all these years later if he kept all the information on his old authors.

The female police officer returned with a crowbar that she inserted in between the lock and lid of the metal box. She snapped through the lock easily, the lid popped up, and she stepped aside.

Tanika looked into the box.

"OK, we've got some old papers," she said as she reached inside.

She pulled out a small pile of paperwork and went through it.

"So here's Geoffrey's birth certificate, his NHS card—this is just ancient paperwork."

One by one, she dropped the pieces of paper onto the desk, and everyone could see how inconsequential they were. Becks picked up an old card for Marlow library that had expired in 2003.

"Why would a burglar want to break into this box?" she asked.

"Hold on, what's that," Judith said, looking inside.

At the very bottom, there was a sheet of black paper they hadn't noticed. Tanika reached in and pulled it out. Unlike the other pieces of paper, it looked brand new, and they could see it was folded over. She opened it up.

Someone had cut letters out of different magazines and glued each of the individual letters to the paper so that a message could be read.

STOP WHAT YOU'RE DOING OR I'IL TELL EVERYONE YOUR SECRET

The women looked at each other, amazed.

Becks was the first to speak.

"Geoffrey was being blackmailed," she said. "Wasn't he?"

"Told you," Suzie said, her face breaking into a broad grin.

"Geoffrey Lushington wasn't perfect after all. He had a dark secret—a secret someone thought it was worth killing for."

Chapter 18

AS THE WOMEN LOOKED AT the blackmail letter, Suzie had an idea.

"I know who's behind this," she said. "Someone who'd be the first to resort to blackmail. Someone who'd then be prepared to do a little breaking and entering to get the blackmail back. Someone who recently had his plans smashed by Geoffrey."

"Who?" Tanika asked.

"Ian Maloney, the property developer."

"What makes you think of him?"

"Let's just say his name has cropped up as part of our inquiries."

"It hasn't, really," Becks said.

"Shh, Becks," Suzie said. "It has."

"We've not come across him in any of Geoffrey's emails, or phone calls," Tanika said.

"That doesn't mean anything. Men like Ian Maloney don't leave a trace. And I don't doubt for a second he'd kill you if you got in his way."

"It's an interesting thought," Tanika said. "As it happens, we've had Mr. Maloney in for questioning a few times, but we've never been able to make anything stick. He's too fly. And he's got no history of violence."

"Would you say he was of average height and build?" Judith asked.

"As it happens, he is. And before you ask, he's also got blond hair."

"There you are!" Suzie said excitedly. "Ian Maloney is our man."

"That's still quite a leap," Tanika said.

"You need to bring him in for questioning."

"On what grounds? That he has blond hair and is of average height?"

"Yes—and that he's recently had a planning application turned down by Geoffrey and the committee."

"I imagine there's a long list of people who've had applications turned down. Are you expecting me to question everyone who's of average height and build?"

Suzie felt deeply frustrated. How could they discover whether or not Ian Maloney was involved if the police didn't talk to him?

Judith suggested that she and her friends leave Tanika to process the new evidence, but as soon as they were outside, she announced that if the police weren't going to talk to Ian Maloney, then they should. Fortunately for Becks, who wasn't as convinced as her friends that it was a good idea, when they started asking around, they couldn't find him. They tried ringing his office and were told that he was on a work trip to Dublin. After a few days, they realized they were being fobbed off, so they went to his business address in High Wycombe only to find that it was a serviced office with a virtual switchboard.

In the end, Suzie decided to use her Sunday-night radio show to ask her listenership if they knew of a way of meeting up with Ian Maloney. No one rang in to give her any tips, which she didn't find much of a surprise. It had always been something of a long shot. However, when she finished her shift, she found that someone had slipped a handwritten note through the letter box of the station. It said that Ian Maloney could be found most afternoons fishing on the stretch of the Thames between Marlow and the nearby village of Bourne End. Reading the message, Suzie smiled to herself. Sophia might have a bigger listenership for her podcasts, but nothing beat local radio for engagement.

The following day, Suzie decided that she'd take her Doberman, Emma, and some miniature schnauzers she was dog-sitting on a riverside walk from Marlow to Bourne End. She invited Judith and Becks to meet her at the church and explained the purpose of their walk once they'd set off.

"I still don't see why you think this Ian Maloney person is involved," Becks said.

"We'll have a better idea if we can speak to him," Judith said. And then, to change the subject, she asked, "So, how's your mother-in-law?"

"Oh, God," Becks said with a shudder. "Her latest scheme is to suggest we all go on holiday."

"And that's bad?"

"She's convinced Sam and Chloe we should all go to Disney World in Florida."

"Ouch," Suzie said. "That's a lot of money."

"And she won't contribute a penny. Which is particularly bad when you're adding an extra Marian-shaped member of the family. If we went, there's no way she'd have the patience to queue for hours on end; she'd want to pay through the nose to get to the front."

"Then say no."

"I have, but it doesn't stop her. And she's reminded the kids that I made a load of money last year—it's always about money to her! You know I wouldn't mind if she cared about the children, or even about Colin, but she just wants to spend our cash."

"Are you still going through the old council records as a way of getting away from her?" Suzie asked.

"Guilty as charged," Becks said sadly.

"But you must have finished going through all the papers by now."

"I have. And so have the police. In fact, Tanika's pulled the other officers back to other areas of the case. After all, 'follow the money' could refer to anything, really. We know it's not Geoffrey Lushington's money—and now it doesn't look like it's the council's money either—so maybe it's someone else's money. But I can't help feeling it's to do with the council, given that Geoffrey was murdered during a council meeting."

"You should stop hiding at the police station," Suzie said, "and take Marian on."

"No one should feel unwelcome in their own home," Judith said in agreement.

"Of course," Becks said. "I agree. But what can I actually do?"

The women walked on in silence while Judith tried to think of a way to help her friend, but she soon found her thoughts drifting to the view. She loved this stretch of the river. Even though it was a cold afternoon, there were still people out on boats, and walking or cycling the towpath. And she was delighted to see that so many of the hedges and bushes had come into bud. The promise of summer was in the air. It was still a way off, perhaps, but it was around the corner, she could feel it.

"By the way, Becks," Suzie said, "I've been thinking about what you told me. About how I shouldn't hustle for everything. And just enjoy my life. It feels wrong, and I don't know how I'll do it, but I'm going to give it a go. I'm going to try and accept I'm happy—like you said—and leave it at that."

"I think that's a very good idea," Judith said.

"It's always a good idea to decide that you're happy and leave it at that," Becks said.

"It's weird, though. Not having a side hustle to focus on. Oh, look," she said, indicating a man off in the distance who was standing on his own by the riverbank with a fishing rod in his hand. "Hold on, I think that's Ian Maloney."

As they got nearer, Judith could see that the man was in his thirties, of average height and build, and he had a glossy head of blond hair that swept back from his forehead and fell below his ears. But there was something about his manner as he looked at them—the dark sockets of his eyes, the slight downturn to his mouth—that Judith thought made him look like the sort of person who'd step out of a dark alley, knife you, drop the knife, and then get on with his day entirely unconcerned with what he'd done.

Ruthless, that's what it was. He looked ruthless.

"Mr. Maloney?" Judith asked as they approached. "You're a difficult man to track down."

"You can't have tried very hard," Ian said.

"What are you fishing for?" Becks said, trying to improve Ian's mood.

"Carp. Pike. Whatever I can get."

Ian turned back to look at the river, and Judith decided that if Ian was going to have no manners, then she could join him in that game.

"We're working for the police," she said.

That got Ian's attention, although he sneered a smile.

"You three?"

"Actually, we're civilian advisers," Becks said, before her friends overplayed their hand.

"Bloody community policing," Ian muttered to himself. "I remember when I could expect to be interviewed by the proper Bill."

"I understand you've had a few run-ins with the police," Judith said.

"Don't worry, ladies, that's all in the past. My name won't even appear on a computer anywhere."

"How's business?" Judith asked, quietly fuming that Ian had patronizingly referred to her as a lady.

"Booming."

"I understand you're trying to develop Wiley's Field."

"Sure. I've had my eye on that plot since I started in the development business. That's prime housing land, that is. It has its own access, a primary school five minutes' walk away—and on that side of town, you're ten minutes' drive to the M40 and High Wycombe."

"A primary school that's already oversubscribed," Becks said.

Ian shrugged. "If the families who move in overcrowd local services, that's the government's fault, not mine. There's a housing crisis, didn't you know?"

"Although your development got rejected, didn't it?" Judith asked.

"With a list of objections as long as your arm," Becks added.

"You don't know what you're talking about."

"Then how about you enlighten us?"

"Look," Ian said, resentment oozing, "the first rule of any application is you ask for the moon. OK? You shrink gardens, you raise the roofline, you skimp on building materials. It's an opening bid, that's all. And sometimes you get away with murder," Ian said with a chuckle.

"An interesting choice of words," Becks said.

They all saw the moment when Ian understood why they were talking to him. He put his rod down on its stand and looked directly at Judith. Judith stared straight back.

"You think I'm connected with Geoffrey Lushington's death?" Ian said.

"His murder," Judith corrected.

Ian laughed—just outright laughed.

"You think he put poison in his own cup, do you?" Judith said with a confidence she wasn't feeling.

"No idea, do I? But if you think I was involved, you're barking up the wrong tree."

"He turned your planning application down."

"So what?"

"Which is why you started blackmailing him."

"What are you talking about?"

"You threatened to reveal his secret, didn't you? Unless he backed your development."

"Blackmail?" Ian said, taking half a step toward the women in an attempt to intimidate them. Becks instinctively took half a step back while Judith and Suzie held their ground. Becks winced an apologetic smile at her friends before inching back to join them, although she stayed behind their shoulders.

"Why would I need to blackmail him?" Ian continued, "I was expecting the committee to turn down my first application. They gave me a list of changes I needed to make before I could resubmit, and you know what? I still managed to sneak a few shortcuts past them. But that's how it goes. They've got a load of applications to sift through, and I'm only concerned with one. I'm always going to win in that battle. When my architect's finished addressing their concerns, I'll resubmit the plan and it will get through this time."

"Are you sure?"

"You ask anyone in this town. I've never been rejected twice by the planning committee. My proposal was going to get through next time. Bloody hell!"

Ian's focus was suddenly on the river as his float vanished underwater. He grabbed up his rod, released a catch on the reel, and the line screamed as it ran out.

"You've caught something!" Suzie said, thrilled by the excitement.

"First you let your victim run," Ian said, his eyes sparkling with the joy of the hunt. "Let the fish think they can swim where they please—that they're not on the hook. Then, oh so slowly, you reel them in."

The line had moved downstream, and Ian started to wind the reel on his rod.

"Which is the hard bit," he continued. "The battle of wills. So, if you don't mind, I'll get back to this. I think I've answered your questions."

Judith and her friends were happy to get away from Ian as he landed his fish, and they headed back toward Marlow. Before they left the field, Judith turned and looked back at Ian one last time. He'd caught the fish and had it flapping helplessly under his hand on the grass. His other hand lifted a cosh and smashed it down into the fish's head.

He tossed the dead fish into a bucket.

Judith's phone started ringing. She pulled it out, saw the number was "withheld," and answered the call.

"Hello," she said into the handset.

"Have you done it?" a deep and distorted voice asked.

Adrenaline rushed through Judith. It was her anonymous caller! She took a quick look back at Ian Maloney. He was washing his hands with a bottle of water, so it couldn't be him.

"Done what?" she asked into her phone, and then hit an icon on the screen to turn on the speakerphone feature.

"Have you followed the money?"

"We've tried," Judith said. "Geoffrey's completely in the clear. The police say there's no financial irregularity. But is this connected to why he's being blackmailed?"

The voice on the end of the line didn't immediately answer.

"It is, isn't it?" Judith said, triumphantly.

"I don't know anything about blackmail. But you have to follow the money. Not Geoffrey's. The council's."

"But that's what I've been doing!" Becks said into the speaker.

"Who's that?"

"Sorry," Becks said, realizing she'd misstepped. "Becks Starling. I'm the vicar's wife."

"Check the petty cash," the voice said, and then hung up.

"Oh, God, I'm so sorry," Becks said.

"Don't worry," Judith said as she dialed 1471. A voice spoke from the phone, telling the women that the phone number of the person who'd called was withheld.

"Come on," Judith said, picking up her pace as she headed out of the field.

"Where are we going?"

"The hockey club. We know he uses the phone box down there, and with luck we'll catch him before he's finished wiping it down. We can ring Tanika on the way to update her, we can't let him get away!"

Chapter 19

SUZIE'S VAN BUMPED DOWN THE unmarked road that led to the hockey club.

"What sort of person does that?" she asked. "Disguises their voice and then only gives cryptic messages. One or the other! We don't know who he is, why not just come out and tell us what he knows?"

"There has to be a reason," Judith said. "Even though it seems mad to us, whoever it is thinks they're acting rationally."

"When is making anonymous phone calls ever rational?"

"And what did he mean 'check the petty cash'?" Becks asked. "I've checked the petty cash, it's the first place we looked."

As Suzie reached the phone box outside the hockey club, she slammed on the brakes, the van came to a juddering halt, and the women climbed out.

There was no one in the phone box.

And there was no one else nearby.

"Bugger," Suzie said.

"Well, look," Becks said. "Why don't we split up? Maybe we can find someone who saw who just used this phone."

Becks's phone started ringing, and she fished it out.

"It's Tanika," she said as she answered the call. She listened for a short while, the others could see her frown, and then she said, "I'm with the others, we'll go and see what we can do," before hanging up.

"OK," she said, "Tanika's traced the call to the phone box opposite the vicarage, by the bridge. That's why she rang me. She thought I might be nearby."

"Then let's get going," Judith said as she headed back to Suzie's van.

Once they were all in, Suzie carried out what her friends felt was a punchy two-point turn into the hedge on the side of the track and bombed back toward the center of Marlow. Turning right at the little roundabout at the bottom of the High Street, Suzie drove up to the phone box that stood before the bridge—the church and vicarage on the other side of the road—and mounted the pavement. She and her friends flung the doors of the van open and ran to the phone box.

It was empty.

"I'll stay here," Judith said, "and make sure no one else comes along and uses the phone. We need to protect the scene. You two spread out—see if you can find someone who saw the person who used this phone!"

"I'll take the church side of the road," Becks said, crossing over to the pavement on the other side of the road. Suzie saw a young mother with a child in a pushchair nearby and dashed over to talk to her.

Judith turned her attention to the phone box. The door wasn't fully closed, so she took a hankie from her handbag and prized it open further so she could enter. Once inside, she tried to ignore the fetid smell of the thousands of bodies who'd gone before her. Instead, she focused on the black handset that sat on top of the main body of the phone. The year before, she'd used the icing sugar from a tin of sweets to reveal whether a glass jar had any fingerprints on it, but she could see for herself that the phone handset was entirely clean of any smears of fingerprints. It was the same for the silver numbers on the main body of the phone. Someone had recently wiped the unit clean of prints. The metal sparkled in the sunlight.

A police car roared over the bridge, barely slowed down as it slipped through the traffic-calming bollards, and pulled up by the phone box. As Tanika got out, Judith went to meet her.

"Becks and Suzie are looking for witnesses," she said, "and I'm making sure no one contaminates the scene."

"We'll make a detective of you yet," Tanika said.

"No, thank you," Judith said. "I'm quite happy helping out, but that's as far as it goes."

Having seen Tanika's arrival, Suzie and Becks returned. "Find anyone?" Judith asked.

"I ran around like a blue-arsed fly," Suzie said. "Not a sausage."

"It's the same for me," Becks agreed. "Not that I ran around like any type of fly."

"So our anonymous caller's got away with it again," Judith said.

"Not necessarily," Tanika said. "Maybe he left forensic evidence behind this time."

"I had a quick look," Judith said. "The handset and main unit look like they've been wiped clean again."

"And it's a public phone box," Suzie said. "You find anyone's DNA in there—or any other evidence—and whoever's it is will just say sure, they used the phone before now."

Tanika was about to agree when she noticed that Becks was looking up at the spire of All Saints Church.

"What is it?" she asked.

Becks looked from the spire back to the phone box, and then she pulled her phone out of her handbag.

"You know what?" she said. "I think I'll be able to show you who our mystery caller is. Courtesy of a pair of nesting kestrels. Hold on."

On her phone, Becks opened a web browser. Her friends crowded round as she then navigated to the home page of All Saints Church.

"A few months ago," she said by way of explanation, "one of the church wardens spotted two kestrels coming and going from the parapets of the spire. When we investigated, we discovered they'd built a nest and had two eggs, so we installed a webcam. We've been live streaming the birds twenty-four hours a day ever since."

As she spoke, Becks navigated to a live video feed that filled the screen.

"They're gorgeous!" Suzie said, as they all looked at two kestrel fledglings in their nest.

"How marvelous," Judith agreed.

"But if you look carefully," Becks said, "just over the parapet, you can see down the High Street. That's us," Becks said, indicating on the screen where they could see the three of them standing by a bright red phone box.

Suzie looked up at the spire and waved a hello. On the iPhone, they could see Suzie waving.

"Oh, this is really very good," Judith said.

"Better than that, the webcam buffers the last twenty-four hours of footage, so you can see what the birds have been doing since the last time you logged on—it's particularly useful when you want to see what they get up to at night, which is when they go hunting." Becks put her finger on the slider at the bottom of the screen and dragged it to the left. "What time did the anonymous call come in, Judith? Two thirty?"

"A little after," Judith said.

"Well let's see," Becks said, and lifted her finger from the phone. The time stamp read 14:31.

On the screen, there wasn't much to see. Just people coming and going, and no one went anywhere near the phone box. Although that wasn't quite true, the women realized. There was a person on a mobility scooter who was heading along the road toward the phone box. The scooter was being driven by a man. As he reached the phone box, the scooter stopped by the pavement, and the man hefted himself off it, looked about him, and then approached the phone box. As he opened the door, Becks paused the playback. Even though he was so small on the screen, it was possible to see that the man was significantly overweight. His hair was dark and messy, he appeared to be wearing tracksuit bottoms and a thick jacket of some sort, and there was a distinctly unhealthy look to him.

"That's him?" Suzie asked in surprise.

Becks pressed play, and the women watched as the man went into the phone box. Through the glass, they could see him lift the handset and dial a number.

"Do any of you recognize him?" Tanika said.

"No," Judith said for all of them. "I've never seen him before. And I can't think of anyone involved in Geoffrey's life who even begins to look like that, I think we'd have noticed."

On the screen, the man put the phone down and then got out a handkerchief. He wiped the phone down, put the cloth away again, left the phone box, and once again looked about himself to see if anyone had noticed him.

Becks pressed the side buttons and took a screen grab of the image.

On the screen, the man had a bit of a coughing fit, and then got back onto his mobility scooter with an effort and drove off slowly.

The women didn't know what to say.

This was Judith's mystery caller, but who on earth was he?

Chapter 20

"WE NEED TO FIND OUT who that man is," Tanika said.

"I'll email you the screenshot I took," Becks said. "But I'm guessing you can get hold of the footage yourself by logging on to the church's website."

"Don't worry, we'll be able to rip the video from the hard drive."

"But now we've got him, how do we work out who he is?"

"That shouldn't be hard," Suzie said. "All we have to do is ask everyone if they know a fat man who goes everywhere on a mobility scooter."

"You can't call him fat," Becks said.

"Why not? What do you want me to say? He's got heavy bones? No, he's fat—dangerously so, if you ask me—let's call it how it is. But we should see if anyone on the planning committee knows him," she added, although she noticed Judith flash a warning glance at her.

"Of course," Tanika said, thinking the idea over.

"But first you'll have to get an official printout from that video," Judith said. "Something that will be admissible in court and doesn't mess up your precious chains of evidence. And I'm sure this whole phone box needs forensics officers to do their business as well."

"You're not wrong there," Tanika agreed with a sigh. "If you don't mind, I've got some calls to make."

"Come on, ladies," Judith said, "how about we visit that new pottery shop on the High Street."

"Nah," Suzie said, "I'm having too much fun here."

"I said," Judith said more insistently, "how about we visit the new pottery shop on the High Street."

"Yes, let's," Becks said, having picked up on Judith's subterfuge.

"Oh, right!" Suzie said, finally realizing that Judith was maybe speaking in code. "Let's go and check out the new pottery shop on the High Street."

The women walked back along the High Street.

"We aren't checking out the pottery shop, are we?" Suzie whispered to Judith.

"Of course not," Judith said. "We're going to Percival's estate agents."

As Judith spoke, she looked to see if Becks would object, but was gratified to see that, for once, Becks seemed as intent on getting to the bottom of what was going on as the rest of them.

After a short walk, the women entered Percival's, a glass and chrome office with overly bright flat-screen monitors on the walls showing expensive houses with swimming pools, often set in woods, or with extensive river frontage. There were half a dozen estate agents all working at their desks, the latest touch screen computers in front of them. At the back of the office, there was a glass-walled meeting room. Inside, Ian Maloney was chatting amicably with Marcus Percival.

Marcus got up, shook Ian's hand with a smile, and then ushered him to the door of the glass office.

"Ian can't see us!" Judith hissed, and plonked herself down at the nearest desk—Becks and Suzie following suit and sitting at other desks in the office. The startled estate agents on the other side of the three desks didn't know what to say to the women who suddenly arrived and started talking to them, but it bought Judith and her friends the few seconds they needed to blend into the background of the office, and Ian didn't notice them as Marcus showed him to the door.

Once he was outside, the three women thanked their respective—and very baffled—estate agents and converged on Marcus.

"Good afternoon, Marcus!" Judith said.

"Oh," he said, surprised to see the women. "Where did you all come from?"

"We could well ask the same question of Mr. Maloney there," Judith said.

"Why shouldn't I see Ian Maloney?"

"You recently turned down his application to build a new housing estate on Wiley's Field," Becks said.

"That's right. It wasn't a serious document."

"How do you mean?"

"Developers like Ian have to be watched like a hawk. If they can cut a corner, they cut it clean off."

"So why were you meeting him just now?"

"Because I'm an estate agent. Ian's one of my first points of contact when I want to find out what's coming on to the market, or what trends in the wider development community will soon be sweeping into Marlow."

"You trade information with each other?" Judith asked.

"I'll be honest, ninety-nine percent of being a good estate agent is about having the best information. So yes, we trade information. For example, right now, he was telling me about the three houses he's building for the rugby club. They'll be ready to market by September, and that will be three more families helped onto the housing ladder. If it makes you feel any better, I don't much like him, but he does more good than bad in this place. Unpopular opinion, though, that is."

"So will the planning committee reject his next proposal for the development at Wiley's Field?"

"I don't know. Ian always sails close to the wind. But he's not in any rush. He'll keep changing and then resubmitting applications until we finally give him consent. Which is all quite normal. Planning is a conversation, there's often back-and-forth. Unless there's some calamity about the site, like it's contaminated—which I can tell you it isn't—he'll get his planning permission in the next few months or so."

"Do you benefit?"

"How do you mean?" he asked.

"Financially. From the development of Wiley's Field."

"No, can't say that I do," Marcus said, but for the first time, the women could see that he wasn't entirely comfortable. "Now I'm sure you didn't come here to talk to me about Ian Maloney. How can I help?"

"We were wondering if you'd be able to help us identify someone?" Becks said as she pulled out her phone and got up the screenshot she'd just taken of the overweight man by the phone box.

"Do you recognize this man?" Judith asked.

Judith watched Marcus carefully, but he seemed nonplussed as he looked at the screen.

"Sorry," he said. "Can't say that I do."

"Are you sure?"

"I'm sure I'd remember meeting him if I had, he's quite—er—*distinctive* looking, isn't he? Is that everything?"

"Do you know who might know him?"

"I've answered your questions, I think we can all agree I've been helpful, but I really must get on with my day. Houses don't sell themselves."

With a smile, Marcus returned to his desk at the back of the office. Judith and her friends realized they had nothing more they could achieve, so they showed themselves out onto the street. "Did anyone notice how uncomfortable he was when we asked if he benefited from the development of Wiley's Field?" Judith asked.

"You think he could be in cahoots with Ian?"

"It's possible. Although I suppose it's also like he said—a local estate agent is always going to be a bit in the pocket of a local developer, and vice versa."

"You scratch my back, I'll scratch yours," Suzie said.

"Exactly."

"So, who are we seeing next?"

Judith explained that Marlow Wealth Management was around the corner on Little Marlow Street; they'd be able to find Debbie Bell there. When the women arrived, they were met by a rather severe-looking woman who was guarding a door that led into the office area. After Judith explained that they wanted to see Debbie Bell, the woman reluctantly disappeared into the interior of the building. As the door opened and closed, the women got the briefest glimpse of a smart bar area with a gleaming coffee machine and comfortable sofas.

"How the other half lives," Suzie said.

After a few moments, Debbie came out, wearing a brown tweed skirt and cream blouse, her hair up in a ponytail. She was dressed like the sort of teacher who had taught Judith at school, she thought to herself. And like many of them, Judith noticed, the hem to the skirt was frayed. Clearly, Debbie didn't get paid the sort of money that would allow her to use the services of the company she worked for.

"What are you doing here?" Debbie asked.

"Don't worry," Judith said, "this won't take long."

And it didn't. Almost as soon as Becks showed Debbie the screenshot of the man by the phone box, she said she didn't recognize him.

"Are you sure?" Judith asked, surprised at how quickly Debbie had responded.

"Quite sure. Was there anything else? No? Then I'm afraid I really have to get back to work."

Next, the women went over to the Globe industrial park to see Jeremy, but he came to the same conclusion as Marcus and Debbie. He didn't know the man, he was sure of it.

"Actually, I'm glad of the chance to talk to you," Judith said. "You see, we've been to Geoffrey's house and checked his whisky collection."

"It's rather fine, isn't it?" Jeremy said.

"But there was no bottle of Kyoto Gold."

"There wasn't?" he said, a touch awkwardly.

"And none of the other bottles were even half-empty. He wasn't a fast drinker."

"Oh, he was," Jeremy said, and then licked his lips. "When the whisky was right. Or maybe he gave it to a friend?"

"I think you've been lying to us," Judith said. "Your argument with him after that meeting at the Rotary wasn't about whisky—when he said he wouldn't 'give it back to you.' I think you need to tell us what he was referring to."

"I've told you, it was about a bottle of whisky. Or have you considered, maybe he dropped the bottle on the floor and it smashed?"

"We'll find out the truth. You know that, don't you? We always do."

"I'm telling you the truth. I promise."

"He's not bloody telling the truth," Suzie said as soon as they left Jeremy's office.

"But how to find out what was really going on?" Becks asked.

"We'll work it out," Judith said. "You mark my words. We'll find a way. Next stop—Sophia."

This time, when they visited Sophia's house, she answered the door.

"What do you want?" she asked suspiciously.

Judith explained that they wanted her to look at a photo of a man.

"Do you know him?" Judith asked as Becks handed over her phone.

"I've seen him before," Sophia said, trying to access her memories. "That's it!" she said more confidently, "Oh, God, he's that guy."

"What guy?" Suzie asked.

"He's a freelance IT guy. He installed the cables and mics in my podcast studio a year or so ago. I can't say I liked him, he gave me the creeps."

"Do you remember his name?"

"It was Dave something—now what was it? Sorry, I'm not sure I remember. Dave Butler!" Sophia suddenly added, delighted with herself. "That's it, his name's Dave Butler."

"Hold on," Becks said, pulling her phone and firing up her search engine.

"What do you mean, he gave you the creeps?" Judith asked Sophia.

"I don't want to be too judgy, but I'm always suspicious of people who are that overweight. They can't be trusted."

"I beg your pardon?" Suzie said.

"It's very simple. I find it upsetting to be near people who've let themselves go. He barely managed to get up the stairs to the studio. Imagine not being able to get up a staircase?"

"And that's you *not* being judgy?"

"You asked, I'm just telling you the truth."

"Did he do a good job?" Judith asked tartly.

"I suppose so."

"For a reasonable price?"

"That's why I chose him."

"In the amount of time he said it would take?"

"I know how I sound," Sophia said, uncomfortable enough to try to drop the subject, but not uncomfortable enough to recant, "but our bodies are temples—Mother Earth's greatest gift—and I can't help it if I'm offended by people who don't respect that fact."

"Got him," Becks said, thrilled with herself. "Dave Butler, Marlow IT Solutions, 8 Avenue Gardens, Marlow."

"That's right," Sophia said. "I remember the letterhead on his invoice. He lives in Avenue Gardens."

Judith turned to her friends.

"Then I think we need to pay a visit to Mr. Butler at 8 Avenue Gardens."

Chapter 21

AVENUE GARDENS WAS A LITTLE development on the western edge of Marlow above the Henley Road. It was a close of new-build houses, but it had beautiful views down to the Thames and Winter Hill beyond.

"You can see your house from here," Becks said to Judith as they got out of Suzie's van.

Judith looked and could see that, while her house itself was hidden from view by the clump of trees that surrounded it, it was possible to make out the shape of her boathouse at the bottom of the garden. She had a brief qualm that her naked swimming in the river could be seen from the houses up here, but she had to remind herself that she was currently standing about a mile away. And besides, who'd be looking?

Dave Butler lived in a squat bungalow behind an unruly hedge. There was a wooden five-bar gate, but it was rotten, and the garden in front of the main entrance was overgrown with weeds. However, Suzie and her friends could see that Dave's maroon mobility scooter was plugged into an electricity socket by the wall.

"Bingo," Suzie said, indicating the mobility scooter. "He's in."

Judith led her friends to the front door, where there was a modern-looking doorbell that had a camera built into it.

"Can't stand these things," Judith said as she went to press the doorbell—and then she paused, her finger hovering over the buzzer.

"I think I can hear a TV," she whispered. "Or radio. He's definitely in."

Judith pressed the button, the unit flashed with a blue light, and there was a tuneful chime inside the house.

"Shouldn't we have told him we were coming?" Becks whispered.

"And spoil the surprise?"

Judith put her ear to the door.

"What is it?" Suzie asked.

"Shh! I can't hear the TV. I think he's turned it off."

Judith bent down to the doorbell and looked straight into the camera.

"Mr. Butler!" she said to it. "We know you're in, we can hear you."

Judith waited and listened.

There was no sound from inside.

Judith went over to the nearest ground-floor window. The woodwork was grimed with moss, and the curtains were drawn.

"There are no lights on," Becks said, indicating the upstairs windows.

"He has to be in," Judith said. "We saw how much difficulty he had walking. If his scooter's at home, then so is he."

"Let me see if I can get around the side," Suzie said, and headed back out onto the street.

Judith returned to the front door and rapped her knuckles on the hard wood.

"Mr. Butler, please come to the door, this is the police," she called.

Becks frowned at the white lie, Judith flapped her hand at her friend to stop fussing, and then she put her ear to the door again. She still couldn't hear anything.

They waited for another minute, but the door remained closed.

"Maybe it wasn't a television you heard," Becks said.

Judith pursed her lips, frustrated.

"Oh, he's in, all right," Judith said and headed back to the road. Becks followed her and saw Suzie approaching along the pavement.

"There's no way around the back," Suzie said. "The gardens of these houses back onto the gardens of the next street along."

An old station wagon turned into the house next door to Dave's, and a young woman got out.

"Come on," Judith said, and strode over to the woman.

"Sorry, can I ask you a quick question? It's about your next-door neighbor, Dave Butler."

"Is he all right?" the young woman asked.

"I don't know. We're trying to get hold of him."

"You and everyone else. He keeps himself to himself at the best of times, but my husband reckons we've not seen him this last year. We know he's there, his lights are sometimes on and sometimes off, but we've not seen him in person."

"But he must go out from time to time to do his shopping," Suzie said.

"He gets everything delivered."

"Or to do his job," Becks added.

"I don't know. Maybe he does it remotely."

"You've really not seen your neighbor at any time in the last year?" Judith asked, having difficulty believing it could be true.

"He's a recluse," the woman said. "But why are you asking?"

"We're concerned friends," Becks said quickly, before Suzie could whip out her lanyard.

"And we think he's been out of his house at least a few times. For example, this afternoon."

"Of course," the woman agreed. "It makes sense I'm not seeing his every coming and going. I've been at work today."

Judith thanked the woman for her time and she and her friends returned to the street.

"We've got to get him out of his house," she said.

"We could set it on fire?" Suzie offered.

"I don't think Tanika would be happy if we did that," Judith laughed. "I was thinking more of getting her to issue a warrant to gain access."

"Good thinking," Suzie said. "And I dog-sit for Mr. Peat over there," she added, pointing at the house opposite Dave's. "And three doors down are the Greens, and my Amy was best friends with their daughter. I can speak to them, too. I can ask them to keep an eye out for Dave. If he leaves his house, they can tell us."

"Actually, you're right," Becks said. "I know Wendy Brown at number 17. She helped tutor Sam for his maths GCSE and did a brilliant job. I can ask her to keep an eye on the house as well."

The women returned to Judith's house, and while Becks and Suzie started phoning the people they knew who lived near to Dave, Judith rang Tanika and informed her that they'd identified the man who'd phoned her anonymously.

"I'll send an officer around to speak to him."

"I think you're going to need a warrant to get into that house."

"Unfortunately, I can't apply for a warrant at this stage. There's nothing we've found so far that links him directly with Geoffrey Lushington, or anyone else on the planning committee. He's just someone who's made a strange phone call to you. At best he's merely a person of interest."

"But what happens if he doesn't answer the door?"

"We'll visit him a second time and send him a letter inviting him to the police station. And when we've explored all other avenues, *then* we can get a warrant."

"How long will that take?"

"He'll be offered fourteen days to make contact with us."

"That's far too slow!"

"I agree, it's frustrating. But it's correct procedure, my hands are tied. And don't worry, we know where he is now. We'll talk to him sooner rather than later, you have my word."

Judith felt deeply frustrated as Tanika ended the call, and her mood wasn't improved when she heard the clatter of the letter box as the day's post arrived. Judith ignored it.

"Aren't you going to see what that is?" Suzie asked.

"I know what it is," Judith said. "It's the post."

"But don't you want to know what it is?"

"Really," Judith said tetchily, "must you boss me around the whole time?"

Judith got up from her chair in a huff, went to the front door, picked up a letter from the floor, looked at the envelope, and then put it off to one side. Suzie was watching carefully and could see that the envelope was blue.

"Happy now?" Judith said as she returned.

"One hundred percent," Suzie said, a plan forming in her mind. It wasn't a clever plan, or cunning in any way, which was why she liked it.

"Can we talk about Dave Butler?" Becks said. "Because I was wondering if there's any way we could flush him out of his—"

Suzie jumped out of her chair and raced over to the front door, where she grabbed up the blue envelope.

"Suzie!" Judith called out, but it was too late.

"I knew it!" Suzie said as she returned holding the letter. "It's from the same person."

"What's that?" Becks asked.

"It's the same handwriting as the last letter. Why won't you open it?" Suzie asked Judith.

"I will," Judith said defensively.

"Then open it," Suzie said, handing the letter over.

"I'll do it later."

"What's so special about it?" Becks asked.

"Very well," she said with a sigh, pretending the whole conversation was of no particular consequence, "if you must know, it's from Matthew Cartwright."

"And who's he when he's at home?" Suzie asked.

"He's an old school friend. From the Isle of Wight."

"An 'old school friend'?" Suzie asked, raising an eyebrow.

"We never stepped out, if that's what you're asking. In fact, I mostly lost touch with him when I was sent away to boarding school on the mainland."

"You 'mostly' lost touch?"

"We still saw each other in the holidays and at Christmas. Until I went off to university, and he married a nice local girl from Ventnor called Sally, and then went and worked for JCB in China. He did very well for himself and made a lot of money."

"So why's he writing to you now?"

"I believe he's back from China. Has been for some time, in fact."

Becks and Suzie could tell that there was something Judith wasn't saying.

"And...?" Suzie asked.

"And last year his wife died."

"He's *propositioning* you?" Suzie said.

"Hardly! He's writing to say hello. To let me know his news." Suzie knew that Judith was lying.

"*And?*" she asked again, even more insistently.

"And he's also asking if we'd like to meet for a cup of tea," she added, finally revealing her secret.

"But that's lovely," Becks said. "So why won't you open the letter?"

"Because I'm not interested in letting a man back into my life," Judith said, folding her hands in her lap.

"What?"

"I've worked hard to get everything 'just so' in my life. I've got a wonderful house, a job I love, and good friends. Why would I let a man ruin all that?"

"It wouldn't ruin all that," Becks said, but without complete conviction. All three women knew that letting a man into your life always risked ruining *all that.* "Are you sure that's actually what he wants?"

"Oh, yes. I mean, he doesn't couch it in those terms. He just said it would be nice to catch up over a cup of tea."

"Then what are you worrying about?" Suzie asked.

"There's no such thing as 'just a cup of tea,'" Judith said darkly. "Especially at my age. You know how it will go. He'll be nice and charming, and then the moment he gets through my front door, he'll want someone to cook his meals, do his washing, and generally run around being a maid of all works, and I really don't want that in my life, thank you very much."

"Hear, hear to that," Suzie said.

"Although it's nice to have someone to laugh with," Becks said.

"What's that?"

"I know Colin's not perfect. But we'll be going on all as normal when he'll say something out of the blue that'll really make me laugh. Generally it's because he gets the wrong end of the stick. Or he'll make a reference to something that happened to us in our twenties. Or we'll be sitting on the sofa watching the telly, and he'll hold my hand. In those moments, it feels lovely to be with someone. Although it could just be Stockholm syndrome on my part, and my marriage is basically a hostage situation."

"Don't listen to her," Suzie said. "You're right, you've got your life set up perfectly. Why would you risk that for anyone?"

"Thank you," Judith said. "Anyway, have you both phoned all the people you know who live near Dave Butler?"

Suzie and Becks agreed that they had no more calls to make, and Becks said she had to get back to the vicarage to cook supper and Suzie had to go and dog-sit a black Labrador in Bisham village, so Judith showed her friends out.

Once they were gone, she returned to her sitting room, but all she could see was the blue envelope by her wingback armchair. She sat down and tried to ignore it. Instead, she made herself think about Dave Butler and why it was that he'd phoned her anonymously, but she couldn't stop thinking about how sad it was that he lived on his own, locked up inside his house.

Judith picked the blue envelope up, slit it open with her finger, pulled out the letter, and started reading.

Chapter 22

THE FOLLOWING MORNING, JUDITH WOKE with a sore head. She hadn't meant to drink so much whisky the night before, but as she looked at her bedside table, the presence of the empty cut-glass decanter and tumbler reminded her that that's precisely what she'd done.

Padding downstairs, she knew there was only one thing for it. By the front door, she took off her nightie and threw on her cape, although there was a sharp stab of pain in her shoulder as she did so. Bette Davis had been right, she thought, getting old wasn't for sissies.

Judith went through her front door and strode to her boathouse. There was dew on the grass and mist rising from the river, but the sky was a sparkling blue and Judith could tell it was going to be another beautiful spring day. As she approached her boathouse, she realized that Dave Butler could be spying on her with binoculars from his house, but she tried to ignore the thought. Instead, once inside, she hung up her cape and stood for a moment, completely naked, in the darkness. Her skin goosebumped in the cold air, and then she walked down her slipway into the silky embrace of the water and swam out under her boathouse doors into the wider river.

Judith swam upstream. She had a lot to think about. Her feelings had been churned up by what she'd read the night before in Matthew's letter. In many respects, it was the worst possible outcome for her: he'd been entirely reasonable. Neither too gushing, nor too reserved. It was polite and respectful. As Matthew explained, he'd written twice before, but he wanted to make one last attempt at reaching out. What with the postal service being what it was, he couldn't be sure that his previous letters had arrived.

He went on to explain that while he'd loved his life as an expat in Shanghai, when it came time to retire, he and his wonderful wife Sally knew they had to come home to the Isle of Wight. And then, when Sally got sick and died, he'd entered a period of mourning that had been very dark. He wrote that he'd loved her for as long as he'd known her, and with her passing, she'd taken his heart with her. However, he'd continued, that was some time in the past now, and he'd realized as he started to look at his life in a world that had no Sally in it, because he'd been abroad for so many years, he'd lost touch with his old friends back in the UK. It hadn't mattered while he'd had Sally, but he didn't have her anymore. So he was writing to all of the old crowd who he still thought fondly of, and just wanted to make contact. He quite understood if Judith hadn't thought of him in years, or indeed had no inclination to meet up, but if that was so, he wanted to wish her well and hope that she was living a fruitful life.

"Of course I'm living a fruitful life!" Judith had muttered in irritation as she'd finished reading the letter. But now that she was swimming, she found her mind drifting in and out of thoughts of sharing her house with someone. Sharing her life with someone. No, it wouldn't do, she told herself. Who was she kidding? She loved living on her own—not that she did, of course, she had her cat Daniel, and Judith was very much of the opinion that a cat was all the company a person needed.

There was something else as well. While the Matthew Cartwright in the letter was self-evidently a thoughtful soul, that wasn't quite her memory of him before she'd been expelled from their school for organizing a sit-in protest against a particularly brutal teacher. Matthew had had a girlfriend at the time, a nice girl called Ellie, Judith remembered. Ellie had changed her look when she and Matthew started dating. And had put her hair up when before she'd worn it to her shoulders. And got her ears pierced—that was right, it was all coming back to Judith. For all his fine words, Matthew wasn't the sort of man who could accept someone for who they were. He wanted to change them. Improve them.

Judith stopped swimming and realized that while it was lovely to be remembered fondly, her instincts had been right the first time. She'd be mad to let a man like Matthew Cartwright into her life. She was happy. What more did she want?

Letting the current bear her back home, Judith instead turned her mind to the murder of Geoffrey Lushington. It was a far more rewarding topic for consideration. In particular, she wanted to know why Dave Butler had told them to "follow the petty cash" the second time he'd rung. Becks had insisted that all the petty cash was correctly accounted for in the records, as far as she and the police could tell. So what had Dave Butler meant? By the time Judith returned to her house, she realized she needed to know if Tanika had managed to speak to Dave Butler yet.

When Judith rang, Tanika didn't answer immediately, which Judith knew spoke volumes.

"You sent an officer to Dave Butler's, but he didn't answer the door," Judith said as soon as Tanika picked up the call.

"And a good morning to you, Judith," Tanika said.

"I'm right, aren't I?"

"As it happens, you are."

"Then why don't you break the door down and pull him out?"

"We're not allowed to enter a property without the owner's permission unless we believe their life is in danger, or that a crime is in progress. Neither is the case here."

"Have you looked Dave Butler up on the police computer?"

"We have, and background checks haven't thrown up any flags. His mother died when he was fifteen years old. His father remarried an American, and they moved to Dallas, Texas. When Dave was eighteen, he came back to Marlow, and he's been here ever since. His IT company has a reasonable turnover for a one-man band, he's not got any kind of a police record—and no debts to speak of, either. He's vanilla, as far as I can tell, although I did take the liberty of speaking to his doctor at the Marlow Surgery. He said that Mr. Butler has been clinically obese ever since he joined his surgery. And, if anything, he's got even heavier since returning to the UK."

As Tanika finished speaking, Judith heard a voice close to Tanika say "Boss, we've got something."

"One moment, Judith," Tanika said into the phone.

"Of course," Judith said, and then pressed her ear as close to her phone's speaker as possible. She heard the member of Tanika's team say that forensics had finished processing the blackmail letter they'd found in the locked metal box in Mr. Lushington's house. They'd found two separate sets of fingerprints on it. The first, of course, belonged to Mr. Lushington himself. But the second set of prints was a surprise. They belonged to Marcus Percival.

Judith was stunned. *It was Marcus Percival who'd been blackmailing Geoffrey?* How was that even possible?

In Maidenhead Police Station, Tanika was as surprised as Judith, but she also wanted to make sure that Judith didn't find out just yet. She didn't want her running off with the information before she could interview Marcus Percival herself. But when she turned her attention back to her phone, she discovered that the line was dead.

Ten minutes later, Judith pedaled up to Marcus Percival's office on her bike at the same time as Becks and Suzie arrived in Suzie's dog-walking van.

"We won't have long with him before the police get here," Judith said.

"Don't you think—" Becks said.

"No, we don't," Suzie said, interrupting. "Come on. This is the break-through we've been looking for all this time. The proof that Geoffrey was up to no good—seeing as he was being blackmailed. And now we can speak to his blackmailer in person," she added as she opened the door for her friends.

Marcus looked up from his desk with a smile as Judith and her friends approached, but his smile vanished when he saw the looks on their faces.

"Ladies…?" he said by way of an opening.

"You've been blackmailing Geoffrey Lushington," Judith said.

Marcus looked as though he'd been slapped in the face.

He tried to recover his poise as he stood up and said, "How about you come into the breakout room?"

Marcus led the women into the glass office where they'd seen him talking to Ian Maloney. He didn't sit down.

As soon as he closed the door, he said, "What on earth are you talking about?"

"You're the person who's been blackmailing Geoffrey."

"I'm not."

"So you agree he's being blackmailed?" Judith asked.

"That's not what I said."

"You weren't surprised when we told you," Suzie said. "You didn't say 'what blackmail?'"

Marcus had no immediate answer to this statement.

"Let me tell you what I think happened," Judith said. "Because it's always struck me that the hardest part of poisoning someone is to get them to ingest it. Especially if you're in company, as you were at the committee meeting. But there was one thing, from a poisoner's point of view, that presented itself. Geoffrey would always take a cup of coffee. You could put poison into his coffee capsule. But that presents two problems, doesn't it? Firstly, how can you be sure that he will drink that specific capsule of coffee and not another? You could, of course, poison all of the capsules in the basket, but, as Debbie demonstrated, she also used the machine. You wouldn't want to end up killing two people when you only ever wanted one dead.

"So how to make Geoffrey choose the one poisoned coffee capsule out of the many that weren't poisoned? It's quite the conundrum. I'm thinking, what if there was in fact no poison in Geoffrey's coffee capsule? Instead, he made himself a nice cup of coffee entirely innocently and then, as you were finally forced to admit, you offered him a cube of sugar, knowing he always had sugar, and it was this one sugar cube that was laced with aconite. The aconite then dissolved into his coffee when the sugar dissolved, Geoffrey drank from the cup, and died. You then removed and hid the jar of sugar—because I never bought the idea that an innocent person would remove a key piece of evidence from a murder scene."

"You're babbling, woman," Marcus spluttered.

"And then you did a rather clever misdirection. It would have been easy to have saved an old coffee capsule that Geoffrey had used at a previous meeting. After all, fingerprints don't really age, do they? And you could just as easily have laced this used coffee capsule with traces of aconite before the meeting. Then, in all the confusion following his death, you whipped the Kilner jar away—the real murder weapon—and hid it where you thought it wouldn't be found. And then you went over to the coffee machine, removed the innocent coffee capsule

Geoffrey had used, and replaced it with the old capsule you'd laced with traces of aconite to make it look like it was the capsule that had poisoned him.

"It's a rather neat murder all round. Geoffrey died from aconite poisoning. Aconite was found in his coffee and in a used coffee capsule in the coffee machine. But, as I've often told my friends here, when you're trying to be logical about something, it's important to remember that correlation isn't causation."

"I'll be honest," Suzie said, "I've never heard her say that before."

"No, she has," Becks said. "She says it all the time."

"Sorry, I'm not always listening."

"Not that I know what it means," Becks added. "I still don't," she added for Marcus's benefit.

"Shut up," he spat, his body quivering with a sudden rage.

"I'm sorry?" Suzie said.

"If you repeat any of what you're saying to me in front of witnesses outside this room, I'll sue. Do you understand? As an estate agent, my name is everything, and you blacken it in any way, I'll come after you for every penny you've got. I'll destroy you in the courts."

"But it was you who was blackmailing Geoffrey. And he'd worked it out, hadn't he? Which is why you killed him—before he could tell the police."

"OK, this is where you're going to have to listen very carefully. I didn't send that blackmail letter to him."

"Then explain your fingerprints on it," Judith said.

Marcus took a deep breath, steadying himself.

"I was the person it was sent to."

"Say that again?" Suzie said.

"I'm the person who's being blackmailed. That's why my fingerprints are all over it."

Chapter 23

BECKS WAS THE FIRST TO recover.

"Why was the blackmail letter sent to you?"

"I've no idea," Marcus said tightly. "'Stop what you're doing or I'll tell everyone your secret'? I mean, what does it even mean? What am I doing that's so wrong? You look into my life. Get the police to look into my life. All I do is work—that's it. Seven days a week. And I wasn't joking when I said my reputation is everything. There's no way an estate agent would last for as long as I've done if they were dodgy in any way. All I can think is the person who sent it has got me confused with someone else."

"You really think so?" Judith asked skeptically.

"Someone's doing something dodgy, that much must be true. And it's got to be something that some other third party thinks I'm behind, when I'm not. Why do you think I took the letter to Geoffrey in the first place? I didn't know what to do with it. If I'm honest, it freaked me out. I didn't dare go to the police. And Geoffrey's a wise old bird, and someone I trusted implicitly. I wanted his advice. Little good it did me."

"Why's that?"

"He insisted on keeping the bloody thing. He said he'd have a good think about it, but in the meantime he wanted to keep it safe in his box file. He said it could prove to be evidence in a blackmail trial, and it would be better all round if he kept hold of it. As an independent person unconnected with the whole thing—and a person who had some standing in the town. But that was Geoffrey all over. He always did the right bloody thing. I realized I should never have taken the letter to him. He was always going to want to keep it, and I should have known."

"It was you who broke into his house," Judith said, suddenly realizing.

Marcus had the good grace to look ashamed.

"I didn't mean to," he said quietly.

"How do you mean, you 'didn't mean to'?" Suzie asked. "You're saying the door came off in your hands by mistake when you smashed through it?"

"But that's what I'm saying. I didn't mean to smash through anything. I used Geoffrey's spare key to get in."

"Ah," Judith said in appreciation. "That explains why the bolts at the top and bottom of the door had broken, but the mortise was unlocked."

"Geoffrey keeps his back door key in a little bird box by his garden shed. Always has done. It's proved critical plenty of times. You know, when there's a big event on and he realizes he's left something at his home. The mayor can't slip away, so he'll send one of us back to his house. The point being, when he died, I was in a real panic about the police finding the letter. I knew my fingerprints were all over it and they'd come to the wrong conclusion that I was blackmailing Geoffrey, when I wasn't."

"That's why you came over and talked to us in the street that first time we met you, wasn't it?" Judith said. "You were trying to find out if the blackmail letter had been found yet."

"I was seriously worried, if you must know."

"You hid it well."

"How can we believe anything you're saying?" Suzie asked.

"I'm helping you with your inquiries, aren't I?" Marcus said.

"You're revealing information only when you can't keep it hidden any longer. If you were really helping, you'd have said all of this much sooner."

"You're right, it's always better to come clean, isn't it? But I was so worried about that letter. It was like having a ticking time bomb. What if it was found? But I began to realize, it was my property. There was nothing stopping me from getting it back. Especially seeing as I knew where the spare key to Geoffrey's house was. It wouldn't even be breaking and entering. I could just let myself in and take it back."

"So you dressed in black and put on a hat," Suzie said.

"I didn't want to be recognized. There are other houses that overlook Geoffrey's back garden. I was doing the police a favor, that's what I decided. It was my duty to remove that letter from the house so they didn't find it and waste their time going down a pointless rabbit hole."

"How very public-spirited of you," Judith said.

"I know you won't believe me, but I know what my motives were, and I'm telling you how it was."

"So what happened?"

"It basically went wrong from the start, that's what happened," Marcus said, running his hand through his hair as he remembered the horror. "I got the key, unlocked the door like normal, but then I found I still couldn't push it open. It's an old door, and it's been quite rainy of late, so I wondered if it had swelled a bit and jammed in its frame. So I pushed on it as hard as I could. It didn't budge. It was so weird. I could see I'd unlocked it, so I gave it a real heave with my shoulder and got it open. That's when I discovered someone had put new bolts at the top and bottom of the door. It put the fear of God into me, I can tell you. There was me wanting to leave no trace, and I'd only gone and torn through the woodwork. But it was about to get worse, so much worse. When I entered the house, a bloody alarm started screaming. I didn't know what was going on, Geoffrey doesn't have an alarm system. He always said he didn't have anything worth stealing other than his books, and who'd steal books?

"So now I'm in a blind panic, and I figured I'd grab the paper out of his box file before I got out of there, but that's when the next disaster hit me. Seriously," Marcus said ruefully, "I do *not* recommend burglary, it's terrifying. But when I got to Geoffrey's box file, the thing was locked. This was a man who'd never cared about security his whole life, and now there were suddenly locks on his door, a new alarm system, and he'd locked a box file I very definitely saw hadn't been locked when I watched him put my letter in it. And if my actions up to this point could be explained away if I was caught, even if it would make me look pretty stupid, here's where I went badly wrong. But I wasn't thinking straight. That bloody alarm, I was in a panic."

"You tried to break into the box file."

"Geoffrey had a metal letter opener on his desk. A vicious thing. Anyway, I figured I could use it to lever the lid up and pop the lock. Which I tried to do, but the damned thing wouldn't open. And with each passing second, I was getting more and more freaked out. I reckon I was only at it for ten seconds, the siren blaring, until I couldn't take any more of the stress. I just dropped the letter opener and fled. But that's the story in all its gory details of how I ended up breaking into Geoffrey's house."

"And the Kilner jar of sugar?" Judith asked like a disapproving maiden aunt.

Marcus looked down at his feet, ashamed.

"You're right," he said, "it was me who put it in the filing cabinet."

"I knew it!"

"But it was only because my fingerprints were all over it—from offering Geoffrey sugar before he died. Because once he'd drunk his coffee and collapsed, I knew it was something in his coffee that had killed him. And I didn't want anyone looking too closely at me. So, in all the confusion after his death, I hid the jar with my fingerprints on it, hoping no one would go searching for it. And I know how this is looking, but it's like I said—would I really have hidden the jar of sugar so badly if I was behind his murder? You have to believe me."

"No way," Suzie said. "Why would we believe anything you say? Seeing as you're the sort of guy who hides key evidence in filing cabinets while a man's dead on the floor, lies when you're asked about it later on, and then breaks into the dead man's house to steal his property."

"It wasn't his property, it was mine—but I admit, it's not a good look," Marcus conceded.

"But then, nor is being blackmailed," Judith added. "Because let's not forget the blackmail letter you're now admitting was sent to you in the first place. You can try and pass the blame all you like, but you're up to no good. Someone knows about it. And wants you to know that they know."

"But I don't know why I was sent that letter," Marcus pleaded, and for the first time, Judith detected a desperation—and vulnerability, perhaps—she'd not seen in him before. "It's a mistake, it must have been."

"But it's connected to Geoffrey's death."

"As it happens, I don't think it can be."

"That doesn't make any sense. If you don't know why that letter was sent to you in the first place, how can you know it's not linked?"

"Because…" Marcus took a deep breath before continuing. "I've received another letter since Geoffrey died."

Marcus went over to a little safe that was sitting on a shelf of files. He pressed the numbers on the keypad, a light in the corner lit up green, and he swung the door open. Reaching in, he pulled out a brown envelope and handed it to Judith.

"You shouldn't be touching that," Becks said to Judith.

"Oh, well," she said as she opened the envelope, "it's a bit late for that, and Tanika's got my fingerprints on file. She can exclude them. So what have we got here?"

Judith pulled out a folded-over sheet of black A4 from the envelope and opened it. Once again, the message was made up of letters that had been cut out of various newspapers and magazines. This time it read:

i TOLD iOU tO STOP Or eLSe

"Can I look at that?" Suzie asked.

"Why, what is it?"

Judith held the letter open for Suzie.

"Just thought I recognized the font of that T. The second letter of 'stop.'"

The letter was thick, a deep maroon in color, and serifed.

Suzie looked at it for a few more seconds, then shook her head in frustration.

"No, maybe I don't. It would be mad anyway, wouldn't it? Being able to recognize a font."

"I've got to be honest," Marcus said. "The two letters have really scared me. I've no idea what they're referring to. It's like I'm being gaslit or something. There's nothing I'm doing that I need to stop doing!"

Sincerity radiated from Marcus, but Judith no longer believed him, if only because she'd seen the spike of fury he'd briefly revealed at the beginning of their conversation. Even though he went on to control himself, she now knew he wasn't the smooth businessman everyone believed him to be; there was a rage inside him. She didn't doubt for a second that he was capable of committing murder. And Suzie was right, he'd been lying to them from the start about pretty much everything. In particular, she believed that Marcus knew full well why he was being blackmailed and was still lying to them. But how could they get him to tell them the truth?

Chapter 24

AFTER JUDITH AND HER FRIENDS handed the second blackmail letter over to Tanika, and Marcus had amended his original statement to admit to his break-in at Geoffrey's house, the case once again stalled. This was especially true when Tanika reported back to Judith that the only fingerprints they'd been able to lift from the new blackmail letter belonged to Marcus and Judith. And no matter how hard the police looked, they could find no evidence in Marcus's life that suggested that he was up to anything nefarious. What if he was telling the truth and the letters were being sent to him by mistake?

Judith felt deeply frustrated. The evidence they were piecing together seemed to be so bitty—with major developments being hard won, and all of them just making the circumstance of Geoffrey's murder all the more puzzling. Assuming Marcus was still lying to them—which seemed likely—who was blackmailing him and why? But then, who had phoned Alec Miller and asked him to stand down, if not Sophia? Who had been the blond-haired man in the kitchenette when Geoffrey had died? And what was Dave Butler's connection to Geoffrey that made him leave his cryptic messages, and why was he still refusing to come out of his house?

With the case stuck, Becks decided that enough was enough, she was going to follow her friends' advice and force Marian out of her house. And so "Operation Marian" was born, not that Becks ever said the words out loud, or told anyone that that's what she was calling it. Her plan at first involved low-grade attempts to make her mother-in-law feel less comfortable in her home, but what she couldn't quite believe was that whatever she unleashed on Marian, she seemed instinctively to be able to head off at the pass, or use to her advantage.

Becks turned the thermostat on the radiator down in the spare bedroom, and Marian announced how much better she was sleeping. She encouraged her son Sam to throw a pizza party—which Becks knew would get out of hand—and Marian plied Sam and his friends with gin cocktails, joined in with their PlayStation dance competition, and took the boys' side when an increasingly rattled Becks asked them to turn the noise down at midnight.

Everything Becks tried to do to get rid of her mother-in-law failed. She announced one day that she, Colin, and the children were planning a big holiday to Europe, so it would probably be time for Marian to move out. Marian was baffled. Didn't Becks know the statistics of houses that were robbed while the owners were away on holiday? The very least Becks needed was to have a house sitter during their absence—and, what's more, as a gesture of thanks, she wouldn't charge anything for the service.

Next, Becks revealed that, very sadly, they were going to have to redecorate the house, but Marian phoned Becks from the paints section of Homebase to ask what paint colors she wanted her to pick up. Her bluff called, Becks couldn't answer with any conviction, and then Marian spent the next few days teasing her in front of Colin about her desire to redecorate the house without having a color scheme sorted first. For his part, Colin was confused, first by the news that the house was going to be redecorated, and then by the news that it wasn't. But then, he'd been just as surprised by the development that they were all going on holiday, so nothing was new there.

Things reached a particular nadir for Becks when she was drawing herself a lovely hot bath, and she found herself idly wondering if she should block up the overflow pipe, flood the house, and then use the excuse of a damaged house to finally boot Marian out.

Her failure to get Marian to leave her home meant that instead of spending less time at Maidenhead Police Station, she was now spending even more.

"She's at the police station," Suzie said to Judith when they once again discovered that while Marian was in the vicarage, Becks wasn't. "This is crazy.

Imagine going to a police station the whole time to get away from home. We need to help her."

"I agree. But there's only one way of stopping her going to the station. We need to prove once and for all what Dave Butler meant when he said 'follow the money,' and 'follow the petty cash.'"

"But how? Becks and the police have been going through those documents for weeks and found nothing."

"Then we'll just have to roll up our sleeves and work even harder."

When Becks arrived at the police station the following day, she found Judith and Suzie already in the archive room, arms deep in all the old minutes, accounts, and piles of receipts.

"What are you doing?" Becks asked.

"We're staging an intervention," Suzie said.

"How do you mean?"

"We're going to find out what 'follow the money' means so you can go home once and for all and deal with your mother-in-law."

"That's very kind of you, but I've tried and she's unbeatable, I'll never get rid of her."

"Well, let's see about that," Judith said. "First let's solve the mystery of 'follow the money.' What have you got so far?"

"It's like I said. I keep hunting, but everything adds up, everything's accounted for. The only thing I've noticed since the last time I talked to you both is that there's a pile of letters from our mystery phone caller, Dave Butler."

"What sort of letters?" Judith asked.

"They're not quite 'green inkers,' but you can feel he's pretty angry in them. He mostly complains when correct procedure isn't followed—he's something of a stickler. Like making sure correct notice periods are given before decisions, that sort of thing."

"Does he ever accuse the council of mismanaging their money?"

"Not once, which I found a bit odd. The moment they step out of line, he fires off a letter of complaint, but he's never suggested that they mismanage their money."

"Then why is he suddenly ringing up and telling us to look at the council's petty cash?"

Becks sighed.

"I've no idea," she said.

"And you really haven't found anything dodgy at all in the petty cash?" Suzie asked.

"I've been through every single receipt for the last seven years. And there are thousands of them. But if you add them up for each tax year, you get the figure that's listed in the accounts. About the only thing that comes close to looking suspicious is the fact that the total of petty cash that's been taken out each year has been a bit more in the last three years than it was in the previous seven."

"It's gone up recently?" Judith asked.

"But it still all adds up. It's just a larger amount, that's all."

"How much by?"

"Off the top of my head, I'd say by about two thousand pounds per year. In the previous years, the petty cash total hovers at about nine thousand pounds, but these last few years, it's been more like eleven thousand pounds."

"So, it's more, but not by that much," Suzie said.

"I don't know I'd agree with that," Judith said. "That's an increase of just under twenty-three percent on the previous years. Have you been through the receipts for these most recent petty cash claims?"

"Of course," Becks said, going over to a pile of boxes in the corner of the room. "They're all in here."

"Then I think we should go over them again."

A few hours later, Tanika stuck her head through the door to say she'd heard that the three friends were in the building and she was wondering how they were getting on. She was shocked to discover that every inch of the main desk in the room—and the shelves and floor—was covered in receipts. Thousands of them, all laid out side by side.

"Don't open the door!" Judith said.

"We've been banned from moving for the last half hour," Suzie said from the corner of the room where she was standing marooned with Becks on a tiny bit of carpet that had no receipts on it.

Judith carefully picked her way among the receipts, bending down to look at them individually, and then stalking over to look at others elsewhere in the room.

"What's going on?"

"We don't know," Suzie said.

"That's not true," Becks said. "Judith explained what she was about to do."

"So what's she doing?"

"I didn't really understand," Becks confessed.

"OK," Tanika said. "I'll leave you to it."

As she closed the door, Judith called out "Don't create a draft" without looking up.

Suzie and Becks exchanged glances. How much longer were they supposed to wait in the corner like this? As it happened, the answer was, not much longer at all.

"Seven pounds seventy-seven," Judith said, out of the blue.

"What's that?" Becks asked.

"It's quite an odd number," she said, picking up a receipt. "Literally, of course, but also figuratively. What costs seven pounds seventy-seven?"

"Something that costs seven pounds seventy-seven," Suzie said, by way of explanation.

"Oh!" Judith said, ignoring Suzie and instead picking her way over to the opposite corner of the room.

"What is it?" Becks asked.

"I know why that number rang a bell," Judith said as she got down on her hands and knees and started scanning the hundreds of receipts in her line of vision. "I know you're here, come on, where are you?" she muttered to herself. "Got you!" she eventually called out as she reached down and picked up another receipt. She compared it to the receipt in her hand.

"How interesting," she said. "These two receipts are for different months, but they're for the same amount. Seven pounds and seventy-seven pence."

"Why's that interesting?"

"If Dave Butler has been saying we need to check the petty cash, but Becks says the numbers all add up, there's still a way both those statements can be true. Someone's been taking petty cash out—to the tune of an extra two thousand pounds a year for the last few years—and then faking a load of receipts to make it look like the numbers still add up. And if I were faking two thousand pounds' worth of petty cash receipts, I'd get bored making up numbers and maybe just keep my finger on the same key on the keyboard, which is how you end up with a receipt for seven pounds seventy-seven."

"That's quite a leap if you ask me," Suzie said.

"But the price on this receipt resonated as I remembered I'd seen that precise figure before." Judith held up the second receipt she'd picked up off the floor. "Seven pounds seventy-seven paid to Hunt's Hardware Store on Station Road."

"Hunt's?" Suzie asked.

"Yes, Hunt's. Is that interesting?"

"What date is on that receipt?"

Judith explained that the payment had been made in the October of the previous year.

"That's not possible," Suzie said, picking her way across the room and taking the two receipts from Judith.

"Careful where you're treading," Becks said, but neither Suzie nor Judith was listening to her.

"Why's it not possible?" Judith asked her friend.

"Hunt's closed in the summer," Suzie said. "So how come it's still issuing receipts in October?"

"Dear heavens," Judith said. "Am I right? This is how our embezzler's been getting hold of their cash? They've been submitting fake petty cash receipts?"

"But who's claimed that expense?" Becks asked, now striding across the room with scant regard for the receipts she was displacing as she went.

Judith looked down at the two receipts in her hand.

"It's the same name on both receipts," she said. "And I could tell you, but I don't think you'd believe me."

Chapter 25

IT TOOK JUDITH AND HER friends the rest of the day to prove how the embezzler had operated, but once they'd got their evidence together, they headed back to Marlow and knocked loudly on the culprit's front door.

After a few seconds, it was opened by Debbie Bell.

"You've been stealing money from the council," Judith said.

"I'm sorry?" Debbie said.

"You can act innocent all you like, but we've worked it out," Judith added as she pushed past Debbie into her house, Suzie following on her heels.

"What are you doing?" Debbie asked in mounting panic.

"May we come in?" Becks asked somewhat redundantly from her position outside.

Debbie ignored Becks and followed Judith and Suzie into the kitchen. Becks came in last, and when she got into the kitchen, she saw that Suzie was laying out all of the receipts from Hunt's they'd spent the afternoon collecting.

"You only made one mistake," Judith said by way of explanation. "You carried on faking receipts at Hunt's after it had closed."

Fear slammed into Debbie's face.

"How…?" was all she could manage to say.

"It's only these three receipts here that are dated after it closed," Suzie said, handing over three receipts to Debbie. "I guess you'd not heard it stopped trading at the end of the summer and carried on making up fake claims."

Debbie's eyes darted from the women to the receipts and back to the women again. She had nothing to say.

"But these receipts really look like the real deal," Suzie said in appreciation, picking one of them up. "Although I suppose it's not that hard to fake receipts with the computers we all have these days."

"Mind you, it took some chutzpah on your part to put all of these receipts through in your name," Judith said. "I'd even say it was somewhat foolhardy. But then, I suppose, as an accountant, and the person who's trusted with ordering and storing the regatta ducks and Santa Fun Run outfits, your colleagues think you're entirely trustworthy. Which you're not, I hasten to add."

"It's for private doctors' appointments," Debbie blurted. "You're right. Some of the council's petty cash has made its way to me. I never meant it to, and it's not that much anyway. Not compared to the budget of the council. Which runs into the millions. And you're right. I used Hunt's and a few other shops as my cover. You've no idea how shocked I was when I found out it had closed. It brought me back to my senses, and I vowed I'd stop what I was doing. Not that you'll believe me, I'm sure. Or the reason why I had to take the money in the first place."

"Then why don't you try us?" Suzie asked.

"Very well. That first time we spoke, I told you how Geoffrey had helped me with a health scare I'd had, but I didn't tell you what it was. It wasn't a scare as such. It was more that I was part of my way through my forties, my brain had turned to fog, and my life was falling apart. I didn't know what was going on."

"Ah," Judith said, understanding coming to her.

"Tell me about it," Suzie said in solidarity.

"I couldn't remember things at work. Whole conversations. I thought I was going mad."

"When I first got menopausal," Becks said, "I'd start talking about something, forget what it was within seconds, and then I'd have to ask the person I was talking to what I was talking about."

"You're still a bit like that," Judith said.

Debbie relaxed, believing that her audience were on her side—which they weren't—but it didn't mean they didn't have empathy.

"And the most terrible hot flushes," Debbie added.

"Bloody hell, yes," Judith said in agreement. "First thing in the morning, last thing at night, and all the times in between. I could be sitting in a chair doing nothing, and suddenly I'm sweating like a dray horse. I found carrying one of those Chinese fans in my handbag worked wonders," she added kindly.

"It was impacting my work. To do my job, I've got to be able to concentrate on a lot of numbers. And remember them. When I tried to talk to my boss, he just told me to sort it out."

"You mean Paul De Castro?"

Debbie nodded.

"I didn't know what to do. I was at my wits' end. Losing sleep—because of the bloody menopause, but also losing sleep because I was so worried. I was so shattered at work, I was given a formal warning."

"That's disgraceful," Becks said.

"What could I do? Get a job somewhere else? That wasn't possible. Not with how much of a mess I was. Imagine the reference they'd give me."

"When was this?" Judith.

"Three years ago. And I felt bad when Geoffrey offered to help me. I didn't want to tell him what the real problem was when he took me to the hospital for appointments with my consultant. The hospital specializes in cancer and I know he'd put two and two together and make five. But the thing was, I was also a mess. So I might have had cancer for all he knew. I was distracted, depressed, and confused. And he never pried. I could tell he never would. It was simple for him. I needed help getting to and from the hospital, so he dropped everything to be my taxi service, and as for the rest of it, that was none of his business as far as he was concerned. He really was a gent."

Debbie stopped talking as she remembered her friend, and Judith and her friends exchanged concerned looks. There was such fondness in Debbie's words that it was hard to imagine she could be Geoffrey's killer.

"Get to the bit where you steal the council's money," Suzie said.

"No, of course," Debbie said. "I knew I had to do something, but I didn't know what. I tried talking to my GP, but he was unsympathetic. Every time

I tried to get any kind of treatment on the NHS, it always fizzled out. I got myself on a waiting list, but when I checked back long after I should have been seen, it turned out there'd been a mix-up and I wasn't on any kind of waiting list at all. That's when I snapped. Because the thing is, when I'd been doing my research, I discovered this other health service that's out there. Where they treat you quickly, give you the best advice, and it's all bright lights, the latest hospital equipment, and free coffees in reception while you're waiting to see your specialist."

"You went private," Judith said.

"You just went to their website, booked an appointment for their care package, and then they took charge of everything else. Don't get me wrong, I know it's not how it should be, and they were only offering what I guess the NHS were able to offer when they had more money. But it was so enticing. All I had to do was fill in the form and my life would start improving."

"Although it wasn't that simple, was it?" Judith said. "You also needed to pay them money."

"I've never done anything wrong before, you have to believe me. I'm not a criminal. It makes me sick even thinking about it. But I didn't know what to do. A full package of support from a private specialist was going to cost about two thousand pounds, and I didn't have that sort of money. Life's so expensive, and I've never earned as much as I should. I think I went a bit mad, if I'm honest. My salvation was out there, I knew how I could make myself better, but I couldn't afford it.

"And that's when I realized I could mock up some petty cash receipts and run them through the accounts, like you said. After all, it was my job to prepare the books for the council's accountants. As long as the total of the receipts equaled the amount of cash that had been taken, I figured they wouldn't ask too many questions. And going over budget by two thousand pounds felt more like a rounding error, if I'm honest. Don't get me wrong, it was a lot of money for me—it allowed me to get well—but it barely registers at a council level. I know that what I did was wrong, but you can see the pressure I was under. I only did it to save my health. Under extremis."

"That's not quite true," Becks said. "I can imagine you needing that money to get diagnosed three years ago, but you've been taking out an extra two thousand pounds in petty cash every year since then as well. What are you now spending your money on?"

Debbie flashed a glance at the porcelain figurines on the shelves, and Becks and her friends realized what the look meant.

"You didn't?" Becks asked.

"I, er…" Debbie said, floundering. "Things have been so tough. And I've always loved Lladró figurines. When the accounts went through on the nod three years ago and I realized I'd got away with it, I promised I'd not do it again. But there was still money I had to pay for my HRT treatment. Even if I didn't need to pay for all the diagnosis and tests. So I ended up taking the same amount of money again."

"Theft is theft," Suzie said.

"And murder's murder," Judith said.

Debbie's eyes widened in shock.

"Because Geoffrey found out," Judith continued. "Didn't he? And if there's one thing we've learned about Geoffrey, it's that he was honorable to a fault. He wouldn't have taken kindly to you stealing all that cash from the council."

"But don't you see, that's how I can prove he didn't know. He would have gone to the police, I agree. But he didn't, did he? That's all the proof you need that he never found out. You check the police records, he never told them anything. How could he, he didn't know anything!"

"Or is it that he died before he had a chance to? And let's not forget that two sets of fingerprints were found on the coffee capsule that contained the poison that killed him. His. And yours. Because he found out you were embezzling, didn't he? So you went to Sophia's garden, got hold of some aconite, ground it up, and slipped it into a coffee capsule that you then made sure he used to make his coffee, didn't you?"

"I didn't! You have to believe me!"

Debbie looked so upset that Judith thought it was almost possible to believe she had nothing to do with Geoffrey's murder. Almost.

Suzie's phone started ringing.

"Sorry," she said as she fished it out. "Hold on," she added as she saw who it was. "I think I need to take this."

Suzie listened for a few seconds before replying, "Now that's perfect timing, we were just talking about him. Thanks, we'll be there in five." As she hung up, she said, "That was Alison Green, she lives two doors down from our reclusive friend, Dave Butler. She says a supermarket delivery van's pulled up outside his house about to deliver a shop to him, and the front door's open."

Judith and her friends barely had time to tell Debbie that she'd have to make a full confession to the police before they were leaving her house, climbing into Suzie's van, and bombing across Marlow to Dave's house. Suzie parked beyond the supermarket delivery van that they saw was blocking his small drive.

"OK, so what's the plan?" Becks asked.

"If you ask me, this is a job for you," Judith said. "Because I think we all know that if one of us had to sweet-talk a deliveryman, it would be you. Go on. Go and charm your way into Dave's house. You can let us in afterward. Like Robin Hood letting his Merry Men into Nottingham Castle."

Becks was about to refuse when she realized that she was in fact delighted by the idea of tricking her way into Dave's house.

"Hello," Becks said a few moments later to the older gentleman who was hefting the bags of shopping from his van into Dave's house. "I've come to see Dave. Can I help you with that?"

"Thanks," the older man said, and allowed Becks to pick up a bag of shopping from the red plastic tray of shopping at his feet.

Becks saw that the carrier bag she'd picked up was full of oven chips, meat pies, rich puddings, bars of chocolate, and sweets. A quick glance at the other bags showed a similarly unhealthy selection of food—from high-sugar cereal to cans of fizzy drink. She was quietly appalled as she took her bag into the hallway, although the house she entered was, if anything, even more shocking.

It was the smell that hit her first. The air was dank and rotten, like something was decaying. But if the smell was bad, the sight of the washing in the kitchen sink and food left out among wrappers was even more upsetting. With a tight smile that also allowed her to keep breathing through her mouth, Becks put down her bag of shopping along with the others. The deliveryman thanked her, said he was done, and wished her a good day as he allowed her to show him out.

Becks closed the front door and felt a shiver of ice run down her spine.

She'd gotten into Dave's house, he was almost certainly in a room somewhere nearby, but he didn't know she was there. Had she in fact broken the law, she found herself wondering in rising panic. No, she hadn't, she quickly told herself, she'd come through an open door, that was all.

The doorbell chimed, Becks jumped, and Judith's voice called from outside, "Mr. Butler, are you there?"

Becks threw the door open.

"I hope so," she whispered as she let Judith and Suzie into the house.

"Hey!" an angry voice wheezed from the sitting room.

"Apologies, Mr. Butler," Judith called out, as she went into the room where the voice had come from.

The sitting room was covered in computer equipment, cables, old plates of food, cups that hadn't been cleared away, and there was only one chair at a single table. But what caught the women's attention was the sight of Dave Butler sitting in an old velour armchair, his hand inside a party-sized bag of crisps, a nearly finished three-liter bottle of lemonade on the table to his side.

Up close, Dave looked even bigger than he'd done on the CCTV footage from All Saints Church, and he was wearing a sweat-stained gray hoodie, old black tracksuit bottoms that were smeared in God-knows-what, and he had a dark beard and greasy hair. Not to put too fine a point on it, he looked in terrible shape. Perhaps most shockingly, Judith realized that he was probably only in his late twenties or early thirties. In fact, as she looked more closely at his face, she felt like she could see the younger, thinner version of him somewhere in among the dishevelment. How could someone have let themselves go so catastrophically at such a young age?

Dave had a tablet computer to his side that showed a security camera view of the front of the house.

"Mr. Butler, we meet at last," Judith said.

Chapter 26

"YOU'VE BEEN AVOIDING US," JUDITH said.

"I don't know who you are."

"You do," Judith said. "I'm Judith Potts."

"Not heard of you," he said.

"Are we really going to do this? We've got video evidence of you phoning me from the phone box opposite the church."

"What?" Dave said, shocked.

"There's a video camera on the spire of the church," Becks said. "It's for the nesting kestrels, but it also shows the phone box by the bridge."

"That wasn't me, I don't know what you're talking about, you need to get out."

Dave tried to lift himself out of his chair, but he had difficulty getting purchase and fell back into his seat.

"It's very simple," Judith said. "You either tell us the truth, or the next person to come through your front door will be the police. They won't be as friendly as us. And to be clear, we're not very friendly."

To allow Dave the space to consider the deal she was offering, Judith went and looked at the mantelpiece where there was a faded photo in a battered frame that showed a plump boy, about ten years old, with a cheeky smile, dimples in his cheeks, as he stood by Marlow Bridge with a woman.

"Your mother?" she asked.

Dave scowled by way of an answer.

Judith looked more closely at the woman, and saw an open face, and deep green hazel eyes. Judith saw that Dave had the same hazel eyes.

"She looks lovely."

Dave shifted his considerable bulk, but didn't answer, and Judith remembered what Tanika had told her from the background checks they'd run.

"That must have been hard," she said kindly. "Losing your mother as a teenager. And then being whipped off to a new country. And a new stepmum."

"It was a long time ago," Dave said. "I came back to the UK as soon as I could."

Judith had been wondering what had made Dave such a shut-in, and her instincts were telling her that the answer lay in Dave's past.

"Tell me about your father," she asked.

"I don't want to talk about him."

"Then how about you tell us why you've been phoning me and giving me tip-offs," Judith said. "Now you've had a bit of time to think about it."

"I want Geoffrey's killer caught."

"Believe it or not," Judith said, "I don't believe you."

"It's the truth."

"This is the same Geoffrey Lushington who's been running a council you've written all those letters of complaint to?"

"Jesus!" Dave wheezed. "This is why I didn't want to get involved."

"Why don't you explain?" Becks said again.

Dave shifted himself in his chair so he could sit more comfortably.

"OK—you're right. I've written to the council over the years."

"But why?" Judith asked. "What have the council done that warrants your ire?"

"If you must know, Geoffrey crossed me. Ten years ago."

"He did?" Becks asked. "How?"

"I..." Dave took a deep breath and readied himself for his confession. "I wrote a book. A sci-fi novel. When I was nineteen. Set in the future when the UK's flooded and we're all living in small communities on the land that's high enough. Leeds is the capital city—or what's left of it. London's gone. When I got to Marlow, I sent it out to publishers, starting with Geoffrey. He was this famous local publisher. And he said it was no good. But it was more than that. Everyone else I sent it to rejected it. I reckoned he'd put them off."

"Had he?" Judith asked.

"That's when I started writing those letters. I'd show him the power of my writing. You can see I struggle to get about, but council minutes are always published after each meeting. If you know how to read them, and all of the financial and other reports, there's all the information you need. Between what they publish and reports in the local papers, you can put together a pretty good picture of what's going on."

"Which is how you found out about Debbie Bell embezzling," Judith said.

"What?"

"But you knew that. That's why you rang me and tipped me off."

Dave was amused as much as he was surprised.

"It was the sinister Debbie Bell?" he asked.

"Sinister?" Judith asked.

"It's just a turn of phrase. I think theft's pretty sinister. Not that I knew it was her. Are you sure you're right?"

"She's admitted it," Suzie said.

"Wow. I'd guessed someone was embezzling. The petty cash figure jumped three years ago—after decades of being pretty static each year."

"You noticed?" Judith asked, impressed.

"It went up by just under twenty-three percent."

"That's exactly what Judith said!" Suzie said before realizing that it perhaps wasn't polite, comparing her friend too closely with Dave. "Which is great," she added a touch lamely. "We need people who can do maths."

"The point is," Dave continued, "I couldn't see anything in the minutes of the committees that would explain that extra expenditure. It didn't pass the 'smell test,' you know? Something was up. But I had no idea who was behind it. That's why I tipped you off. I reckoned you'd be able to work it out for me. Because there was every chance the person who was embezzling was behind the murder."

"I don't get it," Becks said. "I thought Geoffrey crossed you. Why did you want his killer caught?"

Dave took a deep breath.

"About a year ago, he got in touch with me. He said he wanted to meet."

"He did?" Judith said, not entirely believing Dave's story.

"He knew I was behind the letters—I make no secret that I'm the person holding the council to account—so I was like you, skeptical. Why did he want to meet up? He said he wanted to visit me at my home, but that was no good. People don't come into my house," Dave said to the women to remind them of their intrusion. "And not everywhere in town has the sort of access or space I need. So we arranged to meet on a bench in Higginson Park. There's good step-free access for my scooter. Down by the pizza barge. And then, when we met, Geoffrey said he had an apology to make. He said that as a publisher you always risk turning down a book that later becomes a big hit. And although he didn't think there was much chance of my book breaking out, he said it hadn't ever left him. It would still pop into his mind every now and again.

"I didn't believe him. Not at first. What if this was him wanting to humiliate me again? I could understand it. But he said that he'd been retired too long. He wanted to get back into publishing. In a small way. By publishing the books he wanted. An 'eclectic' list, that's what he said he was going for. Was I up for it?"

Dave drifted off as he remembered the encounter.

"What did you say?"

"I wanted proof he was on my side. That he wasn't trying to stab me in the back. Again. He was really hurt by that," Dave said with a smile that wasn't remotely kind. "So that's when he admitted I was basically right with all my criticisms of the council. Of course I was," Dave added with a smirk. "Or I wouldn't have sent the letters. He agreed they'd made mistakes over the years—when it came to planning, or breaking covenants for the use of Higginson Park, or not doing the full due diligence when contracts went out to tender—that sort of thing. Basically, he admitted that everything I'd accused them of, they'd done."

"Everything?"

"And stuff I hadn't even known about," Dave added, and then his face darkened. Judith could tell that Dave felt he'd overshared, and she wanted to get him back onside before he closed up entirely.

"So it was a good meeting?" Judith asked.

"Sure was." Dave tried to get out of his chair, his wheezy breath catching as he fell back again. "You see that laptop over there?" he said, pointing at a small desk that had a laptop on it and piles of paper. "There's an in tray. Could you bring it over to me?"

With the practiced smile of someone who was used to helping others, Becks went over to where Dave was pointing and picked up a gray mesh in tray that was brimming with paperwork. She handed it to Dave, who put it in his lap. After rootling through the stack of papers, he pulled out a letter, which he handed to Judith. She saw it was dated almost a year ago.

"Here's the letter he wrote to me afterward."

Judith started reading.

> 13 Highfield Close
> Marlow
> Bucks
> SL7 2BZ
> 14 July 2022
>
> Dear Dave
>
> I thought I'd put into writing what we discussed in the park last week. I don't want there to be any confusion or misunderstanding this time.
>
> I am starting up an imprint called Marlow Press that will publish a small mixed list of fiction. The criteria for publication are simple: that I like the book and think it would do well commercially. Although it's unlikely we'll be able to have much of a presence in any of the major chains, I've already spoken to Marlow Books, the Little Bookshop in Cookham and the Bell Bookshop in Henley, and they're interested in supporting us in whatever way they can. I've also recruited Marcus Percival's son Adrian as a web designer and developer. In this day and age, having a compelling online presence is everything.
>
> So that's my pitch for the business model, but a publisher doesn't exist without books to sell, so I'd like

this letter to be my formal offer to publish your novel, Anthropocene. The advance of £1,000 is very much a token gesture. As I explained, the business model is to split all net profits 50/50. And for the avoidance of doubt, there's every chance that this venture won't make any meaningful money for either of us, but you don't go into publishing with the expectation of making money, only the hope!

The main point is that I think you've written a very important novel that only becomes more and more relevant as each year passes. It would be my honor to be your publisher.

Yours

Geoffrey Lushington

P.S. As for the other matter you mentioned, I've started investigating, but haven't any firm proof yet. I'll let you know when I do.

"Gosh," Becks said as she finished reading.

"It's always been my dream to be published," Dave said. "And now my publisher's dead before my book came out. Can you even imagine how that feels?"

"It won't be published?"

"I spent most of this year doing revisions to the text with Geoffrey giving notes. It was amazing. Being treated like a proper writer. Like I knew what I was doing. And he made it so much better. I was really proud of it. When he died, he was in the process of copyediting it. But all it is is a Word document with corrections."

"I'm so sorry. Could you sell it to someone else?"

"Maybe. But I don't know anyone in the publishing industry, apart from Geoffrey. I don't think they'll be any more interested than they were last time."

"What's that bit at the bottom?" Judith asked, indicating the letter's postscript.

"Geoffrey reached out to me soon after I'd worked out there was a discrepancy in the petty cash account for the council. At that stage, I didn't yet know if it was an honest mistake, or if someone was up to no good."

"Hang on," Suzie said. "Are you saying you tipped Geoffrey off that someone was embezzling council funds?"

"At the end of our meeting in the park. I told him I reckoned something dodgy was going on in the petty cash. Why?"

"What did he say to that?"

"He was shocked—and said he'd look into it."

The women caught each other's eye. *Geoffrey had been looking for embezzlement in the petty cash accounts before he'd died?*

"Why didn't you tell the police about the embezzling?" Judith said as she held up the letter. "And that Geoffrey knew about it."

Dave looked embarrassed.

"I didn't want to get involved."

"Whyever not?" Judith asked, before realizing that the answer lay in every uncleared plate in the room, and in the bag of crisps and bottle of lemonade to Dave's side. He didn't want anyone seeing him, did he?

Dave saw Judith take in the squalor of his room.

"I live like this because I like living like this," he said defiantly. As he spoke, a black cat slinked into the room and rubbed itself against Dave's leg. "And no need to feel sorry for me, I don't live on my own, I've got a cat," he added.

Suzie and Becks realized that they were very carefully not looking at Judith as Dave spoke about how he wasn't living on his own because he owned a cat.

"I've got everything I need to do my job right here," Dave said, indicating the computers around the room, "and my work earns me enough money to do as I want, so why would I share any of that with anyone?"

Becks and Suzie could see that Judith was somewhat on edge as she wound up the conversation with Dave by telling him that his plan had backfired, he was going to have to give a statement to the police, and then she suggested they all leave.

Once outside, Judith waited until they were in Suzie's van before speaking.

"He's the killer, isn't he?" she said before anyone else could speak.

"I think he's certainly capable of murder," Becks said. "But that letter from Geoffrey made it pretty clear that he was going to publish his novel."

"What do you mean 'he's certainly capable of murder'?" Judith asked tartly.

Even Suzie could see that the encounter with Dave had upset their friend more than she wanted to let on.

"I just mean that he comes from a difficult background," Judith said, "and he even confirmed what we'd found out, that he'd written a number of critical letters to the council over the years."

"But I'll tell you this much," Suzie said, "there's no way he was the blond-haired guy I saw in the kitchenette that night."

"Are you sure?" Judith asked.

"God, yes. There's no way the person in the kitchen that night was someone as large as Dave—I'd have noticed. He's not the killer."

This seemed to mollify Judith a bit, but her friends noticed how she didn't join in with their conversation about Dave—and what they'd learned about Debbie as well—as they drove back into Marlow. Instead, Judith asked Suzie if she'd drop her off at her house.

Once home, Judith finally admitted to herself that she'd been much more affected by her visit to Dave than she'd wanted to admit. The fact that he, like her, did all his work remotely. The fact that he, like her, lived on his own with a cat. The fact that he, like her, was the only other person who'd worked out the percentage increase in the petty cash account. And there was something else. Like her, Dave had a tragedy in his past—the death of his mother in his case, rather than the death of an abusive husband in hers—but it was another similarity, wasn't it?

When Judith found herself standing by her whisky decanter, she poured herself a glass. She looked about her—at the mess of her room. At the single wingback chair by the fireplace, her cat Daniel curled up in it asleep.

She went over to her card table and smoothed down the green baize.

She pulled out some paper and picked up a sharp pencil.

She started writing.

Dear Matthew, it was such a surprise to receive your letter.

Chapter 27

THE FOLLOWING MORNING, SUZIE FOUND that she couldn't settle. She kept playing over their encounter with Dave, and Judith's panicked reaction afterward. Suzie could well understand why Judith had been so thrown. She and Becks had talked of nothing else once they'd dropped Judith off the night before.

"Dave and Judith could be peas in a pod," Suzie said to her friend as she drove her back to the vicarage.

Becks, for her part, pointed out that while Judith might be a little indulgent when it came to whisky and chocolate, she didn't willfully overeat like Dave did. In fact, she made it clear that she'd seen nothing in her life that was quite as shocking as the contents of Dave's shopping that afternoon. Since when did pizzas start getting bacon and cheese stuffed into their crusts? And what on earth was a "Hungry-Man Double Chicken Bowl"?

Suzie nonetheless believed that Dave was a possible sign of things to come for Judith, and she couldn't stop thinking about it for the rest of the night and the following morning. Even when she took Emma for a long walk, she couldn't shake the feeling that she should be staging an intervention, despite the fact that she'd promised her friends she'd stop having mini projects. And she knew how angry Judith would be if she thought Suzie was trying to improve her life in any way.

To get her mind off the subject, Suzie decided she'd have to resort to drastic measures. She hunted under the kitchen sink and pulled out the old plastic basket that contained all her cleaning equipment. She'd known for some time that the downstairs smelled of stale cigarette smoke, dust, and dog hairs, and she'd decided it was time to make amends.

She banged the Hoover around the skirting boards, punched the sofa cushions back into life, bullwhipped the TV screen with a duster, and spent the next hour getting the room shipshape. Once she was done, she noted how much better the room made her feel now it was tidy and dust-free, and a good part of her mind vowed she'd very definitely clean her house more often—while a separate part of her mind, at exactly the same time, knew she never would.

But the tidying had put Suzie in a good mood, so she decided to tackle a pile of magazines that were on a nearby table. She couldn't help noticing that each publication represented one of the various fads she'd had over the months and years before only to discover, much later, that she really wasn't interested in freshwater fishing at all. Or investing in penny shares. Or hill running, model railways, and everything in between, she could see. *Practical Photography?* Suzie didn't even remember when she'd thought she'd get into photography. And for every random periodical, there were at least two others on home improvements. *Home and Garden, Woman's Home, The World of Interiors*, she had them all.

God, she thought with a wry smile, she was as bad a hoarder as Judith. But then, she was at least throwing her old magazines out, which was more than Judith had ever managed. Suzie went to the kitchen and brought over her paper recycling bin. With a great heave, she slid the pile of magazines in. As she did so, the beginnings of an idea started to float across her mind—to do with how much better she felt now that she'd had a good clear-out—although it didn't quite arrive as she noticed that a couple of her magazines had missed the bin and fallen onto the floor. Bending over to pick them up, she paused as she looked at the first one. It was a recent copy of *Architectural Digest*. She'd bought it when she'd first thought she was going to build the pod hotel in her back garden. But there was something about the cover that was piquing her memory, not that she could tell what it was. It was more a feeling in her waters that the cover was relevant somehow.

And that's when she realized what her subconscious was trying to tell her. It was the font of the title of the magazine, *Architectural Digest*. The way the horizontal line of the letter "t" was angled.

Suzie grabbed up her phone and opened her video calling app.

On the other side of Marlow, Judith was putting the finishing touches to a crossword she was compiling for the *Observer* newspaper when she heard her mobile phone ring. She was puzzled, as it was a ringtone she'd not heard before. Putting her work to one side, she went over to her phone and saw that she was receiving something that was called a "FaceTime" call from Suzie.

Judith pressed the green "answer" icon and was surprised to see Suzie's face fill the screen.

"I can see you," Judith said, surprised.

"And I can see you," Suzie said with a smile.

"But I look dreadful, you shouldn't be able to look at me like that."

"Sorry," Suzie said, "but this is something you need to see."

In Suzie's house, Suzie could see on her screen that Judith looked panicked at the idea of being dropped in on unannounced—and she saw her friend's finger hover over the screen to press an icon, at which point the image of Judith turned into a cartoon giraffe.

Suzie laughed—a raucous explosion of joy—which made the cartoon giraffe frown. The cartoon giraffe then told her, still in Judith's voice, that she didn't see what was so funny.

Judith as an indignant giraffe was about the funniest thing that Suzie had ever seen, and its increasingly irate face made her cry with laughter.

"If I knew how to end this call, I'd end it," Giraffe Judith said.

"You've pressed a button," Suzie managed to get out, "and it's turned you into a giraffe."

"I can see that, how do I stop it!"

"There's a button at the bottom of the screen. You pressed it."

"You mean this one?" Giraffe Judith said and then turned into a cartoon chicken. Chicken Judith's beak opened in shock.

"Well, I'm glad I'm making you happy," Chicken Judith said sniffily.

Suzie could tell that Judith was about to lose her temper, so she helped her friend put her screen back to normal and explained that she wanted Judith to take her phone through to her incident room and show her the photo they took of the blackmail letters that had been sent to Marcus Percival.

Judith went next door to the incident board and held up her phone so Suzie could see the printouts she'd pinned to the wall of the two blackmail letters.

Back in her home, Suzie held up her copy of *Architectural Digest* next to her phone and compared the letter "t" in the title to the letter "t" that the blackmailer had cut out and stuck to the page to make the word "Stop." It was a perfect match. But better than that, the "g" from the word "doing" was also cut out from the same masthead.

"I was right," Suzie said. "Some of the letters in the blackmail letter have been cut from the title of the *Architectural Digest*."

"Oh, well done, that's wonderful!" Judith said. "Because I can't help noticing, there was precisely one, and only one, architect in the room when Geoffrey was murdered."

Chapter 28

"SO WHAT'S OUR STRATEGY?" BECKS asked as the three women waited outside Jeremy's office.

"Despite his bravado, I think Jeremy's a weak man," Judith said. "An impressionable man. So I suggest we go in there and make the very strongest impression on him as possible."

The door opened to reveal Jeremy.

"Saw you ladies loitering," he said with a smile. "Not with intent I hope?"

"Very much so," Judith said, pushing past him.

"Oh?" Jeremy said, following her inside.

"It's you, isn't it?" Judith said as Jeremy and her friends joined her in the office.

"It's me what?" Jeremy said, trying to keep up his good cheer, but somewhat wrong-footed.

"It's you who's been blackmailing Marcus Percival."

"What are you talking about?"

"Please don't lie to us, forensics have proven it was you."

"They ha—?" Suzie said before ending in a far more authoritative "—ave. They have," she added, just to make sure she'd got her point across.

"What do you say to that?" Judith asked.

Jeremy licked his lips.

"I don't know what you're talking about," he said.

"You shouldn't have cut up the *Architectural Digest* to create some of the letters."

Jeremy looked at the women, could see their resolve, and slumped down on his office chair.

"I don't understand," he said. "I was so careful."

"Not careful enough," Judith said.

"What happened?" Becks asked simply.

The women could see that Jeremy didn't know where to begin, and then the fog of indecision seemed to clear.

"I hate him," he said.

"Geoffrey?" Suzie asked.

"No—Marcus bloody Percival. Always the perfect one. The one the girls liked. We were at school together, but I worked him out in year twelve. Everything he does is always about him, about what makes him look good. Don't be fooled by his charm, ladies. He's a sociopath."

"That's not how he comes across," Becks said.

"That's what I'm saying. He's made it his life's work to pretend to be normal. Marrying that poor woman, it's her I feel sorry for."

"I know his wife, Claire, she's happy."

"You reckon? You ask around. She's living with someone who controls everything about her. What clothes she wears. What perfume! It's always about control for Marcus."

"How do you know all this?"

Jeremy had the good grace to look embarrassed.

"Whenever Claire's around, I always try to listen in on what she and Marcus are saying. Because he's not the same guy when he thinks no one's watching. Not the same guy at all. And there's nothing I can do about it. I've got an architect's practice to run, and he's the number one estate agent in town. I can't cross him—and doesn't he know it. He's always polite to me, but there's a look in his eyes that says he owns me. He thinks he's superior."

"And he's been like this with you…?" Judith asked.

"For as long as I've known to see it. He's a wrong 'un."

"But what's his secret? In your first letter to him, you said, 'Stop what you're doing or I'll tell everyone your secret.'"

The lips on Jeremy's face slid into a leer.

"He runs a Twitter account," he said. "Called Marlow01628. And it spews out the most racist, misogynistic, xenophobic hate you could imagine."

"Are you serious?" Suzie said, pulling out her phone and opening her Twitter app. "What was the name of the account?"

"Marlow01628, like the dialing code."

They all knew that the dialing code for Marlow was 01628.

"Oh," Suzie said as her phone showed her the account's feed.

"Is it bad?" Becks asked.

Suzie's face fell as she scrolled through the tweets.

"This is nasty."

"He's a nasty man," Jeremy said.

"There's a lot of hatred…"

Judith found this chiming with her recent discovery that Marcus had a bottled-up rage inside him, but could Jeremy be believed?

"How do you know Marcus is behind this account?"

"It was Sophia who first brought it to my attention. She'd come across it when it said something particularly vicious about her. But as I was scrolling through the feed, I saw this one tweet where it used the word 'undermime'—with an 'm'—rather than 'undermine.' It looked like an innocent typo. But I know Marcus says 'undermime'—it's always made me laugh. He's learned the word wrong. So when I saw it in a tweet, it got me thinking—not that I could believe he was behind the account. Not at first. But the more I thought about it, the more it seemed to make sense. I'm one of the few people who knows the truth about him—that he's a nasty piece of work.

"So I started going back through the Twitter account to see if there was some other way of proving that Marcus was behind it. There wasn't. There was just that one slip, that one time he'd put his foot wrong. So I decided to see if I could flush him out." Jeremy smiled a lopsided grin at the memory. "After a planning meeting at the beginning of the year, I caught up with Geoffrey afterward and told him I'd heard a rumor that a refugee processing center was going to be set up on the industrial park."

"What did he say to that?" Judith asked.

"He wasn't fussed, and said something like 'Well, if refugees need processing, then there's going to have to be a processing center somewhere.' But the point is, I made sure that we were within earshot of Marcus when I said it. And the following day, guess who tweets about a refugee processing center ruining the town? Marlow01628! I'd spiked him well and good."

"How did you know it wasn't Geoffrey behind the account?"

"Because the man was bloody perfect!" Jeremy said. "There's no way he'd say that sort of stuff. Or even think it."

"I still don't understand," Judith said. "If what you're telling us is true—that Marcus was racist, sexist, a misogynist—why choose blackmail? Why not simply reveal his secret?"

"But how to prove it, that's the problem. If I'd tried to out him, he'd have denied it, wouldn't he? I'd have looked like the person who was in the wrong. Who was vindictive. Jealous. Lashing out."

"All of which you are," Suzie offered.

"And there was something else," Jeremy said, ignoring Suzie's interjection. "I liked the idea of making him squirm."

Judith and her friends exchanged glances. Didn't Jeremy care how he came across?

"That was a far better revenge," Jeremy said. "To know he'd be scared. Worried about where the blackmail letter had come from. Who knew his secret? Who had power over him and could reveal the truth at any time? Because I got to thinking. I knew about his Twitter account, but what if he was up to other dodgy things? Much worse things? That's what got me really excited. I mean, everyone's got secrets."

"You know he showed the first letter to Geoffrey?" Becks said.

"He did, did he? And what did he have to say about that?"

"He took the letter into his safekeeping."

"That's so like Geoffrey. Thinking he's your parent. Or teacher."

"Or at least that's what happened according to what Marcus told us," Judith said, thinking out loud. "After all, there were only two people involved in that conversation, and one of them's now dead, so he can't tell us if Marcus's version of events is true or not."

"Marcus must have been really panicking if he was getting Geoffrey involved," Jeremy said with satisfaction.

Judith looked at Jeremy and realized that she'd rarely disliked anyone more. She decided it was time to shake his self-confidence.

"I don't know why you're acting so surprised," she said. "Geoffrey told you he knew about the blackmail letter, didn't he?"

Guilt slammed into Jeremy's eyes.

"Because that's what your argument with him was really about, wasn't it? It had nothing to do with a bottle of whisky. Geoffrey had worked out you were behind the blackmail letter Marcus had given him. That's what he meant when he said he wouldn't give it back to you. But what I want to know is, how did Geoffrey work it out? Did he recognize the font from the *Architectural Journal* like Suzie did?"

Jeremy's mouth twitched, which was confirmation enough as far as Judith was concerned.

"Thank you," Judith said. "Geoffrey now knew it was you behind Marcus's blackmail—which I needn't tell you is a criminal offense. And we all know how honorable he was; there's no way he wouldn't have told the authorities. You were going to be convicted of a serious crime. So you went to Sophia's garden, got yourself some aconite, and slipped it into Geoffrey's coffee. Before he could tell the police. You killed Geoffrey Lushington."

"I didn't! We were good friends."

"Everyone's told us you weren't, you know," Becks said as kindly as she could.

"And if you were prepared to blackmail Marcus," Suzie said, picking up on Becks's point, "I reckon you wouldn't hesitate to kill someone who could put you in prison."

"Then how did I do it?" Jeremy said, suddenly energized. "Come on, you were there," he said to Suzie. "You saw me. I didn't go near the kitchen, or the coffee machine, or anything that Geoffrey touched. I just walked into that room and sat down in my chair *before Geoffrey had even arrived*. And then I never went anywhere near him. If you think I'm the killer, then I've got one thing to say to you. Prove it."

Jeremy looked at the women, a challenge in his eyes.

"Oh, don't worry," Judith said, deciding to meet fire with fire. "If you're the killer, we will."

Chapter 29

AFTER THEIR MEETING WITH JEREMY, the three friends held a conference in Suzie's van.

"What a horrible man," Becks said, summing up the feelings of them all.

"But he's got a point," Suzie said. "He never went near any coffee that night. If he's the killer, how did he do it?"

"And that was a bit of a bombshell about Marcus Percival, wasn't it?" Judith said. "I'd never have had him down as an online troll."

"We should confront him," Suzie said.

"Like when we confronted him about his fingerprints on the Kilner jar?" Judith said with a sigh. "He'll just deny it like he denied that."

"Then Tanika should get hold of all of his phones and computers and go through them until she finds the proof that he's Marlow01628."

"I'm not sure that would work, either," Becks said. "Sam's got all sorts of social media accounts, all of them attached to different email addresses. All of them are fake."

"And I'm not sure we want to spook him just yet," Judith said. "Since it'll be almost impossible to get a confession out of him. We know he's got this nasty streak, that he's got a dark secret. He's capable of committing murder."

"As is Jeremy," Suzie said.

"You're not wrong there," Judith agreed. "Someone who's prepared to commit blackmail could easily move on to murder."

"So it's disappointing he has such a strong alibi," Becks said.

"Is that true, though?" Judith asked Suzie. "Did Jeremy really never go anywhere near Geoffrey?"

"That's what I remember. He even sat at the end of the table as far away from Geoffrey as it was possible to get."

"It's almost like he's trying to prove he couldn't have done it," Becks said. "Oh, and by the way, you should know, I went back to the council archives at the police station this morning."

"Is Marian particularly bad today?" Judith asked.

"She's sorting the shelves of books in Colin's study."

"Well, that's nice of her," Suzie said.

"She's reordering them all by height. The tallest on the left, moving down to the shortest on the right."

As she spoke, Judith's phone started ringing. She looked at who was calling and saw that the number was withheld.

"Hello," she said into her phone as she answered it.

"It's me," a male voice wheezed at the end of the line. "Dave Butler."

Judith's shoulders slumped.

"I've been thinking about who could have killed Geoffrey," he said. "And I think I've got something for you. You'd better come round. I'll be waiting."

Dave hung up, and Judith knew that her friends had heard who she'd been talking to.

"Well, it looks like we've no choice," Suzie said.

On arriving at Dave's house, the women were surprised when the lock on the door buzzed open the moment they pressed the doorbell, and Dave's voice called out from a speaker, "You'd better come in."

Once inside, the women found Dave sitting in the same chair he'd been in on their previous visit. The mess of old food and dirty plates around him was, if anything, worse.

Judith could see there were beads of sweat on his forehead. Was he nervous, or was he just sweating?

"Sorry, we should have asked last time," she said, before Dave had even spoken. "Where were you when Geoffrey died?"

Dave's eyes widened in surprise.

"You don't think I killed him?"

"Could you answer the question?"

"I was here," he said in a quavery voice.

"Can you prove it?"

"I was on my own, I'm always on my own—of course I can't prove it."

"Then maybe you had an accomplice."

"What?" Dave seemed genuinely baffled by the question. "Who? I never leave this place—you've seen that for yourselves. And I asked you to come here because I think I've got a lead."

"That's really good of you," Suzie said, smiling a warning to Judith to calm down. For her part, Judith drew herself up taller—she wasn't going to calm down for anyone.

"What's your lead?" Becks asked, also wanting to keep Dave onside.

"I was going through everything I know about the planning committee, trying to work out who could have killed Geoffrey. And it doesn't make sense. Thanks to the three of you, I now know Debbie had her hand in the till, but it was only a couple of grand a year, wasn't it? I couldn't see how anyone would commit murder to cover up such small sums. And as for the others—Marcus Percival gives his consent for every development. I've always had the impression he's in the pocket of local developers, not that it's possible to prove; it's just a feeling. And Jeremy Wessel? He's too petty to commit murder. He'd slap a lawsuit against you for sure, but if you look at the planning committee minutes, he always backs down. He's got no backbone. But there's one person I keep coming back to. Sophia De Castro."

"Huh," Suzie said in agreement. "Me too."

"She pretends to be perfect, but she isn't."

"That's what I keep on saying!"

"Do you have any evidence?" Judith asked.

"I worked for her a year or so ago," Dave said. "This was when I was…a bit more mobile. But she rang me in a state. She'd recently installed a podcast studio and there was a hiss on the line whenever she recorded anything. I didn't want to take the job, but she kept upping the money until I couldn't say no. It was a mistake. She never told me about the bloody stairs that went up to her studio. It took me about ten minutes of huffing to get up there. And what I found in her studio was a mess. She had inferior cables, that was the problem. And inferior mics. It turns out her husband had ordered everything, but got cheap versions of everything she wanted."

"He's a cheapskate?" Judith asked.

"And she really went for him. Called him every name under the sun—there was a real intensity to her. She said her studio had to be the best, her podcast had to be the best, and that she always got her way—that's what I remember her saying. She always got her way. I said that for the money she was paying me, she could have the best kit possible, and that's what I ended up doing—installing a really top-end system. But I knew the stakes were high. If I'd given her anything less than perfection, she'd have started screaming and shouting at me like she'd done about her husband."

"Are you really saying she screamed and shouted?" Suzie asked.

"She was spitting at me at one point," Dave said and shuddered at the memory. "Look, I'm not perfect, I know that. I eat too much, I don't do exercise, I can't do anything about it. But if you want to know who on the committee could kill, I'm telling you it's Sophia De Castro."

"Well, that's all rather convenient," Judith said a few minutes later when they left Dave's house.

"How do you mean?" Becks asked.

"Dave Butler suddenly offers up who he believes is the killer."

"I think he was only trying to help," Becks said.

"And he doesn't have an alibi for the time of the murder."

Becks and Suzie knew full well what it was about Dave's solitary existence that was getting under Judith's skin.

"I know what you mean," Suzie said, trying to calm her friend. "But I can tell you he wasn't in the room when Geoffrey died. Or in the kitchen just beforehand. I seriously would have noticed if our blond-haired man was the size of Dave Butler—and he wasn't."

"And the thing is," Becks added, "I think the fact that he doesn't have an alibi rather suggests his innocence to me. Any killer worth their salt would make sure they had an alibi for the time of the murder."

"I still don't believe him," Judith said, as though this was the last word she expected any of them to say on the matter.

Seeing the skeptical looks on her friends' faces, she continued, "Very well, if you're not going to believe me, there's an easy way to find out if he's been telling us the truth about his relationship with Geoffrey."

"There is?" Becks asked, worried about where Judith's logic was taking her.

"He showed us a letter that purported to be from Geoffrey, but what if it was a fake? Why should we believe it's real?"

"OK…?" Suzie said, and like Becks, she was wondering where Judith was going with her line of thinking.

"Geoffrey has box files for all of the authors he's published. If Dave's been telling us the truth about their relationship, then there'll be a box file for him that's full of their correspondence. Their *real* correspondence."

"But we don't have access to Geoffrey's house," Becks said.

"And yet I couldn't help noticing that when we all left his house the last time, Tanika didn't turn the alarm back on."

"But we don't have a key to get in," Becks said, before remembering the truth. "There's a spare key in the bird box out back, isn't there? We can get into his house using it."

"Yes, we can," Judith said.

Chapter 30

"MAYBE MARCUS DIDN'T RETURN THE key to its hiding place," Becks said as she and her friends entered Geoffrey's garden through the back gate. "Oh," she added, as Suzie lifted the lid on the little bird box and fished out a mortise key.

"Are we *sure* Tanika didn't set the alarm?" Becks said as they approached the back door.

"Well, I'll tell you this much," Suzie said as she inserted the key into the lock and gave it a turn. "There's only one way to find out."

Suzie pushed the door open and entered the kitchen.

There was no sudden blaring of an alarm.

"There we are," Suzie said, and theatrically stepped aside so her friends could enter. "So where do we start?" she asked.

"In his study," Judith said. "That's where he keeps his author files. But I also want to have a poke around for ourselves. Try and get a better sense of the man. We didn't have a proper nose around when we were last here."

"Good thinking," Suzie said.

"So how about you go to his study?" Judith said to Suzie. "See if you can find Dave Butler's file. Becks, how about you take the rest of downstairs? I'll see what's upstairs."

"What are we looking for?" Becks asked.

"Oh, you know," Judith said airily as she headed toward the stairs, "evidence of betrayal, jealousy, hate, murderous intent—the usual."

Once upstairs, Judith crossed a corridor and entered what she soon realized was Geoffrey's bedroom. It was spotlessly clean. There was a double bed with a checked blanket neatly laid across it, shirts and trousers on hangers in a recess in the wall, and photographs in frames on the one bedside table. Judith went over and saw that the photos were of a younger Geoffrey with a woman. This must be his wife, Judith thought. In each picture, Geoffrey and the woman looked radiantly happy. Both were dead now, she realized. It was so very sad.

Judith refocused her attention on the room. She got the impression that Geoffrey had been a neat and tidy man who was comfortable living on his own. She recognized the signs—for example, the fact that there was only a single bedside table on one side of the bed.

Remembering the new locks that had been installed downstairs, Judith went over to the window and saw a brand-new lock on the frame. It was something of an oddity, wasn't it? Why had Geoffrey recently put in new security measures? It was a question no one had adequately managed to explain as far as Judith was concerned. Was it just a coincidence, or had something specific prompted it? As she turned to leave, she saw a tiny flash of light under the bed. The room was otherwise so tidy, she was surprised that Geoffrey had left something on the floor.

She went over and got down on her knees, and was able to see there was indeed something small and shiny nestling in the carpet. In between the bed and the wall. She picked it up.

It was an earring.

Looking at it more closely, she could see that it was a short silver chain that had a small hoop of silver at the end. Now who could have left that there? Judith stood up with a grunt of effort and took the earring to the window so she could see it more clearly. It was rather pretty, she thought. Judith remembered the photo of a woman in a lacy bra that had been sent to Geoffrey, and found herself wondering if Suzie's instincts had been right along. Was it the case that Geoffrey hadn't been as loyal to his dead wife as he'd told everyone? In fact, she realized, the earring rather proved this fact. Although, thinking about it, it didn't seem possible that Debbie would have an affair with Geoffrey, and nor did it feel probable that Sophia would, either. Sophia was at least twenty years Geoffrey's junior, and where he was short and pudgy, she was strikingly beautiful. Surely, if she were to have an affair, it would be with someone more obviously attractive than Geoffrey. So was it Debbie's earring after all?

Either way, the earring suggested that Geoffrey had been having a relationship with someone. Judith just had to work out who it was. She slipped the earring into her pocket, headed downstairs, and found Becks in the kitchen. Before she could ask her how her search was going, they saw a flash of red at the window as the postman, Fred Smith, parked his trolley in the driveway.

"Quick, down!" Judith said, grabbing Becks by the sleeve and pulling her to the floor.

"What is it?" Becks asked.

"It's Fred, he's outside!"

Fred had helped the women following the murder of Stefan Dunwoody, and Judith knew that he'd want to know what they were now doing in Geoffrey's house. And once he knew, he'd tell everyone. There was nothing Fred liked more than a good natter on the doorstep.

"Go and warn Suzie!" Judith hissed.

"What?"

"She has to get away from the window. Go and tell her—but don't let Fred see you."

Becks took a moment to gather up the tiniest scraps of her dignity, and then she scurried out of the room on her hands and knees like a spider. As she went, a very large part of her wondered how she, a law-abiding vicar's wife, was now finding herself scuttling across the floor of a murdered man's house.

She crawled across the hallway as Fred's shadow loomed at the glass of the front door. As she entered the study, Becks saw Suzie at the window, holding an open box file in her hands and looking out at Fred's trolley. She was startled to see Becks appear on her hands and knees in the room but was doubly surprised when she started waving to her to get down on the floor.

Understanding came slowly to Suzie, but when it did, it arrived in a rush, and she dropped to the floor like a sack of potatoes.

"Bloody hell!" she whispered, as she realized how close she'd come to being spotted in Geoffrey's house.

"Shh!" Becks hissed.

"Sorry!" Suzie said just as loudly.

The letter box clattered as something was posted through, and then they heard Fred's footsteps return to the street.

Becks and Suzie both lifted their heads to peek out of the window and saw Fred head over to his cart and start to push it away.

"We got away with it," Suzie said, standing up.

Judith entered, holding a pile of post in her hand.

"You can't go through his post," Becks said.

Ignoring Becks, Judith went over to Suzie.

"What have you found?" she asked.

"You were right," Suzie said. "There's a box file on Dave Butler. It contains his original novel all printed out—with Geoffrey's comments written down the side of every page. But there's also dozens of letters between them both. About changes Geoffrey wants to make."

"Can I see?" Becks said, taking the box file to Geoffrey's desk.

"And I'm sorry to say, as far as I can tell, Dave and Geoffrey had a really good relationship. Dave's almost groveling, if I'm honest."

Becks started reading from one of the letters.

"'I'm so lucky to have an editor who knows what they're doing,'" she read. She picked up another letter. "'This is a dream come true, finally being taken seriously.' Let's see what Geoffrey says," Becks added, turning to the next letter in the box. Here we go: "'This process is reminding me why I got into publishing in the first place. To uncover new talent. There's no doubting, you're a rare talent.'"

"OK, so Dave appears to have been telling us the truth," Judith said, as though she weren't in fact admitting she'd been in the wrong. "But it's lucky we came here to check, because look what I've found."

Putting the various fast food and gutter-cleaning flyers on a side table, Judith held up a brown envelope with the address of the sender printed on the top left-hand corner. It said "Environment Agency."

"I wonder why the Environment Agency are writing to Geoffrey," she said.

"I imagine they don't know he's dead," Becks said. "We'll need to get this to Tanika, only she'll be able to open it."

"Why?"

"It's against the law to open someone else's post."

"But is it?"

"Yes, it is," Becks said firmly.

"Even if they're dead?"

"*Yes,*" Becks repeated.

Judith ripped through the flap of the envelope with her thumb.

"What are you doing?" Becks asked in a panic.

"Oops," Judith said. "Butterfingers."

"You have to put that letter down right now."

"It would be a shame not to look at it now it's open," Suzie said, perfectly happy with Judith's decision.

Judith opened the letter so they could all read it together.

> The Environment Agency
> Solent and South Office
> 40 Queen's Road
> Reading
> BERKS
> RG1 4PQ
> 17.04.23
>
> Dear Mr. Lushington
>
> Thank you for alerting us to Mr. Alec Miller's concerns about a possible housing development on Wiley's Field in Marlow. I attach our report and invoice for the work carried out. Please pay within 30 days.
>
> Our findings in summary:
>
> WILEY'S FIELD, MARLOW
>
> We sent a surveyor to the site and can confirm there is a colony of Myotis Bechsteinii (Bechstein's Bat).

The Bechstein bat is a UK Biodiversity Action Plan species, which means it's a conservation priority on both a local and national scale. It is also listed on Annex II of the EC Habitat Directive. It's therefore one of the most protected animals in the UK.

It is our ruling that there can be no development of Wiley's Field. The only person able to overturn this decision is the Secretary of State for the Environment.

Thank you for bringing this matter to our attention.

Yours sincerely
Sean Farrell
Director, Environment
Agency (Solent and South)

"There are bats at Wiley's Field?" Suzie asked.

Judith turned to the next page and saw that the Environment Agency had billed Geoffrey £3,000 for the survey.

"And Geoffrey had taken on a three-thousand-pound bill to find them," Judith said. "Although that's not what's jumping out at me. According to Mr. Farrell here, the whole process was started by a Mr. Alec Miller."

"You mean the guy who serves the tea and coffees?" Suzie asked.

"Who *normally* serves the tea and coffees," Judith said. "Remember, he wasn't there the night that Geoffrey was killed. I think we need to talk to him about this letter. Don't you?"

Chapter 31

WHEN JUDITH AND HER FRIENDS knocked on Alec's door, he answered looking even more rumpled than he'd done the first time they'd talked, if that were at all possible.

"Hello, Alec," Judith said. "A quick question. You spoke to Geoffrey Lushington about getting the development of Wiley's Field stopped, didn't you?"

Alec's mouth opened in surprise.

"How do you know about that?" he asked.

"Why don't you tell us yourself? Set the record straight."

Alec frowned—it was obvious to the women that he couldn't work out where to start—and Judith remembered something he'd said to them the first time they'd spoken.

"You've lived up here your whole life," she said.

"Man and boy," Alec agreed.

"Bet you've seen a few changes over that time," Becks said, picking up on Judith's strategy.

"Down in the main town, but here's stayed the same. You see what nature gets up to if you leave a place alone. I've seen nightjars, hawfinches—last week I saw a wood warbler, and you normally only get them in Wales."

"And bats?"

"Sure. There are bats. Everywhere has bats."

"But you happen to think there's a colony of Bechstein's bats up here, don't you?"

"Don't just think it, I know it. Not that Geoffrey bloody Lushington believed me."

"That's interesting. You mentioned the bats to him?"

"He said he couldn't get involved in individual cases. He was the chair of the committee, he couldn't be seen to take sides. I disagreed with him, violently. This field is the last remaining sanctuary for wildlife in this town. It was his duty to get the development stopped."

"You disagreed with him 'violently'?" Suzie asked.

"That's just my way of talking. I don't mean I wanted to hurt him, but the developer was breaking all the rules, someone had to stop him."

"Do you mean Ian Maloney?"

"That's right."

"How was he breaking the rules?"

"Coming up here with his shovel. Looking for orchids and other rare flowers he could remove. Fool. I know every inch of that field, there's only grass and common flowers. But he knows that if there's even one rare plant, the whole development gets stopped in its tracks. But I chased him off, so that was something."

"What happened?"

"I went over to him and told him to get off the land. In no uncertain terms."

"Violently?" Judith asked innocently.

Alec chuckled.

"You could say so. I had a camera with me, so I told him if he planted his shovel in the ground even once, I'd photograph him. But that man's dangerous. You can tell. He came right up to me, and he said the houses were going to be built whether I liked it or not. He had the chair of the planning committee in his pocket. That's what he said. In his pocket. What did I think of that? And he turned around and stalked off. It's why I was so angry when I went to see Geoffrey. I've known him for years. Always liked him. Or thought I did. But if he was doing dodgy deals with men like Ian Maloney, he needed to be told what for. That's why I was a bit aggressive when I saw him."

"How did Geoffrey take it?"

"He didn't know what to think. I could tell no one had gone for him in years. Suppose that happens if you're the mayor, everyone kowtows to you. But I don't, not to anyone," Alec added proudly.

"What happened when you accused him of doing dodgy deals?" Suzie asked.

"He got really upset. How could I say that about him—you know, all that malarkey. But if you ask me, he was only angry because I'd caught him out. He was guilty, he had something to hide. I was sure of it."

Judith fished in her handbag and pulled out the letter they'd retrieved from Geoffrey's house.

"You should know Geoffrey asked the Environment Agency to check Wiley's Field for Bechstein bats."

Alec's hand shot to the doorframe to steady himself. "Wh-what?" he stammered.

"It turns out Geoffrey did what you asked him to."

"He said he couldn't!" Alec said, agitated. "That he wasn't allowed to!"

Judith handed over the letter, and Alec read it, all the fight going out of him.

"Is this a problem?" Becks asked, just as surprised as her friends to see Alec so wrong-footed.

"He told me there wasn't money in the council budget for any kind of special survey," Alec said, still trying to make sense of what he was reading.

"It looks like he was going to cover the three-thousand-pound cost of the survey himself," Becks said. "Which is good news, isn't it? There'll be no development."

Alec didn't say anything, and Judith realized that she found his response to the letter deeply puzzling. Why wasn't he happy? As she tried to imagine why this might have been, she realized there was a question they'd not yet asked him.

"Where were you on the night Geoffrey died?" Judith asked.

"What?"

"We know you weren't at the planning committee meeting. Where were you?"

"I was in the Duke of Cambridge," Alec said, although he didn't sound entirely convincing.

"What time?"

"I don't know. I normally have my tea at about six thirty, and I reckon I'm in the Duke by about seven. Or just gone seven."

"You normally arrive at that time?"

Alec shrugged.

"But is that what happened that night?" Judith asked.

"Yeah. Sure."

Judith decided to change tack. "You live up here on your own?"

"That's right."

"But you spend a lot of time in the field and the woods all around."

"Of course. The natural world's the only one we've got."

"So I suppose you know all about the various edible plants and mushrooms out there."

Alec smiled.

"Any country boy would," he said.

"And where aconite grows? It's a wild plant, after all. I bet it grows somewhere in the woods around here."

"There's some up in the woods just beyond Wiley's Field. But you can find it all over the place. Down by Higginson Park—in the scrubland by the hockey club. If you know what to look for, you can always find it."

"Then one last question and then we'll be on our way," Judith said. "Do you have an answerphone for your landline?"

"What sort of question is that?"

"How about you tell me whether or not you do, and then I'll tell you what sort of question it is."

"All right. Sure. I've got an answerphone. What of it?"

"Now that's interesting, because that's the one bit of the puzzle I otherwise can't make fit. How you managed to make the phone call. Which you've kindly solved."

"You're talking in riddles."

"OK, then how about I tell you a story? After all, we've been chasing around trying to work out how the killer got the poison into Geoffrey's coffee, when the one thing we've always known for sure is that aconite was found in the coffee capsule he used. A coffee capsule that was set out by the person who was serving that night."

"I told you, a woman rang me that morning and said the meeting was canceled. That Sophia woman."

"Although, if my memory's correct—and it is—you only identified Sophia after we'd played you a clip from one of her podcasts and told you her name. All the police records show is that *someone* made a phone call that morning to your landline from the council office that lasted thirty-seven seconds. Which would be easy for you to do. Just slip into the council building and cut the cable to the security camera that covers the public phone. Then, use that phone to call your home number. Your answerphone picks up the call, you then stay on the line long enough to make it look as though a short conversation has taken place. Thirty-seven seconds as it happens. You then hang up. And that evening, all you now have to do is disguise yourself."

"What are you talking about?"

"There are all sorts of fancy dress shops you could get a blond wig and false goatee beard from."

"I was in the Duke of Cambridge that night."

"I don't believe you. And you can drop your country yokel act. Because your plan was rather clever, if you ask me. After all, the teas and coffee were all set up as per normal on the night Geoffrey died. No one noticed any difference between how you normally did it and the blond-haired man that night. So isn't it the most logical conclusion that it was in fact you who was serving? Only, you were wearing a disguise."

"Why would I do that?"

"So people wouldn't realize it was you who'd killed Geoffrey."

"But it wasn't Geoffrey I had a problem with! I mean, I did, I admit it, but he wasn't the person trying to destroy the field. That was Ian Maloney. If Ian died, sure, you could make a case I was behind it. I hate everything he's doing to this town. But what had Geoffrey ever done that meant I'd want to kill him?"

"You believed that Geoffrey was in the pocket of Ian Maloney. That he'd approve the development of Wiley's Field. That because of Geoffrey, your precious field you've lived next to, as you say, 'man and boy,' and which gives you so much pleasure, was about to be concreted over."

"You're putting words into my mouth. None of that happened," Alec said angrily, before pushing the letter into Judith's hands, going back into his house, and slamming the door.

"Mr. Miller!" Judith called after him.

The women took a moment to recover.

"Wow," Becks said. "You'd already worked all that out about how he could have phoned himself?"

"I'll be honest, it came to me as I was talking."

"Amazing."

As they got into Suzie's van, Suzie asked, "So come on, then, what do we think? Is he our killer?"

"I don't know," Becks said. "Is he really clever enough to come up with a plan where he impersonates himself?"

"If you were desperate enough, sure," Suzie said.

"But you also said the killer was of average height. And Alec is tall, isn't he?"

"You're right. He can't have been the blond-haired server that night, he's far too tall."

"Are you sure?" Judith asked.

"Very definitely."

"Well, that's no good, is it? Although, if he's too tall, it makes me notice there's still one person out there who'd have been just as furious as Alec if he'd found out Geoffrey had commissioned a report from the Environment Agency. Someone who we already know has violence in him."

"You mean Ian Maloney," Suzie said.

"And I can't help recalling that he's already blond-haired and very much of average height and size."

"But how can we find him?" Becks asked. "He's impossible to track down, we discovered that last time."

"But since then, Marcus Percival told us Ian's company is building some new houses down by the rugby club."

"So?" Suzie asked.

"So, I think I know *exactly* how we can smoke him out."

Chapter 32

IAN MALONEY'S FOREMAN WAS A burly thug who'd started in the building trade at fourteen and had worked his way up by being tougher than everyone else he met. On this day, though, he was rattled. Upset, even. As a gleaming, lime-green sports car pulled up at the building site, he went over to it as the door opened and Ian Maloney got out.

"What do you mean you don't know what to do?" Ian barked.

"Boss," the man said, "there are things I've done for you—we both know what they are—but I don't know what to do about this."

"Go on, then, where are they?"

The man led through the building site to where a JCB digger was idling, black smoke belching from its exhaust.

Judith Potts was lying down in front of it.

Becks and Suzie were standing a little way away with their phones out, filming every second.

"What the hell's going on here?" Ian called out, Becks's and Suzie's cameras swiveling to take him in as he arrived.

"Ah, there you are!" Judith said from her position in the mud.

"It's you?" Ian asked contemptuously.

"And because of what I'm doing, I can also say, 'It's you,'" Judith said in satisfaction.

"You delay my workers anymore, there'll be repercussions."

"Oh, don't worry, now you're here, I can get up."

"Then go on, then."

Judith didn't move.

"Becks?" she eventually called out. "Suzie?"

Becks and Suzie realized that Judith had gotten a bit stuck on the ground and went to their friend.

As she was helped up, Judith was impressed that she barely let out an "oof." She dusted herself down while Ian looked at her and her friends in contempt.

"I must say," Becks said, trying to take the heat out of the situation, "these houses are going to be lovely."

Ian just looked at her.

"When they're finished, of course," Becks added.

"I'm surprised the rugby club want to develop their land," Suzie said.

She indicated the Marlow Rugby Club sign near the building site, and they could all see the single-story clubhouse on the other side of the asphalt car park.

"This is nothing," Ian said. "They've got acres of land they could sell off for development."

"I see," Judith said. "You do these houses well enough, and they might let you build elsewhere on their land. Who's your architect?"

"What sort of a question is that?"

"His or her name will be on the plans you submitted to the council for these two houses, but it would be easier if you told us."

"I'm not going to—"

"Is it Jeremy Wessel?"

Ian blinked in surprise.

"He wasn't my choice," he said. "He was the rugby club's. He was already doing some work for them."

"Is Jeremy also designing your development up at Wiley's Field?"

"No. Why are you even asking?"

"I'm trying to work out how far your tendrils reach. Because I can't help feeling that there's one person who connects so many elements of Geoffrey Lushington's life, and that's you."

"I had nothing to do with him."

"Even though he opposed the development at Wiley's Field."

"Jesus!" Ian said, snapping. "You need to get off this site. Come on. Off with you."

Ian held his arms wide, and Judith and her friends had no choice but to allow themselves to be shepherded to the side of the road.

As they went, Ian explained.

"I told you, the council always pushes back against the first application. It means nothing that Geoffrey bloody Lushington opposed it."

"But it was more than that, wasn't it? He told you he was getting the field checked out for bats, didn't he?"

Ian stopped in his tracks.

"How do you know that?" he asked.

"The Environment Agency have made their ruling," Judith said, pulling the letter out of her handbag. "And they're slapping a protection order on the field."

"That's not possible," Ian said, grabbing the letter from Judith and reading it greedily. "The bastard did it, he really did it!"

"Maybe you should tell us in your own words what happened," Becks said kindly. "Set the record straight."

"He was so full of himself," Ian said, unable to keep a lid on his fury. "Always thinking he was right. He decided Wiley's Field shouldn't be turned into a housing development. Full stop. Some old git up that way said there were bats—it's always bloody bats, or newts. I mean, Jesus Christ, people have got to live somewhere, and are we really saying a bloody newt is more important than a human?"

"So he told you he was contacting the Environment Agency?"

"He couldn't wait to tell me, and how he was going to fund it himself, the smug bastard."

"And I bet you already knew about the bats."

"What? No, what are you talking about?"

"We know you've been up in Wiley's Field looking at the wildlife there."

"Taking a shovel to remove any protected plants," Suzie added.

"We've spoken to Alec Miller," Judith said, by way of explanation. "The 'old git' you were referring to. He told us he'd had to confront you."

"Another bloody do-gooder, that one. But so what? I didn't find anything that would stop the development."

"I don't think that's true. I think you found bats, or knew they were nearby. So, the moment Geoffrey told you he'd commissioned a report, you knew the whole development was sunk. Your life's dream, as you told us the last time we spoke—and a serious amount of money—it was over. And Geoffrey was to blame. So you killed him."

Ian didn't say anything, but the women could see he was struggling.

"How dare you?" he eventually spluttered.

"You couldn't help yourself. He'd ruined your plans, you needed to exact revenge."

"I didn't!" Ian shouted, stepping forward to spit the words into Judith's face. She winced but didn't take a step back. Instead, she held his gaze, Ian breathing heavily through his nose like a bull getting ready to charge.

"I was glad he died, I'll admit it," he said. "Is that what you want me to say? He deserved to die. For what he did to me."

"You knew about the bats," Judith said.

"I knew about the bloody bats," Ian said. "OK? The moment he told me he was going to pay for a survey, I knew he'd stopped the whole development dead. But think about it, how does killing him help me? The report's still been commissioned, it still says the development's not going to go ahead. Whether Geoffrey's alive or not, the project's dead in the water."

"That assumes you knew that he'd already contacted the Environment Agency. And all you've said so far is that Geoffrey told you he was *going* to contact the Environment Agency—he was *going* to fund it himself. Until you saw that letter, you didn't know that he'd already done it, did you? In fact, when you saw the letter just now, you said, 'The bastard did it, he really did it.' It was as much a surprise to you as it was to us. Which means you've got a motive. Mr. Maloney, I think you killed Geoffrey Lushington to stop him from contacting the Environment Agency."

"You do, do you?" Ian said. "Then you should know I was at a jazz night at the British Legion that night."

"You were?" Suzie scoffed. She couldn't imagine someone less likely to be at a local jazz night. "Who was playing?"

"A guitarist. I like guitar music."

"Remember his name?"

"John Dunsterville, but he goes by the name 'Dusty.'"

"Almost sounds like you've rehearsed your answers."

"You ask anyone who was there. The gig started at about seven p.m., ended at about ten, I didn't leave at any time. So you can claim I killed him all you like, but I was with dozens of witnesses all night."

Ian held Judith's gaze until he realized she had nothing more to say, and then he turned and headed back to his foreman on the building site. As he went, he called, "And where would I get a load of aconite from anyway?"

"How do you know it was aconite that killed him?" Judith called out to Ian's retreating back.

"Everyone knows it was aconite," he shouted without missing a step.

"What a nasty piece of work," Becks said.

"Agreed," Judith said. "And with a copper-bottomed motive to want Geoffrey dead."

"And it would have been easy for him to put on a false beard and wig to poison Geoffrey from the kitchen," Suzie said. "He's the right size to fit the man I saw that night. So let's hope he's lying about being at the jazz club. Because if he is, I think we've maybe just found our killer."

Chapter 33

WITHIN MINUTES OF ARRIVING AT the Royal British Legion Hall, Judith and her friends discovered that Ian Maloney had indeed been at the jazz concert for the whole evening that Geoffrey had been murdered. In fact, one of the old dears they spoke to, a lovely woman called Penny, said she'd sat next to Ian the whole evening. He'd not left at any time, except to go to the bar to get the odd drink. He was barely gone for longer than a few minutes at a time.

The three friends were still trying to come to terms with the news as they entered Judith's makeshift incident room.

"One of these people killed Geoffrey Lushington," Judith said, indicating the index cards that were pinned to the wall. "But who? And why? And how?"

"Tell you what," Becks said, "how about we have a nice cup of tea and some biscuits, and we can go through the suspects one by one. See if we have any inspiration."

"Good idea," Suzie said.

"Sadly," Judith said, "I finished off the packet of biscuits you brought last time."

"Never mind," Becks said and left the room. A few minutes later, she returned with a pot of tea and cups on a tray, and a plate of chocolate Digestives.

"Where did you find those?" Judith asked, indicating the biscuits.

"I knew you'd eat any biscuits I left behind, so I hid a second packet in your grand piano," Becks said, as she poured out the teas.

"That's really very clever of you," Judith said.

"Thank you. Now, how about we start with Marcus Percival, the smooth-talking estate agent?"

"Good idea," Suzie said. "A man who knows his whole career collapses the moment the world finds out he's behind that troll Twitter account. Although I still can't believe it's him."

"I can," Judith said. "He was always too glossy for my liking. And he'd have had a motive if Geoffrey had uncovered his secret identity. Because there's no way a man as honorable as Geoffrey would have kept quiet about it. And I can well believe that someone like Marcus could kill to protect his reputation—his status—his money. But did he do it?"

"I know what you mean," Suzie said. "Because if I killed someone with a poisoned sugar cube, I wouldn't leave my fingerprints all over the murder weapon."

"Then maybe he killed Geoffrey with a poisoned capsule in the coffee machine after all?" Becks said. "He could have lined it up while he was making himself his cup of tea."

"But if he killed him with a coffee capsule, why hide the Kilner jar?" Judith asked. "I can't quite square that circle. And until then, I think we have to presume he's not our prime suspect."

"But it's the same for Debbie Bell, isn't it?" Becks said.

"How do you mean?" Suzie asked.

"We've been able to pin actual criminal activity on her—embezzling council funds, something you could go to prison for—but, as with Marcus, we don't know for sure that Geoffrey knew about it."

"We know Dave Butler tipped him off that *someone* was embezzling," Suzie said. "And that was months ago. It's totally believable Geoffrey had worked out Debbie was behind it. It only took us a few weeks. I bet Geoffrey did as well. We just have to prove it."

"I'm not so sure," Judith said. "Because Debbie was right when she said that the moment Geoffrey worked out she was behind the thieving, he'd go straight to the police. Which we know he didn't do."

"Then what if he'd only found out that day?"

"I still think he'd inform the police within minutes of finding out that money was being stolen from his beloved council."

"So he didn't know she was the culprit, which puts her in the clear?" Suzie asked.

"This isn't going very well, is it?" Becks said.

"And I'm afraid it's rather the same for Jeremy Wessel, isn't it?" Judith said. "Because, like Marcus, I believe he's capable of committing murder."

"He's already committing blackmail," Becks said. "And I think we can presume Geoffrey had worked it out for himself. That's what he meant when he told Jeremy he wouldn't 'give it back' to him. He was talking about the blackmail letter he'd taken from Marcus."

"But that's good news," Suzie said. "It makes Jeremy our number one suspect!"

"Which is when we come to a small problem," Judith said. "According to you, it's like he told us and Jeremy never went near the coffee machine or the serving hatch, he just went and sat straight down at the table. And once there, he didn't interact with Geoffrey's coffee cup, either."

"It's true," Suzie agreed. "Geoffrey stayed well out of reach the whole time."

"So he may have had a motive, but he didn't have the means—he's in the clear," Judith said. "Which means we've got reasons why Marcus, Debbie, and Jeremy might have wanted Geoffrey dead, but we can't quite pin the murder on any one of them."

"I don't suppose they carried it out together?" Becks asked.

"The way those three complain about each other," Suzie said, "I don't see any of them working together."

"Which leaves Sophia De Castro," Becks said. "And she arrived last of all—and like Jeremy never went near Geoffrey or his coffee. In fact, she had the least opportunity of anyone."

"Yup," Suzie said. "She'd barely got down to the others before Geoffrey died. And we've not found a motive for her, either."

"So she's doubly in the clear," Becks said, summing up for them all.

"It's the blond-haired guy in the kitchen!" Suzie said, going to the board and plucking down his index card. "He's always looked like our killer, it has to have been him!"

"I know what you mean," Judith said. "Because if he isn't, I can't imagine what he was doing there that night."

"So who was he?" Suzie said, taking a step back to look at all the index cards on the wall. "There are only three other people who've become part of our inquiries: Alec Miller, Ian Maloney, and Dave Butler—and we can discount Dave, there's nothing average about Dave's size, so that leaves only two possible killers."

"Ian Maloney or Alec Miller."

"And it can't have been Alec Miller—he's too tall," Suzie said.

"Then it has to be Ian Maloney!" Becks said.

"But Ian Maloney has an alibi," Judith said. "He was at a jazz concert that night. So to sum up, we all agree that it's hard to see how any one of the planning committee could be the killer. And of the three people who might have been our blond-haired kitchen server that night, one is too tall, another is too large, and one is the right size and height—and has the right colored hair—but has an unbreakable alibi."

"It's not really ideal, is it?" Becks agreed.

"But *someone* was in the kitchen that night," Suzie said. "Who was it?"

"It's the million-dollar question, isn't it?" Becks said before sneezing loudly. "Sorry!" she said, pulling a hankie from her handbag. "It's all the dust in the room."

Becks indicated the piles of newspaper that still dominated the further half of the room, and Suzie suddenly finished the thought that she'd started when she'd been cleaning away the magazines in her house.

"I could help you get rid of all that junk," she said to her friend.

Judith didn't understand.

"What's that?"

"I know it's none of my business, and I tried to take your advice and stop thinking of side hustles—but it doesn't work. I always need something to keep me busy. A hobby. And I think I know what my new project should be. I should help you finish what you started with Becks over a year ago. We should help you clear out this room."

"That's very kind of you," Judith said primly, "but no, thank you."

"But think how great it would be. We could really go for it. You know, clear the rest of this room, and all of next door, and then give the whole thing a lick of paint."

"And get new carpets," Becks added, swept along by her friend's enthusiasm.

For her part, Judith could feel herself starting to panic. She didn't want to get rid of her archive. She'd spent so many years collecting these papers, they represented who she was—where she came from, her whole history—and the idea of losing that support terrified her.

But she saw looks of such sympathy in her friends' eyes that she was reminded—with a jolt—of how they'd looked at Dave Butler. Realizing this, the fight went out of her. She still couldn't imagine the circumstances where she'd ever get rid of her archive, but that didn't mean she couldn't meet her friends halfway.

"You know…I've agreed to a cup of tea," she said.

"What's that?" Suzie asked.

"Matthew Cartwright."

"You contacted him?!" Becks said, delighted.

"I wrote him a letter."

"What did you say?"

"That I remembered him. I tried to stay as matter-of-fact as possible. But I included my phone number in the letter. And then, the other night, he rang."

"You've spoken to him?" Suzie said in glee. "What was he like?"

"I didn't recognize him, if I'm honest. I don't know what I was expecting, but this deep gravelly voice wasn't it."

"Was he nice?" Becks asked.

"He was polite. But he told me how much money he'd made. Not exactly, but in so many words. He's got a flat in Bordeaux, if he came over to see me he'd bring his two-seater Jag, that sort of thing."

"Sounds to me like he just wanted you to know he wasn't a no-hoper."

"I don't know."

"He's coming over to see you?" Suzie asked.

"I knew that when I wrote to him, I was pushing a domino over. There are always other dominoes."

"But this is wonderful news!" Becks said.

"Doesn't sound as if you liked him," Suzie said, reading the situation more astutely.

"No, that's not it," Judith said, trying to make sense of her thoughts. "He seemed kind, and he was interested in me. He was delighted when I told him I set crosswords—he's got a very attractive laugh, and he said I always was the cleverest person he'd ever met, so he's not threatened by smart women."

"Good," Suzie said. "So when are you meeting up?"

"Next Tuesday."

"No way!" Becks said. "That soon?"

Judith nodded. Unsure.

"How exciting."

"It is," Judith said, although her friends could see she wasn't quite as sure as her words were suggesting. "The thing is," she added, "I don't want to meet him."

Suzie and Becks didn't know what to say.

"OK," Suzie said, wanting to sum up the situation. "You don't want to meet rich men who want to see you. You don't want to clear out your old rooms of junk."

"I like my life how it is," Judith said. "I do exactly as I please, I've got good friends and gainful employment. Why do I need to change anything?"

"Don't you feel…" Becks started, but didn't have the heart to continue.

"Lonely?" Judith asked. "Sometimes, I suppose. But not often. Every now and then I have what I call 'blue days.' But they pass, and for the rest of the time, I'm happy. Maybe I'm selfish?"

"Or maybe it's as you say," Becks said, "and you've got your life sorted exactly how you like it."

"That's it. I have everything 'just so,' and why would I risk that?"

"Then cancel on him," Suzie said.

"He's back in China for a few days. Visiting friends. He says he's coming to see me straight from Heathrow on Tuesday. I can't cancel this late in the day."

"Then go for your cup of tea with him," Becks said. "Where's the danger in that? Dazzle him with your stories of catching killers, setting crosswords, and living in a mansion on the Thames."

"Actually, do you mind if we don't talk about it?"

"Of course," Becks said. "If it makes you feel uncomfortable. What would you rather talk about?"

"Murder," Judith said, turning back to face her makeshift incident board. "Because it occurs to me—since we've ruled everyone out—there is one final person we've not properly considered."

"Who?" Becks asked.

"Paul De Castro."

"But he can't be our killer," Suzie said. "He's got an alibi. He was at the cinema that night."

"But was he?"

"Tanika says he was."

"If I remember rightly, her officers found cinema workers who said they remembered him because he spilled his drink on the way into the screening."

"That's right," Becks said. "He made them give him a replacement for free."

"Which all feels like attention seeking to me—like he wanted to be noticed as he went in. And we all know what cinemas are like. Once it goes dark, there's nothing stopping you from slipping out, getting into a disguise, going to the town council, setting up the tea and coffee, poisoning Geoffrey, taking the disguise off, and then slipping back into the screening before it's ended. Who'd even known you'd gone? And there's something else about Paul De Castro I can't help noticing. He must be very cunning if he's head of a wealth management company."

"And this is a cunning murder," Suzie said.

"But more than that, there are two other qualities about him that mark him out as a possible killer. He's average in both height and in weight. I think we need to talk to him, don't you?"

Chapter 34

THE FOLLOWING MORNING, JUDITH AND her friends met outside Marlow Wealth Management.

"How did you get a meeting so quickly?" Becks asked.

"I said I had a large amount of money I wanted Mr. De Castro to invest," Judith said.

The women went into reception, where the young man behind the desk told them that Mr. De Castro would be ready to meet them soon. As they sat down in the comfortable chairs to wait, the door opened to the office area and Debbie Bell came over.

"What are you doing here?" she asked, worried.

"We want to speak to your boss," Suzie said.

"Paul doesn't come in until ten a.m.," Debbie said, looking at the watch on her right wrist.

"We rang ahead," Becks said. "He's coming in early."

"But why do you want to see him?" Debbie took a step closer to the women and whispered, "Is it about me?"

"It's nothing to do with you," Becks said.

"Because I've been thinking, what if I return the money?"

"That you took from the council?" Judith replied, and Debbie looked over her shoulder to make sure the receptionist wasn't listening. He was taking a phone call from a client.

"It was an accounting error," Debbie said desperately.

"I don't think that will wash."

"But it was such a small amount of money!" Debbie whined. "I needed medical help, why don't I deserve the same as everyone else!"

Judith was startled by Debbie's sudden intensity, but then she realized that in Debbie's professional life, she was surrounded by untold wealth. It must be hard working day after day for the rich while you were only getting the sort of salary that meant you wore skirts with frayed hems.

But there was something else about Debbie that gave Judith pause. There was a nagging sense on the edge of her thoughts that was telling her she'd just gleaned important information. She recognized the feeling as almost a physical tingling inside her—akin to when she realized that a word had a tasty anagram buried within it. But what was it? Judith replayed the conversation, trying to find what it was that had pinged the radar of her subconscious, but she was interrupted by the receptionist calling over to them.

"Mr. De Castro will see you now," he said.

"I don't think repaying the money will help," Becks whispered to Debbie, and Judith's focus returned to the room. She'd have to try to work out what it was later on.

Becks continued, "You've repeated what you did every year since then. I don't think anyone could dismiss that as an accounting error. I think your best bet is to go to the police and make a full confession. They'll be more lenient if you hand yourself in."

"I'll be disbarred, I won't be able to work again, and all I've got is my work!"

"Ladies?" the receptionist called over again.

"No, of course," Judith said. "Just coming."

As she and her friends went through the door into the main office, Judith looked back at Debbie. She had slumped into one of the visitor chairs underneath a framed photo of a bright red sports car. She had her head in her hands, and her shoulders were shuddering. She was crying. Judith resisted feeling sorry for her. Debbie was a crook, pure and simple—and she only had passing sympathy for someone who felt regret only once they'd been caught out.

Judith followed her friends and the receptionist through a large, wood-paneled office that had a plush carpet on the floor and half a dozen heavy wooden desks behind which smartly dressed young people in dark suits and neat haircuts were working. They approached a thick wooden door, the receptionist knocked once—waited until a gruff "enter" was called out from inside—and then opened the door.

Paul De Castro sat behind his desk, his hands pressed down on its top as though he were about to leap to his feet.

"I haven't got long," he said without acknowledging the receptionist, who left, silently closing the door behind himself.

"Then we'll drop the pretense," Judith said.

"We're from the police," Suzie said, holding up her lanyard. "We've a few questions."

Paul laughed. The idea of three women, none of them younger than middle age, interviewing him didn't make any sense to him.

"We're investigating the murder of Geoffrey Lushington," Judith said.

"Like hell you are," Paul said as he rose from his desk and closed the distance to Suzie, before whipping the lanyard from around her neck and taking it back to his desk.

Paul had been so swift that Suzie hadn't even had time to take a step back.

"Let's see what this is," Paul said, putting on a little Bluetooth headset that had a microphone running down the side of his cheek. Judith could see that Paul was inordinately proud of his hi-tech phone. He tapped his earbud and self-importantly read out the Maidenhead Police Station phone number from Suzie's card.

While the call waited to connect, Judith noticed there were a number of framed photos on the wall that showed Paul at various black-tie events. In some of them he was smoking a cigar with other middle-aged men, and in others he had his arms around the waist of beautiful younger women. He clearly thought himself quite "the man about town," Judith noted.

"Hey," Paul said into his mic, "I've got three women running around Marlow with fake IDs—thought you'd want to know."

It was much to Paul's surprise when he read out the warrant number on the card that the person on the end of the line was able to inform him that Suzie Harris was indeed working as a civilian adviser, and he should offer her his assistance. He jabbed at his earbud to end the call and dropped the lanyard onto the table.

Suzie picked it up and protectively put it back around her neck.

"This country's going to the dogs," Paul said.

"I'm sure we can all agree on that," Judith said, looking directly at her foe. "And I appreciate your time is valuable, Mr. De Castro, but it really will be much quicker for you if you answer our questions."

Judith could see that Paul was clenching his jaw.

"How did you meet your wife?" Becks asked, as ever correctly divining that they needed to take the tension out of the room.

"How's that your business?" he asked.

"It isn't," Suzie said, holding up her lanyard. "It's police business."

"Jesus!" he said, running his hand through his dark hair. "We met at a dinner party. OK?"

"Go on," Becks said.

"This was ten years ago. I'd recently got divorced, and there was this girl at the end of the table—pretty much the most attractive woman I'd seen, and I decided I had to have her. That's all there is to it, OK?"

"You 'had to have her'?" Judith asked, channeling her inner Lady Bracknell.

"I always get what I want."

"Always?"

"I got Sophia, didn't I?" he said with a smirk.

"And how's that going?" Suzie asked.

"Great," Paul said.

"Is that all you have to say about your relationship?" Judith asked.

Paul shrugged.

"I don't get it," Suzie said. "You're so... What's the word I'm looking for?" she asked her friends.

"Successful?" Becks offered, knowing that Suzie was looking for something far more Anglo-Saxon.

"OK—successful," Suzie said. "So rich—running this company, living in that big house on the river—you're all right, Jack. But your wife's into plants and wellness and yoga and all that."

"That's women's stuff."

"Then how do you feel about a woman accusing you of murder?" Judith asked.

Paul didn't really understand the question.

"What film were you watching when Geoffrey Lushington died?"

"I've been through this with the police."

"What was the name of it?"

"It was a superhero flick."

"You go to the cinema on your own to watch superhero films?"

"Not normally, but I've always liked Spider-Man, and the Everyman in Gerrards Cross was showing the most recent one. I'd not seen it in the cinema before."

"What was it called?"

"*Spider-Man: No Way Home*. What is this, a quiz?"

"Oh, God!" Becks said before she could stop herself.

"You know it?" Judith asked Becks in surprise.

"Heavens, no. But I remember when Sam and his friends saw it. I had to pick them up from the cinema afterward. They talked about it all the way home. Apparently all of the actors who'd previously played Spider-Man were in it at the same time. Something to do with the multiverse—it all sounded like gobbledygook to me."

"It was great," Paul said.

"Although they really banged on about how it was sad that Doctor Octopus wasn't in it. Seeing as all the other baddies were brought back as well."

"They're right about that," Paul said. "I thought the same thing."

"You did?" Becks asked again.

"I said, didn't I?"

"Hold on—sorry—I've got that wrong," Becks said with a lethal smile. "They said they *loved* how Doctor Octopus was brought back."

Paul's face fell and Judith beamed, thrilled with Becks's subterfuge.

"You don't remember this character?" Judith asked.

"I don't always follow all the ins and outs of Marvel movies."

"But he was the big baddie at the end," Becks said. "Are you really saying you don't remember him?"

"Look, it's possible I nodded off."

"In the middle of the big battle that always ends those films?"

"I remember now, I was knackered from work. I fell asleep and only woke up at the end."

"That really doesn't seem very plausible," Judith said.

"It's what happened, OK?"

Judith decided she'd had enough of Paul.

"I don't suppose you've bought anything from a fancy dress shop recently?" she asked.

"What sort of a question is that?"

"Or bought any wigs or false beards online?"

"OK, this meeting is over."

"We decide when it's over. Why did your wife ring Alec Miller?"

"Who the hell's he?" Paul asked sharply, but the women could see the tiniest dent in his confidence.

"You don't know?" Judith said, to test Paul's defenses.

"Just tell me who the damned man is!" he spat at the women.

Judith guessed what was behind Paul's sudden anger and decided to risk prodding the bear.

"What would you say if I said he's your wife's lover?"

"I knew it—the ungrateful bitch! I've given her everything she has. *Everything*! And this is how she repays me?"

"You've suspected for some time, haven't you?"

"This last year, she's been evasive. Up to something. I could tell. I came home at lunch a few months ago, and she wasn't in. Or in that stupid recording studio of hers. I didn't think anything about it and went back to work. That evening, I asked her how her day was, she said she'd been at home all day, and when I said I'd returned home at lunchtime and not seen her, there was this look in her eyes…"

"What was it?" Becks asked.

"Guilt. Pure guilt. I went for her. Bloody hell, but I went for her, demanding she tell me the truth, but she wouldn't change her story—she kept saying she'd been home all day—even though I knew it was a lie."

"I bet you accused her of sleeping around," Suzie said with an edge.

"Damned right I did—she was married when I met her, did I tell you that? When she and I got together, she'd already betrayed one husband, so what if she was doing it again?"

"And what did she say about that?"

"That's when she looked guilty."

"So you've known for some time she was having an affair?"

"I've guessed as much, but I didn't know who with. Now I do."

"By the way," Judith said. "It's not Alec Miller. I just wanted to give you a name and see how you reacted. However, it does rather beg the question, who is she having an affair with?"

Paul spluttered, uncomprehending, and Judith decided to leave him to stew. She went over to the photos on the wall to look at one in particular. It showed Paul with Sophia and a very smart-looking woman in her seventies wearing a ball gown with some kind of official insignia and ribbon pinned below her left shoulder.

Judith's breath caught as she saw something else in the photo, and she yanked it off the wall to look at it more closely.

"Hey!" Paul said.

"Not now," Judith said to silence him as she peered even more closely at the photo.

Becks and Suzie joined her.

"What is it?" Suzie asked.

"What do you notice about this photo?" Judith said, still trying to process what she was seeing.

Suzie frowned. "I don't know."

"The earrings Sophia's wearing."

"What about them?"

Judith reached into her handbag and pulled out the single hooped earring she'd found in Geoffrey's bedroom.

In the photo, Sophia was wearing the same earring.

"Mr. De Castro," Judith said, spinning back to look at Paul. "You've just admitted you suspect your wife's been having an affair for the last year."

"I'm not talking to you anymore."

"I've got a question I need to ask you, and it's very important you think very carefully before you answer. Does your wife by any chance have a diamond-shaped birthmark on her side underneath her left breast?"

Paul was thrown by the question.

"How on earth do you know about that?" he asked.

"Just answer the question."

"Yes. Yes, she does."

Chapter 35

"I THINK I ADMIRE HER," Becks said as she and her friends banged out of the front door of Marlow Wealth Management. "Having an affair with a man who must be twenty years her senior."

"He looked like a gnome!" Suzie said, uncomprehending.

"But think about what he offered," Becks said. "He was kind, everyone says that. And considerate. These are attractive qualities."

"Sorry," Suzie said, "what part of 'he looked like a gnome' aren't you getting?"

"But maybe it's like Marilyn Monroe and Arthur Miller," Judith said. "A woman who people dismiss because she's beautiful is liable to be attracted by qualities other than looks in men."

When Judith and her friends arrived at Sophia's house, she didn't answer the doorbell, and she wasn't in her recording studio, either. They eventually found her in her poison garden, picking tiny pink flowers from the tips of nettles.

"What do you want?" she asked, dusting the dark earth from her knees as she stood up.

"You lied to us," Judith said. "You've been lying to us from the start."

"What a horrible thing to say. I've been nothing but helpful."

"About having a birthmark under your left breast," Suzie said. "Meaning it was you who sent that racy photo to Geoffrey."

"Which is hardly surprising," Judith said, pulling the silver earring out of her handbag. "Because you were having an affair with him, weren't you?"

"I wasn't," she said.

"It's too late for that," Becks said. "Judith found your earring in Geoffrey's bedroom, and we know the provocative photo you sent Geoffrey was of you."

"You don't understand," Sophia said.

"Then why don't you tell us?" Becks said, and there was such kindness in her voice that Sophia softened. But it was also obvious that she didn't know where to start her story. And then they all saw the moment her indecision cleared.

"I loved him," she said simply. "I loved him, but he wouldn't have me."

"I'm sorry?" Suzie asked.

"I fell for him, you're right about that. I didn't mean to. I mean, why would I fall for someone like Geoffrey?"

"I know," Suzie said before Becks dug an elbow into her ribs to be quiet.

"He was so old, and not even a bit attractive." Suzie said.

This time a warning glance from Becks was enough to keep Suzie quiet.

"It was when he helped me out with that awful situation with the graves. All those years ago. He refused to blame me. He said it was his fault if it was anyone's. He'd given me the job, I hadn't asked to do it, and I'd done my best, hadn't I? That's what he kept saying. As long as I'd approached the job with a good heart, then that's all that mattered.

"I got the most terrible crush on him. At that time, I wasn't attracted to him physically, it was more the idea of him. Someone who saw me, who cared about me."

"He really was a saint," Suzie said.

"He was," Sophia agreed. "And over the years, I noticed that he wasn't just kind to me, he was kind to everyone he met. He lived for them. And before too long, I realized I was looking forward to our planning meetings far more than I should. The whole thing crept up on me, I don't know how."

Sophia lost herself in her memories.

"We've spoken to your husband," Becks said to help Sophia.

"Then you know I wasn't entirely truthful the last time we spoke. My home life's far from ideal. Paul's..." Sophia tried to put into words her relationship with her husband and failed. "Everything with him's transactional. If he does anything for me, he wants something in return—and he only thinks of me as someone he can parade on his arm. He wouldn't care who was on his arm, I genuinely believe he'd be happy if he paid for a female escort to accompany him to events as long as they were pretty and he could show them off."

"I'm so sorry," Becks said.

"I don't get it," Suzie said. "How come we found an earring in Geoffrey's bedroom if you weren't sleeping with him?"

"You know how you can get fixated on something? Or someone. It's been building for some time with me. Last year I had to confront a shocking truth. I'd become obsessed with Geoffrey. But I knew I couldn't have him, and that tormented me even more. In the end, I just came out with it and told him how I felt."

"When was this?" Judith asked.

"Six months ago. I invited him here when I knew Paul would be away. Made up some story about wanting to speak to him for my podcast. And as soon as he was through the door, I kissed him—threw myself at him like a teenage girl, I couldn't help myself."

Sophia didn't say anything else, and Judith and her friends were wise enough to give her space.

"He pushed me off," Sophia said, facing her greatest shame. "He wasn't interested. I didn't know what to think. I'm not used to men not finding me attractive. He explained he was surprised, and 'flattered'—that's the word he kept saying, he was flattered by my interest, but he couldn't cheat on his wife. I didn't know what to think. His wife was dead, she'd been dead for the last twenty years! And here I was, offering myself—to a man with no ties—it was me who was risking everything, not him. Me who risked looking like a fool if people found out. Me who was risking my marriage—but he wouldn't listen. He pushed me away and left the house. I've never felt so humiliated. How dare he turn me down? There was no way I could go to the next planning meeting, not with him claiming he could resist me. He had to know what he was saying no to. So instead of going to the meeting, I let myself into his house."

"Using the key in the bird box," Judith said.

"That's right—and went upstairs to his bedroom. And…I took my clothes off and lay on his bed. And took that photo of me in my underwear. I sent it to him at the end of the meeting."

"I get it!" Judith said, understanding finally coming to her. "*That's* why Geoffrey got the new bolts and fancy alarm system installed in his house. It was after you'd let yourself in."

Sophia ducked her eyes, ashamed at having her secret revealed.

"When he got back, I was available—his!—but he was furious, said I was being disrespectful, that I was harassing him. He made me get dressed, I was scrabbling around for my clothes like a common tart."

"Which is when you lost your earring," Judith said.

"Yes!"

"That must have been so humiliating for you—him tipping you out of his house."

"It bloody was," Sophia said, her shame turning to fury.

"Which is why you killed him."

"What? No! I loved him!"

"I don't think that's true. You were obsessed with him—that's the word you used. It was obsession, pure and simple. Not love. And when he rejected you, that obsession curdled into hate. The humiliation of being rejected, it was too much for you. And let's not forget, you're the one person in Marlow who knows about poisons. You also knew that Geoffrey always made himself a coffee before each meeting. Because you couldn't risk him telling anyone that you'd thrown yourself at him. Or that you'd sent him a photo of your breasts. Imagine the shame, then? Paul would leave you—you'd lose your comfortable house and your perfect reputation."

"I was right the first time, wasn't I?" Suzie interjected. "There *was* an odd vibe between you and Geoffrey at the planning meeting. It was because you knew you were about to murder him."

"I didn't!" Sophia sobbed. "You have to believe me, I didn't!" she added, but there was a pleading tone to her voice. And there was something else about Sophia's words, Judith and her friends could see. Sophia was riven with guilt.

"And I was the last person to the meeting," Sophia said. "Geoffrey had already got himself his coffee—he was sitting down with it. I never went anywhere near him."

"You noticed he already had his coffee, did you?" Suzie asked.

"Of course I did—it was the first time I'd seen him since he'd thrown me out of his house. I noticed everything. That's why I was strange with him, I felt so embarrassed. But don't you see? I admit I have access to aconite, but there's no way I could have poisoned him."

"When we last spoke to you, you said you arrived late at the meeting because you had a puncture. And you had to take your car to Platts to get the tire changed."

"That's right."

"So if we go and speak to Platts garage right now, they'll say you brought in your car that evening?"

"Of course they will. Why would I lie to you about that?"

Once again, the women heard the words Sophia was saying, but all they saw was the guilt on her face. And luckily for them, they knew a quick way of proving whether her story was true or not.

Suzie drove herself and her friends straight from Sophia's house to Platts garage in the center of Marlow. After a couple of inquiries, they learned that Sophia had indeed brought her car in on the night Geoffrey was killed, and that a man called Leonard had dealt with her. Leonard was an elegant young man with a tidy mustache—not the sort of person the women expected to find working in dirty blue overalls in a garage.

"Yes, I remember Mrs. De Castro," he said, wiping his hands on a dirty towel. "She was pretty rattled when she came in. She said she risked being late for a meeting, but there was something else going on, if you ask me. She was really distracted."

"Did you have any idea why?"

"None. But she was definitely worried about something. Like she had something on her mind."

"What was wrong with her car?" Suzie asked.

"That was an odd one. She said she had a puncture in the front driver's side wheel, and I could see the tire was flat. But when I checked it over, there wasn't a puncture. Someone had let the air out of it, that was all."

"Are you serious?"

"I've never had that happen to me before. A tire that wasn't damaged in any way."

"What did you tell her?"

"There was nothing I could say. The moment she dropped the car off, she left on foot, saying there was somewhere she needed to be, and then I didn't see her again until the following morning. And that was weird as well. When she picked her car up, she made a big play of being surprised that her tire hadn't been punctured at all. The whole thing felt 'off.' Almost false. You know?"

"Hang on," Judith said. "She dropped off her car at six thirty?"

"That's right."

"Saying her tire had been punctured, even though it wasn't—someone had just let the air out of it?"

"That's right. It took me about five minutes to fix."

"And she left on foot as soon as she arrived?"

"Got it in one."

Judith and her friends looked at each other. They all knew it was only a ten-minute walk from the garage to the town council building. So why had Sophia lied to them about her tire being punctured? And what had she done between leaving the garage and her late arrival at the planning meeting just after 7:30 p.m.?

Chapter 36

"SOPHIA'S THE KILLER," SUZIE SAID as she and her friends got back into her van. "It was her poison, Geoffrey had recently rejected and humiliated her, it was her who phoned Alec to tell him not to come in that night, she vanished for an hour before the murder—and we've all seen how deranged she was, making up stories about having flat tires when her tires were all OK."

"But how can she be the killer?" Becks asked. "It was you who said she never went anywhere near Geoffrey."

"Maybe that was the whole point?" Suzie suggested. "Her arrival was a performance where she created the *impression* she couldn't be the killer."

"But if she never went near him, it's still impossible," Becks said.

"That's not quite true," Judith said. "You're forgetting the blond-haired man who was serving in the kitchen."

"I don't see how he can be connected to Sophia," Suzie said.

"Tell me," Judith asked Suzie, "did the man in the kitchen leave before or after Sophia arrived?"

"I don't know."

"Then think back to the murder. When Sophia came through the door, was the blond-haired man in the kitchen?"

"No," Suzie said, searching her memory. "He'd definitely gone by then. Actually, now you mention it, he left not long after Jeremy arrived. I remember seeing him go through the fire door and thinking he must have known to get out before Jeremy started being difficult, fussing about biscuits."

"Excellent!" Judith said. "So he left just after Jeremy got there. Now, who was next to arrive?"

"I don't know. Jeremy chatted for a bit with Marcus, and then…that's right, Geoffrey came in. He asked why I was there, and we chatted, which took a bit of time, and that's when Geoffrey went to the hatch and got himself his coffee—his poisoned coffee—and then he went and sat down. That's right. He was sitting down with his coffee when Sophia then arrived."

"So a good few minutes had passed between our blond-haired friend leaving and Sophia arriving?"

"I suppose so."

"Then I think we need to go to the town council building."

Judith wouldn't explain her theory as they drove to the council building. As they got out of Suzie's van, Becks said, "We won't be able to get into the debating chamber, will we? It'll be locked."

"I don't think we'll need access," Judith said, as she headed around to the back of the building where the fire door was located. "But let's see if we can't work this through. As you just reminded us, Suzie, it was Sophia who phoned Alec Miller to tell him not to work that night. He identified her voice when you played one of her podcasts to him. So let's keep this as simple as possible. The reason why Sophia wanted Alec to stay away that night was because she wanted to poison Geoffrey with aconite."

"Are you saying Sophia is our blond man?" Becks asked.

"Let's say she was. After all, the goatee beard would have been a good way of suggesting that it was a man in the kitchen. And we already know that no one on the committee really paid attention to the person who was serving. No one mentioned him in their original statements."

"You really think Sophia was able to disguise herself as a man?" Suzie asked.

"It wouldn't have been that hard. All that lovely blond hair could have been hidden under a man's wig—and it would explain why the man was blond. She'd want to keep the color as close to her own hair as possible. The shorter, straight hair—and the blond goatee beard—would be enough to suggest she was a man, if you ask me. And she's of average height, we can all agree on that. As for her shape, I'm sure that if she wore tight-fitting clothes, she could have hidden her breasts, even if it would have been uncomfortable for her for a spell."

As Judith spoke, she was looking out over Higginson Park.

"So what are we doing here?" Becks asked.

"Looking for somewhere for her to have got changed out of her disguise, and fast," Judith said as she strode to a little toilet block on the edge of the car park only ten yards away.

"You think she got changed in the toilets?" Suzie asked.

"She couldn't go around the front of the building and risk bumping into someone who knew her. If I were her, this is where I'd do it."

The toilet block was made of three individual unisex toilets on one side, and another three on the other. The friends poked their heads into each cubicle, but there was no way of telling whether or not Suzie had gotten changed in there.

"Becks?" a voice called out, and the friends saw a woman approaching.

It was Marian.

"What on earth are you doing lurking by toilets?"

"This is my mother-in-law, Marian," Becks said by way of explanation to her friends.

"Oh!" Marian said, as she looked from Becks to the toilets, and back again. "So is this what you mean when you say you're doing 'police work'?"

"It's not all hanging around public conveniences," Becks said, trying to make a joke of it and failing.

"I'm pleased to hear it. And I'm glad to bump into you, the Meat Hook have been in touch. They say they won't extend any more credit to you until the bill is paid."

The Meat Hook was a very fine butcher's at the top of the High Street.

"I don't have an account at the Meat Hook," Becks said, confused.

"You do! I set one up for you."

"You've been buying food from there?"

"Well," Marian said with a smile, "technically, you have, but yes, I suppose I have."

"I thought you were using your own money when you were bringing food into the house."

"You know I don't have a bean."

"Hold on," Becks said, a terrible thought occurring to her. "Do you have any other accounts around town?"

"No—of course not."

"Good."

"But you do."

"*What?*"

"Just with Strawberry Grove, Lady Sew and Sew, Coopers, and the Cedar coffee shop. Oh, and I've got some jewelry being cleaned at Wellington's—I couldn't bear to see how tarnished it had become. But it belonged to Colin's great-aunt, I know he'll want to see it back to its former glory."

"Did you ask him?"

"His great-aunt Jess was very important to him, I didn't need to."

"We're not made of money."

"Of course not, which is why I always make sure I get value for money."

"And yet I never see you returning to the house with bags from Lidl."

Marian's smile froze. She, like everyone, knew that the town's Waitrose had recently been replaced with a far more affordable Lidl supermarket. Marian took the view, at an almost-atavistic level, that just because Marlow now had a Lidl, it didn't mean one had to talk about it.

"I thought that was a shoe shop," she eventually suggested.

"You did?" Suzie asked.

"The logo's so jolly, I didn't know they sold food. Well, you learn something new every day. I hope you catch your killer!" she offered as she headed off.

Suzie was the first to speak.

"You drove her away by talking about Lidl."

Becks was just as dumbfounded.

"I did, didn't I?"

"Yeah," Suzie said, coming to a decision. "She deserves to die."

"If I'm honest, I don't know how much more of her I can take."

Judith could see how anguished Becks was, and she was reminded of how she'd promised to help her friend rid herself of her mother-in-law. But more pressingly, Marian was right, they had a killer to catch.

"Come on," she said, "there's the last cubicle to look at."

Judith went over to the last door, opened it, and discovered it wasn't in fact a toilet; it was a store cupboard that contained cleaning equipment. Judith noticed there was a wooden stepladder leaning up against a wall by an old mop.

"Now that's interesting," she said. "A stepladder."

"Why's that of interest?" Becks asked.

"Only, I can't help noticing that there's a little hatch in the ceiling."

Judith indicated, and her friends could see it was true. There was a hatch in the ceiling that was covered with a wooden board.

"If I were Sophia and I had to get changed quickly and hide the evidence," Judith said, "I think I'd maybe scoot over to this room, take off my disguise, pull out that stepladder, climb up it, and stuff my costume in the roof void before closing the hatch and then emerging in my usual clothes."

"You think she stuffed her disguise up there?"

"It's a possibility. I don't see anywhere between the exit door of the kitchen and the front of the building that offers a better place for a quick change."

The women looked at the hatch in the ceiling.

"I'm not going up there," Suzie said.

"And I shouldn't have to," Judith said. "Not at my age."

Becks sighed.

"Don't worry," she said. "I'll do it."

"Good," Suzie said as she went to the stepladder and kicked it open so it was directly under the hatch.

"You two hold this thing tight," Becks said. "I'm not having it fall over."

"Got it," Suzie said.

"You promise you won't step away?"

"Why would we do that?" Judith asked.

"I don't know. I think you're both capable of doing that."

"I'm outraged you'd think that," Judith said with a grin.

"I'd definitely do it," Suzie agreed.

"But we'd never do it to a friend," Judith said.

"Damned right," Suzie chipped in.

Becks took a moment to realize that she, the vicar of Marlow's wife, was about to go into the attic space of a public toilet block. Funny how life turns out, she thought to herself as she took hold of the stepladder and started to climb.

Because the roof was quite low, she didn't need to get to the top step before she was able to reach up to the board that covered the access to the attic space.

"Hope there aren't any rats up there," Suzie said.

"Thank you," Becks called down, even though she'd been thinking the same thing.

Becks pushed the board up, turned it in her hands, and brought it down through the hatch. She gave it to Suzie and then reached into her back pocket, where she pulled out her smartphone. Turning on the flashlight, she shone it up into the darkness. She couldn't really see anything.

"You'll have to go up a bit," Judith said.

Becks realized she was going to have to climb up onto the top step after all, and suddenly her fear of looking into a roof void was eclipsed by her fear that she was about to fall off the top of a stepladder.

"We've got you," Suzie said, sensing Becks's concern.

Becks took another step up, the ladder wobbled, and she grabbed at the lip of the roof space with her free hand.

"One more step and you're there," Judith said.

Becks stepped up, the ladder wobbled again, but she held on for dear life, and Judith and Suzie were able to steady it.

"Thanks," she said.

"What can you see?" Suzie asked.

"Hold on," Becks said, moving the beam of her flashlight around the dusty roof space. Luckily for her, there wasn't anything too scary, but her flashlight picked up a carrier bag that was stuffed full.

"There's a carrier bag," she said unenthusiastically.

"What's in it?" Suzie called up.

"Hold on, let me get it." Becks dragged the bag over and saw that it was stuffed with fabric. "I don't know, but it's full of something."

"Chuck it down."

"OK," Becks said and dropped the bag through the hole, being sure to miss the heads of her two friends.

"What else is there?" Judith called up.

Becks peered into the darkness. There were a few mouse droppings and long rolls of gray matter where dust had solidified.

"Wow," she said.

"What is it?" Suzie asked eagerly.

"This doesn't bother me," Becks said, amazed.

"Being up a ladder?" Judith asked.

"The mess. The dust. I don't even want to clean it. Coming down."

Becks took a step down, bent over to steady herself, and came down the ladder. She then banged her hands together to get the dust off them.

"Amazing," she said to herself as she saw the clouds of dust and found she wasn't panicking.

"Well, let's see what's in the bag," Judith said.

She reached in and started to pull out what looked like bandage material about a foot wide.

"What an odd thing to put in an attic space," Becks said.

"Hold on, there's a safety pin on the end," Judith said in mounting excitement. "This could be it!"

As Judith pulled the end of the material out of the bag, they all saw a large safety pin pushed through it.

The material that was now spooled onto the floor was four or five feet long.

"Could this be a bandage she used to bind herself with?" Becks asked.

"I think that's *exactly* what it is," Judith said as she reached into the bag and pulled out a blond wig. She then reached back into the bag and pulled out a blond goatee beard that she held up to her friends.

"We've found it," Suzie said. "The proof. Sophia's the killer, isn't she?"

Chapter 37

TANIKA SUPERVISED THE COLLECTION OF the disguise and bandage herself.

"I don't know how you do it, really I don't," she said.

"Just doing our civic duty," Judith said with a smile.

"Not that you'll tell anyone what you've found," Tanika said, knowing full well Suzie's propensity to brag. "If we can find forensic evidence that Sophia wore this, it's going to play a major part in convicting her. But only if we follow all procedures correctly."

"My mouth's sealed," Suzie said.

Once Tanika had driven off, Suzie said, "Well, I think this calls for a celebration."

She could see that Judith was deep in thought.

"Come on!" she chivied. "This is an amazing achievement—we've put another killer behind bars."

"I don't know," Judith said.

"Or we will when the forensic evidence comes in," Becks added.

"What if she's being set up?"

"Who?"

"Sophia. There's something not quite right about this. It's like when I come up with a crossword clue that works really well—although there's an additional 'and' or 'the' in the question, so it lacks absolute clarity."

"What could be more clear than the fact that Sophia's the killer?" Suzie asked.

"But why would she do it?"

"Because Geoffrey rejected her."

"No, I get that. Of course that would be shameful for her, but he hadn't told anyone about it, had he?"

"He could have done at any moment."

"But would he? Remember what Debbie told us about how he drove her to all of her appointments without pressing her on why she needed to go to hospital."

"She asked him not to ask," Becks said.

"I know, but would you really do all that driving for someone without eventually stepping over the line and wanting to know what was wrong with her? I know I would. And it was the same with Marcus's blackmail letter, wasn't it? Geoffrey took it in because it was the right thing to do, but we've found no evidence that he'd told anyone else about it—or even gone to the police. And he'd still not gone to the police when he'd worked out that Jeremy was behind it. Discretion seems to be his middle name. And Sophia would have known that as well as anyone. So, I agree, she'd humiliated herself in front of him, but her secret was safe, he wasn't going to tell anyone. So why did she need to kill him?"

"Maybe we need to prove that Geoffrey had told Sophia's secret to someone," Becks offered.

"Or maybe the reason why she looks like she's the killer is because she's the killer," Suzie said, wanting to keep things nice and simple.

"I think I'm going to go home," Judith said, suddenly realizing that she needed space so she could think as clearly as possible.

"Seriously?" Suzie said. "In our moment of triumph?"

But Judith was already heading off. When she got back to her house, she went into her makeshift incident room and studied the names of the suspects on the board. She still couldn't put into words what was troubling her; it was really just a sense that there was some aspect of the case that wasn't quite fitting. It didn't mean that Sophia *wasn't* the killer—she was still very possibly the person who'd poisoned Geoffrey—but Judith still wasn't happy with the idea. So she decided to do what she always did when she was stuck with a problem, and that was to go for a swim.

Once in the Thames, Judith found she could drift off into her thoughts as she swam along. Was it really possible to make a case that Sophia was being set up? It didn't seem likely, because the killer would have to be someone who not only wanted Geoffrey dead but also wanted Sophia to be charged with his murder. But who out there hated them both that much? No matter how much Judith considered the suspects, there wasn't anyone who fitted the bill.

However, there was one person who might have wanted to frame Sophia for a murder she hadn't committed, and that was her husband. But just as Judith was beginning to work through how Paul might have done it, a black Labrador ran into the Thames with an almighty splash. Looking over, she saw the dog's owner get ready to throw a stick for the dog to chase in the water. Judith decided that discretion was the better part of valor, stopped swimming, and allowed herself to be borne back home by the current.

Once she'd climbed out of the water and thrown on her cape, she strode back to her house. When she got inside, she was about to hang up her cape when she heard her mobile ring. Still dripping water, she went over to see who was calling.

It was Tanika.

"Congratulations," Tanika said by way of opening. "We've already got results back from forensics. They've been able to lift over a dozen of Sophia's fingerprints from the carrier bag you found the clothes in. They've also found some human hairs inside the wig as well, and they're a DNA match with Sophia's hair. You've done it again, Judith, I can't thank you enough."

"You found Sophia's hair in the wig?"

"Only a few strands. I guess they came out when she took it off."

Thanking Judith once again for all of her hard work, Tanika rang off saying she'd be in touch if there were any further developments.

Judith tried to feel happy, but still found that she didn't quite have a sense of closure. Maybe she was getting cantankerous, she told herself, and didn't like being served the solution on a plate. But that was the point, wasn't it? She couldn't quite shake the feeling that Sophia was being served to her on a plate.

Judith went over to her clothes where they were bunched up on her favorite wingback and decided to get dressed. When she was done, she picked up her watch and put it onto her left wrist—which prompted an idle thought. She wore her watch on her left wrist. Of course she did, everyone did.

But Debbie Bell didn't.

Judith remembered noting the fact when they last spoke. Just before they'd interviewed Paul, Debbie had checked the time by looking at the watch on her right wrist. But why on earth had that particular fact popped into Judith's head? She decided to move on from the memory, it couldn't possibly be relevant, and instead focused on doing up the clasp on her watch.

Her mind wasn't having any of it. There was something of interest about Debbie's watch, she was sure of it—although it wasn't clear what it could be. Aside from suggesting that Debbie was left-handed, what could it tell her that might be of interest?

At that moment a memory sparked—a startling recollection of something she'd heard earlier in the investigation. Her mind instantly resisted following the thought through, it was such a preposterous idea, but she made herself take the next logical step.

"Dear God," she whispered as she realized the implication of what she was now considering. Could it be true?

Judith shivered, but it wasn't from the water drying on her naked skin; she was realizing how brilliant the killer might have been. What about the phone call Sophia made on the morning of the murder? It was very definitely Sophia who'd rung Alec Miller—he'd identified her voice when Becks had played Sophia's podcast to him—but in a rush of excitement, Judith realized the true significance of that moment, and she strode off to her makeshift incident room, barely noticing as her cape slipped from her shoulders to the floor.

Going up to the incident board, she pulled down the suspected killer's index card from the wall and looked at the details. Was it even possible? Judith realized it was, even though it would rely on the most incredible commitment. But if you aren't prepared to commit to a murder, why even bother?

Judith could feel the sugar rush of inspiration running out, and she tried to take an inventory of what she'd worked out: why the CCTV had been cut in the council building for Sophia's phone call, why Sophia had to be late to the meeting, and why aconite from her garden had been used.

But why kill Geoffrey, that's what she couldn't work out—the "why" of it.

It was the same problem they'd had right from the start of the case. Why would *anyone* want to kill Geoffrey? Judith found herself remembering her very first encounter with Sophia, when she said she could never have a motive for killing Geoffrey. He was, as everyone kept saying, a "saint."

And that's when Judith got it.

Impossible though it was to believe, it was precisely because Geoffrey was a saint that he had to die, wasn't it? It was a stunning revelation, but how to prove it? The killer had been so clever.

Judith told herself that no matter how clever the killer was, she was cleverer. She could do this, even though she was standing in a room that was half police incident room and half mad archive of ancient newspapers. An archive that Suzie had so recently told her she had to clear.

Judith turned and looked at the floor-to-ceiling stacks of papers that covered half the room. The first glimmerings of a plan were beginning to fall into place for her. She could use her archive to help catch the killer. It would require creating a fiction, and it would involve a quite considerable sacrifice on her part. But what was a little sacrifice when weighed on the scales of justice? And anyway, she'd live to fight another day whatever happened; the important thing was that the killer was put behind bars.

Standing on her own, completely naked, Judith looked down at the index card she was holding in her hand. She now knew the name of Geoffrey's killer was written on it.

"Got you."

Chapter 38

LATER THAT AFTERNOON, SOPHIA DE Castro arrived at the Marlow town council building. As she put her hand on the door handle, she paused and took a deep breath to steady her nerves. She felt the pressure of her lies—the lies she'd told up until this moment, and the lies she knew she was yet to tell. But she knew she had no choice. She was too far down the road. She was trapped.

She raised her chin and entered the building.

As she walked down the corridor, she tried not to look at the severed cord of the security camera, or the scratched Perspex canopy of the public phone box, and instead she pushed the doors open and entered the debating chamber.

Marcus, Jeremy, and Debbie were already sitting at the conference table with Judith Potts, Suzie Harris, Becks Starling, and Detective Inspector Tanika Malik all in attendance.

"You can't tell us what to do!" Jeremy was saying as Sophia joined them.

"I'm afraid we can," Tanika said. "And the sooner you do it, the sooner you'll be able to leave."

"I'm not cooperating," Jeremy said and folded his arms.

"What's going on?" Sophia asked, even though she knew what was going on.

"It's a bloody reenactment," Jeremy grumbled.

"Not just that," Marcus said, a frown creasing his forehead. "We've apparently got to confess."

Sophia saw that Debbie was looking down at her hands in her lap.

"Confess?" Sophia said with a fake smile.

"Each of you has a confession to make," Judith said crisply. "But it's also very important that you show me exactly what you did when you went to get your teas and coffees from the hatch over there."

Judith indicated the hatch that led to the kitchenette beyond. On it there was the samovar of hot water, the Nespresso machine, the coffee capsules, and tray of tea bags.

"According to your witness statements," Tanika said, "Marcus was the first to arrive, and you made yourself a cup of tea."

"You really want me to do this?"

"If you'd just retrace your steps."

"Very well," Marcus said, pushing his chair back. "When I got here, it was just me and Suzie. And I went to the hatch and made myself a cup of tea," he said as he went over to the hatch, got himself a cup and saucer, plonked a tea bag in, filled it with hot water and a splash of milk, and returned to his seat. "Happy now?"

"And now your confession," Judith said.

"I don't know what you're talking about," Marcus said.

"Marcus is Marlow01628," Suzie said, fed up with the delay. "That's what we're talking about."

"*What?*" Debbie said, stunned.

"It can't be?" Sophia said. "That account's vile."

"And Marcus writes every word of it," Suzie said proudly. "Which is why he was being blackmailed."

"No, no, no," Marcus said, but the guilt on his face made it clear he might as well have been saying "yes, yes, yes."

"And really, you've made this so much harder for yourself—lying to us at every turn when you really didn't need to."

"I can't admit to that account."

"I think you'd better. Because you're a suspect in a murder inquiry, and that means Tanika has just cause to send a team of police officers to investigate every corner of your life—getting warrants to take in all of your computers, your personal correspondence, tear your office apart. Your reputation would be destroyed before they'd even proved the account was yours."

"I've deleted it," Marcus blurted.

"Say that again?"

"After the last time I saw you. I felt so ashamed. I'd let things get out of hand. I've never even believed any of the things I wrote. It was just so…exciting to say more and more outrageous things. It was addictive. I was sick. I'd got sick thinking I could hurt people. Be offensive, it was like a drug. But you look for yourselves, I deleted the whole account. I've learned my lesson."

While Marcus was talking, Suzie had got out her phone and checked on Twitter.

"It says 'account deleted.'"

"I'm shocked, Marcus," Debbie said.

"I'm not," Jeremy said, unable to stop himself from bragging. "I'd worked it out."

"It's not something to show off about," Suzie said, "considering it was you who was behind the blackmail."

Marcus rose out of his chair in fury.

"It was *you?*"

Jeremy held Marcus's gaze.

"Yes," he said, and Judith could feel the decades of frustration in that one word. Frustration at Marcus's ongoing success; frustration at Jeremy's feeling of inadequacy.

"Why?" Marcus asked.

"You're the one in the wrong," Jeremy said petulantly.

"Yes—in the wrong—and I've deleted the account. But it was only wrong, it wasn't illegal. Blackmail's a criminal offense."

"You're saying what I did was worse than you?"

"Boys!" Debbie said, "I don't think now's the time."

Jeremy tore his gaze from Marcus and looked at Debbie.

"I can't wait to hear what your confession is," he snapped.

Debbie seemed to shrink in her seat.

"And I've not broken any law," Jeremy said in a manner that suggested he'd played his ace.

"Yes, you bloody did!" Marcus said.

"I didn't ask for anything in return from you—you've got to benefit for it to be blackmail, isn't that right?" he said to Tanika.

"Is this the line you're going to take?" Tanika asked.

"I know my law. Marcus can bring either of those letters I sent him to the police, and you can say they're threatening—in bad taste, perhaps—but no more than that. No law's been broken. Least of all blackmail."

"You always were a rat, Jeremy," Marcus said.

"It takes one to know one."

As the men stared daggers at each other, Judith turned to Debbie, who imperceptibly shook her head.

"I'm sorry, Debbie, but Jeremy didn't get a cup of tea, there's nothing for him to reenact. Although it's good to see that, from where he's sitting, he really was out of reach of Geoffrey and his cup of coffee. Like Suzie's been saying all along. Anyway, you should tell your story to your friends now. It's better they hear from you before Tanika presses charges and they find out that way."

Debbie realized she had no choice. Haltingly, she told the story of how her hormones had started to make her life unbearable, how she'd not been able to think clearly, and how she knew there was a way out for her. The other members of the committee listened respectfully. But when she went on to explain how she'd also stolen money from the council to buy herself porcelain ornaments the following year, and the year after that, their sympathy soon evaporated.

"Well, aren't we a pretty bunch?" Marcus said bitterly. "An online troll, a blackmailer, and a thief."

"Could you get your coffee now?" Becks asked Debbie.

"Seriously?" Debbie asked, looking up.

"It's very important," Judith said.

In fact, Judith knew that this was the moment the whole experiment had been building up to. She watched keenly as Debbie stood up, went over to the coffee machine, and picked up a coffee capsule. She tried to put it into the Nespresso machine, but it wouldn't fit.

"I can't get it in," she said.

"Don't worry," Tanika said, "we wanted to create the same circumstances you found, so I jammed a capsule into the machine before you got here. Like on the night."

"OK," Debbie said as she pulled the front of the machine open, freed the capsule so it fell down into the little hopper, closed the front of the machine, and inserted her coffee capsule.

"I don't know how this can help," Jeremy grumbled.

"Debbie's revealing to us who the killer is," Judith said.

Debbie picked up a cup, placed it under the nozzle of the machine, pressed a button, and then waited while the coffee poured out. Once it had done so, she picked up the cup and carried it back to the table.

Judith and her friends exchanged excited glances, knowing that Judith's theory had just been proven.

Debbie was left-handed.

"You're the secretary to the committee?" Tanika asked.

"I am," Debbie said as she sat down with her coffee.

"So you were making notes during the meeting?"

"Yes."

"With a computer?"

"No, with a pen and paper. I prefer using a pen."

"A pen you use left-handed?" Suzie asked.

"Yes," Debbie said, flummoxed. "I write left-handed, what of it?"

"Really, it's of no importance," Judith said. "Now, Sophia, it's your turn."

"I didn't get myself a cup of tea or a coffee," she said.

"I know," Judith said, "but that still leaves your confession."

Sophia looked from Judith to her friends on the planning committee.

"I fell in love with Geoffrey," she said before she lost confidence. "Years ago. When I got into that mess on the works and buildings committee. He worked so hard to clear my name, I definitely got what we used to call at school a 'pash.' But these last few months, my interest in him grew into an obsession. I threw myself at him—although he resisted. Nothing happened. By the way," Sophia added, turning to face Judith. "I've been going through all the old paperwork I keep in the loft in my boathouse. It turned out Geoffrey had worked out the correct location of every grave and sent me a map of where everyone is buried. I hadn't realized until I looked properly, but every grave's accounted for."

"Thank you," Judith said. "Although it was really only the information about your infatuation with Geoffrey that I needed—you don't get brownie points for clearing up the mess you made in the past. Although I'd very much like to know what you did in between dropping off your car at Platts garage and arriving here on the night that Geoffrey died."

Sophia frowned.

"I…" she said, before forcing herself to continue. "I went for a walk."

"Where to?"

"Through town, over the bridge, I even popped into the church. I was killing time. I didn't want to go to the meeting, it was the first time I'd seen Geoffrey since he'd thrown me out of his house. There was no way I was going to arrive before I had to. I wasn't sure I'd arrive at all. Even at the last minute, I nearly turned away. At the front door to the building, I almost bottled it. But I knew I'd have to see him sometime, so I took my courage in my hands and came into the meeting. Given that I was late, I knew we'd get straight into it without too much chitchat."

"Thank you," Judith said. "And that's everything we needed to see and hear, so thank you, all of you, for indulging me. Although I suppose you're all wondering why we've asked you to do this," Judith added as she moved into the center of the room.

As she spoke, Tanika's phone started to ring. She plucked it out of her back pocket and moved off to one side to take the call.

"Damned waste of our time," Jeremy said.

"Quite the contrary," Judith said. "Because of your help, I can now reveal to you who killed Geoffrey Lushington."

"Judith," Tanika said, interrupting her friend. "It's your house."

"What about it?" Judith asked.

"It's on fire," Tanika said.

"*What?*"

"I'm on the phone to DS Perry. He says there's been a shout for a house fire on the Berkshire side of the Thames. He says it's your house."

Before Tanika had even finished talking, Judith was pushing into the kitchenette and banging through the exit that led into Higginson Park. Her friends—and everyone on the planning committee—followed.

At the end of the park was the River Thames, and half a mile away, just beyond the church of Bisham abbey, the sky was billowing with black smoke, orange flames dancing above the tree line.

Judith's house was on fire.

Chapter 39

GEOFFREY LUSHINGTON'S KILLER KNEW THAT with Judith's house up in flames, no one would be looking at Sophia's house. They were dressed entirely in dark clothes—with black gloves and a black balaclava—and they scurried down the side of Sophia's garden in the direction of the boathouse.

In the distance there was the sound of fire engines, and Geoffrey's killer couldn't help but smile. It had been a glorious moment when the detective inspector had told Judith in front of everyone that her house was on fire. Then, after they'd all gone outside to confirm it was true—and then returned to the debating chamber—it had been even better to see how panicked Judith had been. The unflappable Judith Potts was finally in a flap. The detective inspector had said she'd drive Judith and her friends to her house as fast as she could. Of course she had. They had to see if there was anything they could salvage from Judith's house.

All in all, it was perfect timing. The killer was now free to break into Sophia's recording studio while the police, Judith, and her friends—and all the emergency services—would be at Judith's house trying to save what they could from the conflagration. Even now, the killer could see the dimmest glow of orange on the other side of Marlow where Judith's house was.

The killer raced up the outdoor staircase of the boathouse two steps at a time and pushed into the recording studio, before dashing over to the ladder that led up to the mezzanine floor above. They then scrambled up the ladder as fast as they could and found themselves in among Sophia's boxes of old documents.

The killer started opening the boxes hungrily.

There was a cough from a few feet away—which puzzled the killer. There was no one else nearby, was there?

Judith Potts stepped out from behind a pile of boxes.

"Travel sweet?" she said with a smile.

The killer staggered, knocking a box down onto the floor below, the papers sliding out of the box like guts from a body.

"No?" Judith asked as she held out a tin of travel sweets. She chose one and popped it into her mouth. "I suppose not. And I suppose you're not going to speak, either, are you? Of course not. You're still hoping you can get away with it. You're certainly more nimble than me and can get down the ladder faster than I can give chase, and your identity is well enough hidden behind your balaclava and gloves. In fact—and it's interesting this—you have no unique features as far as I can tell. You are, as we've been saying all along, entirely average in size and height. You could be anyone. Except you're not, of course. I know exactly who you are. So perhaps we can play a game? I think it's the least you deserve after all your efforts. Because I now know that it was you who got hold of aconite from the poison garden just yards away from where we're standing. It was also you who was wearing the blond wig and false beard in the kitchenette on the night that Geoffrey died. And it was you who made sure Geoffrey chose the doctored coffee capsule to make his coffee with—hanging prepositions notwithstanding," Judith added, very much for her own benefit.

She saw a flash of light in the killer's watchful eyes.

"Very well, let's do this. A game of Guess Who, as my friend Becks once explained. So, who killed Geoffrey Lushington and is standing in front of me right now? Well, logically, you can't be any of Debbie Bell, Marcus Percival, or Jeremy Wessel. They were all at the meeting at the same time as you were in the kitchen. But perhaps you're Sophia De Castro? After all, that's what the evidence suggests—that she dressed up as a blond-haired man, murdered Geoffrey from the kitchenette, did a quick change in the nearby toilets, and then arrived rather conveniently late for the meeting. But here's what

I realized—she's not the killer any more than the others are. The evidence against her is only so strong because you planted it to frame her."

The killer shifted their weight.

"That's right, I've ruled out all the people who were at the meeting. As it happens, we eventually discovered they all had secrets—some of them really rather terrible secrets—but none of them had anything to do with Geoffrey's murder. So who does that leave? Well, we can discount Dave Butler, he's never been thin enough to be our blond-haired killer—as you're ably demonstrating as you stand in front of me. Which leaves only three people. Just following the logic, you understand. Although we have to discount Alec Miller, because if Dave Butler is too large, Alec is too tall—again, as is patently obvious as I look at you with my own eyes. Which leaves only two people. Ian Maloney, and Paul De Castro.

"So let's deal with Ian first. Because, I'll be honest, this has never felt like the sort of murder Ian Maloney would carry out. He's already steeped in blood, figuratively of course, but I'm sure we can all agree that if he were to commit murder, he'd do something far more direct. A bungled break-in ending in a bludgeoning, for example. What's more, while I don't believe that poison is exclusively a woman's weapon, it very much isn't Ian's. Added to which, he has an alibi for the time of the murder. He was at a jazz concert. So, despite being the only natural blond, and the perfect height, he couldn't have been our mystery server in the kitchen.

"Which puts you and me at quite an interesting juncture, because I seem to have ruled out absolutely everyone who might have killed Geoffrey—except for one person. One person who knew that Sophia had a poison garden, and would have known where to find the necessary aconite. One person who already treats Sophia with contempt, one person who suspects that she's having an affair, and one person who very definitely has anger management issues. Her husband, Paul."

Geoffrey's killer didn't move.

"But I can't help wondering, why would Paul want to kill Geoffrey as a way of punishing his wife? While I may know about her obsession with Geoffrey, I don't think he did. In fact, when we spoke to Paul, it was obvious that while he suspected his wife of infidelity, he didn't know who the man was. He was happy to believe it was someone called Alec Miller. So Paul might have had the opportunity to kill—his alibi at the cinema is hardly watertight—and he might have been the right shape and size, but what was his motive to kill Geoffrey? He didn't really have one, which once again seems to put us at something of an impasse, doesn't it? Because I keep ruling everyone out. And yet, here you are. So who are you?"

Judith offered her tin of travel sweets again.

"Are you sure you don't want a sweet? I can recommend the strawberry. They're not as calorific as they look—which is important to you, isn't it? Because this is what I finally realized—and it really took me far too long to realize the truth of the matter—that the person who killed Geoffrey Lushington—the person who's standing in front of me right now is Dave Butler."

The killer staggered back half a step.

"That's right, Dave, I know it's you. You might as well take your balaclava off. Come on, reveal your true self. After all, it's such a stunning achievement, you deserve your moment in the sun."

There was a long pause, and then the man raised his black-gloved hand and peeled off his balaclava.

Seeing Dave Butler's face emerge, Judith felt the briefest twinge of sympathy, but she crushed it. Dave was a killer, and he deserved to get his just deserts. Nonetheless, she looked him up and down, admiring his trim figure.

"Gosh, I imagine it took the whole year you locked yourself away to lose all that weight. What perseverance you must have shown. But once you'd slimmed down to your target weight, you knew you could carry out your brilliant misdirection. You'd commit murder as an average-sized man, and then make sure that whenever you interacted with other people after that moment, you'd bulk up your clothes to make it look as though you were still as overweight as you'd always been. Because, while we'd always said a fat person couldn't masquerade as someone who's thin, it *is* possible, with the right padding, for a thin person to pass themselves off as someone who's fat.

"Especially when that person has been so famously large for so many years. Your doctor told the police you were obese when you first returned to the UK and had in fact put on even more weight since then—and Sophia confirmed that fact. As did your neighbors. But then, society dismisses fat people, don't they? Is this person bright, or cunning, or kind? No, society says they're fat. That's the beginning and end of it. It's how they're seen, it's their defining trait, and all they can ever be.

"And my friends and I fell into your trap. When we met you, all we saw was your apparent weight. Although I remember that first time, thinking how your face looked far more youthful than the rest of your body. *Youthful!* I should have realized that what I was seeing was a face that wasn't as plump as the rest of your body appeared to be. As a matter of interest, how did you bulk yourself up? Wearing your old clothes would of course have given you a shape to work to. Towels around the waist and thighs, multiple layers of clothing worn on top of each other? You could have done it any number of ways. Not that it matters, of course.

"The sad truth is that we all saw what we'd been told to see—which seemed even more credible when we saw all the fatty food that was being delivered to your house. But of course your diet was fatty. You weren't ordering bad food because you couldn't stop yourself from being fat, it was because, having killed Geoffrey as an average-sized person, you were piling on the pounds as fast as you could to get back to your old size.

"You of course kept up the fiction that you were still fat and immobile the few times you had to leave your house—to go to phone boxes to make your anonymous phone calls to me. It was so clever, really, and so simple. When we saw the church's CCTV footage of an obese man on a mobility scooter, we took it for granted that we were seeing an obese man with significant mobility issues."

"What are you doing here!" Dave blurted, interrupting.

"I think that's self-evident. Explaining how you killed Geoffrey."

"But your house is burning down!"

"Ah. I see what you mean."

"Why didn't you go and try to save it?"

"Well," Judith said with an airy waft of her hand, "What are worldly possessions compared to justice? You killed Geoffrey, you had to be caught."

"I don't understand. How did you know I'd be here?"

"That's not the right question."

"What do you mean, it's not the right question?"

"The right question is, why have you come to the loft of Sophia's boathouse? By the way, it's a rhetorical question, I know the answer. You see, in all of this, you made one mistake. The first time we talked to you and we mentioned Debbie Bell, you said she was sinister. I remember asking you why you'd chosen the word 'sinister,' and you passed it off as a joke. But it's such an odd word, really. It's not jokey in any way at all. It's rather specific. But sinister also has another meaning, doesn't it? As any crossword solver knows. It's the Latin word for 'left.' In medieval times it was considered evil to be left-handed, so the word sinister became synonymous with evil. At the time, I lodged your use of the word 'sinister' as an oddity. Nothing more.

"When I noticed that Debbie wore her watch on her right wrist—suggesting she was perhaps left-handed—I had the first glimmerings of a connection, but it was still tenuous. Although, when I remembered your use of the word 'sinister,' I found myself wondering if you meant she was left-handed. But how could you possibly know that? When I showed your photo to Debbie, she said you and she had never met. And even if you had, why was it her left-handedness that had stuck in your mind? So I got to thinking about the case from the point of view of Debbie's left-handedness, and I soon remembered that she was the planning committee's secretary. She'd have taken her notes—and drunk her cup of coffee—left-handed. But, again, why had this fact stuck in your mind? You'd never attended a planning meeting, or the committee would have recognized your photo when we showed it to them.

"And then a somewhat surprising thought occurred to me. We've always known that someone had disabled the CCTV camera at the entrance to the council building. What if that same person had *installed* a camera in the debating chamber? A trivial task, I'd imagine, for someone with the right sort of IT skills. Someone who, in fact, ran an IT company—like you. A little camera hidden behind some books, or on a shelf somewhere. Plugged in and accessible from your computer. Just as the doorbell video camera at your house could be accessed by your computer. That would be one way you'd have known that Debbie was 'sinister.' If you'd been watching the planning meeting that night."

"None of this is true!" Dave said.

"Oh, it is, as Tanika and her team will be able to prove in due course. Because the camera's still installed in the debating chamber, isn't it? Of course it is. How could you have gained access to the room after the murder? I'm afraid it's why I staged that reenactment of the planning meeting just now. I guessed that when the police arrived with all the planning committee, the motion sensors in the camera would tell you something was up, and you'd start watching keenly on your monitor. Which is why I decided to set a trap."

"What trap?"

"The one you've so neatly fallen into, Dave. The one that meant you'd come here and reveal yourself to me. But how about I first tell you how you killed Geoffrey Lushington."

Chapter 40

"YOUR PLAN WAS METICULOUSLY PREPARED," Judith said. "As I say, over the past year, you stayed indoors while you lost as much weight as possible. You then purchased a blond wig and goatee beard—from the internet, I'm sure. I imagine someone with your IT skills could create an account the police won't be able to trace.

"You then had to get hold of the poison, but that wouldn't have been hard. Sophia often mentions her poison garden on her wellness podcast. So you risked going out—in the dead of night, perhaps—although how risky was it? Even if you were seen, no one would recognize your new, thinner, body. And you dug up a couple of aconite plants. But that wasn't all you took because, as we saw when Sophia showed us her poison garden, she uses hair from her hairbrush around some of her plants to keep slugs at bay, so you helped yourself to some of her hair as well. And we also saw she used carrier bags tied over some of her plants to keep them protected from the frost. It would have been the work of a moment for you to steal one of those as well. So now you had your murder weapon, and a few handy props as well.

"So, what next? Well, let's stay with the samples of hair and carrier bag. You wanted the police to ultimately believe that Sophia was the killer. And for that, you needed to sell a story. So you scoped around the council building for where you'd be able to suggest Sophia apparently got changed out of her costume, and alighted on the toilet block outside the debating chamber. Better still, you saw that the little cleaning cupboard had a roof void above it. It would be perfect for your plans.

"And now we come to the day of the murder. That morning, you went to the town council building. Were you already in your blond-haired disguise at this point?"

Dave didn't respond.

"I imagine you were—that's what I'd have done. Anyway, the first thing you did was cut through the cable of the security camera so there'd be no recording of the two things you did next. First, you slipped into the debating chamber and found a spot where you could install a secret camera. It would have been easy. The room is unoccupied when it's not being used, and there are plenty of shelves, files, and old equipment behind which you could hide a tiny camera. Again, this would have been child's play for someone who works in IT.

"You then came out and did something that was really very clever indeed. After all, Alec Miller, the normal server for that evening's planning meeting, had to be told not to come in. But how to stop him without implicating yourself? Better still, how could you do it in a way that implicated Sophia? It stumped me how you did it for a while, as it was very definitely Sophia who rang Alec Miller. He recognized her voice from one of her podcasts. And that was when I got the answer! I think you downloaded her podcasts and then used your computer skills to edit together a few words and phrases to create a brand-new and fake conversation where she said that there was no need for him to come in that evening. Didn't you?

"When we asked him about it, Alec said that Sophia had been abrupt when she spoke to him and had then hung up. Of course she'd been abrupt. You only had limited phrases you could get her to say. But you went into the council building that morning, phoned Alec, played the voice of Sophia down the phone telling him not to come in, and then hung up. Mission accomplished.

"And now we come to the grace note: Sophia's flat tire. Because I think you realized you weren't running much of a risk when you got into your disguise and started laying out the coffees for the planning committee that evening. As I say, most of the planning committee had never met you. If they noticed that Alec wasn't serving, you'd be able to explain he had the night off, or maybe sidestep the question altogether. Either way, you'd be able to make sure Geoffrey chose the poisoned coffee capsule and then slip out whether or not they interacted with you. As it happened, none of the committee even noticed you were there—which tells you something about how they treated serving staff, but there you are.

"But if nearly all of the planning committee had never met you before, that wasn't true of Sophia, was it? You'd helped install her podcast studio in this boathouse. Seeing as you were about to frame her for the murder, you didn't dare risk her recognizing you. So you let down one of the tires of her car. You hoped it would delay her long enough for you to carry out your plan and get away from the building before she'd even arrived. This was the one part of your scheme that didn't quite go to plan, as Sophia drove to Platts with her flat tire and got it sorted out far quicker than you'd expected. However, it wasn't all bad luck, was it? Because Sophia was so nervous about seeing Geoffrey again—a fact you couldn't have known—that she had no interest in arriving at the meeting early anyway. So, as you'd hoped, you'd managed to spike Geoffrey's coffee capsule and leave via the fire doors before the one person who might have recognized you arrived.

"Because this was the genius of your plan. From the disguise to the planting of fake evidence, and from the secret camera in the debating chamber to the splicing together of Sophia's podcast into a new speech—even the letting down of Sophia's tire—you hadn't really committed any kind of crime the police would be all that interested in. If any one element failed, you could pull back from killing Geoffrey, regroup, and come up with another plan later on. But everything went perfectly, didn't it? Sophia didn't arrive early enough to recognize you, you'd laid all the breadcrumbs the police would need to later lead to her—and once your existence was discovered by us, you even did something rather daring. You invited us back into your house to tell us that Sophia had a furious temper on her. All lies, I think, but you wanted to make sure the police spotlight would start to fall properly on Sophia. How am I doing?"

Dave scowled by way of answer.

"So that's the 'who' and the 'how' of it. Although you still had one last task to do after the murder. Maybe later that night, or possibly at some point over the coming days, you took the disguise you'd worn and made sure there were none of your hairs or other identifying evidence in it. You then placed a few strands of Sophia's hair that you'd taken from her poison garden in the wig and stuffed it all into one of her carrier bags from her garden along with some crepe bandaging to make it look as though she'd used that to help hide her figure. You then slipped it into the attic space of the toilet block—a feat, I hasten to add, you wouldn't have been able to achieve a year ago, when you still carried all that extra weight. But the new you was able to do it with no problem.

"And now we come to the 'why' of it. You see, yours is a tragic story—not that it excuses what you did. But, just as understanding your current weight was the key to unlocking how you did it, it's also the clue to understanding why you killed Geoffrey.

"Your problems all go back to the death of your mother, don't they? There you were, happily going through your early teens, and then your mother gets ill and dies. A harrowing thing for any child to go through. But then your father finds another woman, marries her almost immediately, and rips you away from Marlow, making you start your life over in America. My heart goes out to you, that must have been terrifying. A new stepmum, a new culture, and I think, if I were playing the pop psychologist, that you anesthetized some of that pain with food. I imagine you also fled into books—I know I did at about the same age. Although, I was more a Flambards and Malory Towers sort of girl, rather than science fiction.

"Either way, it's obvious that you didn't enjoy your teenage years. The moment you turned eighteen, you walked out on your father, on America, and came back to Marlow, perhaps thinking that that would fix your life. But the sad truth is, you can't leave pain behind. It travels with you." Judith smiled sadly and took a moment to regather herself. "But you had dreams when you got here. You were going to write a science fiction novel and become famous. You even had a local publisher you could approach. The only problem was, Geoffrey didn't like your book. He rejected you. And while I'm sure he didn't poison the well for you with other publishers like you told us, I think that if a publisher like Geoffrey turned you down, then it wouldn't be surprising if all the other publishers did the same.

"Rejection hit hard. It hits everyone hard. And I think that's perhaps when whatever reclusive tendencies you had started to come to the fore. Believe me, I know how it can happen. You lose the habit of sociability, you even lose confidence. Life becomes far easier when you can control it, and not going out made sure you were always in control. You weren't any happier in Marlow, your book wasn't getting any interest, and you were having to run an IT company that you didn't enjoy. I think at some deep level, you know that all of your woes stem from the death of your mother, and the fact that you didn't have any chance at closure with her—which I'll get to in a bit.

"But your anger and disappointment started to coalesce around Geoffrey and the way he'd rejected you. That's why you wrote those letters to the council. They weren't offensive like Marcus Percival's tweets, or anonymous like Jeremy's blackmail—and they weren't illegal like Debbie's theft—but they were still critical. Although, your actions had an unintended consequence. It kept your name alive for Geoffrey, and one day he decided to dust down the manuscript you'd sent him all those years ago. And the funny thing is, nowadays, with Britain both hotter and wetter, this time when he read it, he found that it resonated differently."

"He thought it was a masterpiece," Dave said.

"Which is why it's so very sad what you did. But the truth is, while you'd lost hope on the novel years ago, you'd not lost hope on finding the person who was to blame for the loss of your mother."

"What do you mean by 'loss'?"

"You know exactly what I mean. Which is why Geoffrey had to die. But not just that—Geoffrey had to die, and Sophia had to take the blame. They both had to be punished."

Judith waited for Dave to speak, but he kept a watchful silence.

"Very well. This is the reason why you committed murder. Your mother died while Sophia was in charge of the local graveyards, didn't she? I remember Becks's husband, Colin, telling us that while most of the problems of identifying the correct graves were resolved, there was one person whose final resting place was never found. That was your mother, wasn't it?"

Dave didn't dare move.

"I can't imagine the horror of not knowing where the most important person in your life, your own mother, is buried. Lacking the ability to visit her, to feel grounded by her presence—it would have curdled the mind of anyone, let alone a mind that was already as sour as yours. Not that you knew who to blame—not precisely. At that stage, all you knew was that Geoffrey Lushington had been chair of the subcommittee that had messed up the locations of the graves. But you said something very interesting the first time we met you. You said that when you and Geoffrey met, as a way of proving he was on your side, he admitted that all of the things you'd complained to the council about were true—but you also let slip to us that he admitted to you 'more besides.' At the time I could see that you'd felt that you'd overshared and presumed that you were just being introverted, but you clammed up because you'd actually made a potentially dangerous confession. The 'more besides' was Geoffrey telling you the story of how Sophia had messed up the graves, wasn't it? And what poor Geoffrey didn't realize in that moment was that he was signing his death warrant.

"Because now you had a focus for all of your pain. It was Sophia who was to blame for mixing up the plots in the graveyard and not keeping proper records. Although it wasn't only her fault, was it? As Geoffrey was the first to admit, he was the one who'd put Sophia in charge. They were both culpable, but it was Sophia you blamed the most. Was this before or after you'd installed her podcast studio for her? I don't suppose you're going to say, but was it really her idea to hire you or did you in fact go touting for business from her? It never felt entirely believable that someone the size that you were at the time would agree to do a job down a hill and up a flight of steep stairs. But when you were on your own in this studio, you were able to poke around in the paperwork up here," Judith said, indicating the boxes and files that filled the mezzanine. "Not that it did you much good. Whatever it was you found, it wasn't what you were looking for—the definitive proof of where your mother was buried that would release you from your torment.

"I think that's when you had your idea that death would be too good for Sophia. Just as you felt as though you were living a life sentence of pain, you wanted to give her a living sentence of pain.

"And here, finally, I need to apologize to you. When I'd worked out how you'd committed murder—and why—I knew I needed to trick you into revealing yourself. But how, that was the question. Although there was one thing I had over you. I'd guessed that you must have installed a secret camera in the debating chamber, so I tried to see if I could use it against you. That's why I gathered the planning committee there this afternoon, because I knew you'd start watching. All I had to do was have a word with Sophia beforehand and prime her to say that she'd finally found the documents that showed where everyone had really been buried, and that those documents were in her boathouse. It was a lure—a trap—I'm afraid. I knew it would make you desperate to break in at the first opportunity. So all I then had to do was give you the first opportunity—which is why I started the fire at my house."

"It was *you* who started the fire?"

"As I said, I had a murderer to catch. And I knew that the juxtaposition of you discovering that this loft held the location of your mother's grave at the very same time as my house going up in flames would be a temptation too far for you. You'd believe that the police, my friends, and I would immediately be desperately focused on trying to save my house, giving you the briefest window to slip in here and discover your mother's final resting place."

"It's all a lie?" Dave asked.

"I'm afraid it is."

"The document doesn't exist?"

"It doesn't. It may of course be possible in time to work out where your mother is buried, but the answer you're looking for isn't in this loft."

As Judith spoke, Tanika entered the podcast studio on the level below, flanked by two uniformed police officers. As the first police officer started to climb the ladder to the mezzanine, Dave crumbled, tears rolling down his cheeks.

"I'm sorry for my lies, Dave, but you're to blame for all of this. Because Geoffrey Lushington was a good man who'd done no harm in his life. You deserve to be locked up for a very, very long time."

The police officer stepped up to Dave and handcuffed him.

He didn't put up any resistance.

Chapter 41

AS SOON AS DAVE WAS in a police car being driven to Maidenhead Police Station, Tanika drove Judith at speed to her house. They could both see the clouds above the house reflecting orange-black smoke still thumping into the sky. When they arrived, they realized they were witnessing a scene from a hellish nightmare. There were fire engines parked up, hoses snaking out across the driveway; fire officers, their faces blackened with soot, still working hard to get the flames under control.

Suzie and Becks were watching on from a safe distance by Suzie's van. When they saw Judith arrive, they rushed over.

"Did you get him?" Suzie called out.

"Sure did," Tanika said. "Everything came to pass, just like Judith said it would."

"And he made a confession?" Becks asked.

"Not yet," Tanika said. "But he will in time, he'll have no choice but to confess."

"I still can't believe it. Had he really lost all that weight?"

"He had," Judith said. "But how have things been here?"

"Scary," Becks said. "The fire brigade are pretty angry. They say the woods could have caught fire."

"Nonsense!" Judith said. "Not after the wet winter we've had."

A fire officer wearing a white helmet approached Tanika.

"Are you SIO?" he asked.

"I am," Tanika said.

"It looks like the fire was started deliberately."

"It was," Judith said.

"You know that, do you?"

"Oh, yes. It was me who started it."

"You confess?"

"This is my property, I can do what I want here. Even starting fires. Although I should add, sorry it got out of hand."

The fire officer didn't know what to say to that.

"Don't worry, I'll explain later," Tanika said.

"Could we first get a bit closer to see?" Suzie asked.

"If you want to," the fire officer said, now thinking the world had gone mad. "Head around the side of the garden, you'll get a better view from there."

"Thank you," Judith said, and started to cross the long grass to the side of her drive. As they reached the corner of the garden, they looked toward the river and could see the fire raging. It was magnificent, Judith thought to herself. But she also knew that she'd set fire to a part of her life that would now be gone forever. Becks saw her friend's sadness and took hold of her hand. She gave it a reassuring squeeze. Judith was so very grateful to be with her two best friends as she watched the flames stab angrily into the sky.

"Was the house ever at risk?" Suzie asked, looking back at Judith's house as it stood undamaged fifty or so feet away.

Judith hadn't set fire to her house—of course she hadn't. She adored her house. The bonfire that she, Becks, and Suzie had spent the whole afternoon constructing at the bottom of her garden was made up of every single newspaper and old magazine from the secret archive that Judith had collected over the previous forty years.

"Not with the wind in this direction," Judith said. "Although I'm glad to see the boathouse has survived. I was worried some of the burnt paper would fall on its roof and set it on fire."

It had been backbreaking work, it had required many dozens of trips back and forth to fill wheelbarrowfuls with dry-as-dust newspapers, but Judith had been adamant. For her plan to work, it needed to look from Marlow—and from Dave's house—as though her house had gone up in flames. The bonfire of paper they were building had to be as big as possible. That way, when Dave was watching his secret camera showing the debating chamber and saw Tanika receive a call telling her about the fire at Judith's house, he'd be able to go to his front door and see that the news was indeed true.

"I'll tell you what I don't get," Suzie said. "If he was the killer, why did he make those anonymous phone calls to you?"

"I think I can explain it," Judith said. "I imagine he thought those letters he'd been writing to the council would make him a person of interest in the eyes of the police. Him ringing me was his insurance policy. If the police—or we—ever accused him of being behind this murder, he'd be able to point out how he'd tried to help catch Geoffrey's killer by tipping us off."

"Which is exactly what happened," Becks said.

"It explains why his calls were anonymous. He didn't ever want to appear on our radar, but he knew that, if he did, it would be really helpful if he could reveal that he'd been trying to help us from the start."

"Which—again—is what happened," Becks said. "Although, I still can't believe he was the killer. All Geoffrey did was help Sophia cover up her mistake. To think he'd be killed as a pawn in Dave's scheme to make Sophia suffer? It's pure evil."

"I thought the only purely evil person you knew was your mother-in-law," Suzie said with a twinkle.

"Please—the evening was going so well."

"Actually," Judith said. "I've got a plan to get Marian out of your house. It won't happen overnight, but I think there's a fuse we can set a flame to—if you pardon the pun," she added, nodding at the raging fire at the bottom of her garden.

"When did you have time to do that?" Suzie asked.

"Well, sometimes the stars just align," Judith said. "And sometimes you have to make sure the stars align," she added with a nod to the bonfire.

Her friends smiled. They knew only one person who could wrestle stars into alignment, and her name was Judith Potts.

The next morning, a gleaming two-seater Jag with its top down drove up to Coopers coffee bar, and a handsome man in his late seventies got out. He was tall, had a thick hatch of gray hair, and his brown brogues, cords, and sports jacket gave him the air of a movie star from the 1950s.

He entered Coopers and smiled to himself. Judith had chosen the location for their meeting well. The café was bustling with chat and wasn't even remotely formal. A lot like how he remembered Judith. He straightened the white carnation in his buttonhole.

"Can I help you, sir?" a young waiter asked.

"Just looking for a friend," the man said. "An old friend."

The man moved among the tables, but he became increasingly puzzled as he realized he couldn't see Judith. Had she stood him up?

And then he saw her.

Or rather, he spotted an older woman sitting on her own with a white carnation on the table in front of her. She didn't look at all like his memory of Judith, but he knew people's appearance could change over the years. And, as he approached, he saw that her posture was suitably haughty. The man smiled to himself; he'd always found Judith's haughtiness attractive.

"Hello, Judith," he said as he arrived at the table.

The woman looked up at him, confused—but then she wasn't half as confused as the man. In fact, he was realizing that he'd made a terrible mistake. There was no way the woman in front of him was Judith Potts. Even as a teenager, she'd never had such fine cheekbones, and this woman's eyes shone cobalt blue with a sparkling intensity. Judith's eyes weren't blue.

"Oh," he said, losing confidence. "You're not Judith."

"Why would you think I'm called Judith?"

"It's the white carnation," he said, indicating the flower on the table.

"This?" the woman said, now doubly confused. "This belongs to my daughter-in-law. She was here until a few moments ago. She said she had to go to the loo."

"How strange," the man said, looking about himself again. This really was the only table where there was a person with a white carnation on their table. "Sorry, I should have said. My name's Matthew Cartwright. If it's ten o'clock, then I'm supposed to be meeting an old friend here," he said as he checked the time on his wristwatch.

The woman saw that Matthew's wristwatch was a gold Rolex, and then she noticed how elegantly he was dressed, and how handsome he was.

"My name's Marian," she said with her very best smile. "How about you sit down and we can try and work out what's happened together. I really don't know where my daughter-in-law's got to," she added, although Matthew didn't realize, as Marian scanned the café, that she was very much hoping Becks wouldn't return to her table just yet.

As it happened, while Marian and Matthew started chatting, and Matthew was discovering that Marian found everything he said really very interesting indeed, Becks was lurking outside the café with her face pressed up to the glass of the door, along with her two friends.

"She's going for it," Becks said as she peered through the glass.

"She's calling the waiter over," Suzie said.

"I've never seen her so charming. Oh, God, I can't watch this, she's laughing with the waiter now."

Becks took a step away from the door and rubbed her hands together for warmth. It was a lovely sunny day, but there was still a chill in the air.

Suzie and Judith joined their friend, and the three women found themselves looking at Matthew's classic two-seater Jaguar car.

"Are you sure you've done the right thing?" Suzie asked Judith. "Keeping him out of your life like this?"

Judith found herself smiling.

"Quite sure," she said. "Now how about we go back to my house for a nice cup of tea and some biscuits?"

"That sounds lovely," Becks said.

"Although we'll need to pick up some biscuits on the way," Suzie said. "We finished the last pack the other day."

"I wouldn't worry," Judith said comfortably. "I'm sure Becks has some hidden somewhere in my house."

"A box of Fox's Chocolate Originals under your wingback," Becks said.

"Well, there you are," Judith said.

As the women walked back into Marlow, Judith found herself almost overwhelmed by a warm glow of contentment. She knew there were so few moments in life when it was possible to say you were happy, but that was how she felt at this precise moment: truly happy.

"I need to thank you both," she said. "Suzie in particular. I feel so much better today. Lighter."

"You mean, since the fire?" Becks said.

"Since the fire," Judith agreed. "I really should have got rid of all of that baggage years ago."

"We did try telling you," Becks said.

"Yes, well sometimes I get a bit set in my ways."

Suzie and Becks looked at each other and smiled. They knew that Judith, on a point of principle, was *always* set in her ways. But then, they also knew that Suzie would always be looking for a side hustle in life, just as Becks would always feel the need to apologize for everything she did. None of the three friends were ever likely to change, and that's just how they liked it. They wouldn't have it any other way.

Reading Group Guide

1. Most of the book is told from the perspectives of Becks, Suzie, and Judith. What do the differences in their thought processes add to the story?

2. Becks, Suzie, and Judith are seen as outsiders in the police investigation, despite being given permission to help. What are the difficulties in trying to join a tight-knit group? What are the advantages to *being* in such a group?

3. Judith's "archive" is brought up early in the novel, along with the idea that getting rid of it would be like getting "rid of a limb." What causes Judith to hoard all of her papers? Why are they so difficult for her to part with, despite her inability to explain what they mean to her?

4. Characterize Becks, Suzie, and Judith's relationship with one another. How can you tell they are good friends and that they've known one another for a long time?

5. What are the advantages and disadvantages of working a job with your friends?

6. Becks is having trouble with her son and ultimately lands on the side of giving him space rather than forcing him to study. Is it better to give kids space when they're acting out or to be firm?

7. Geoffrey is known by everyone to be an upright, moral, and good man. Do you have someone like that in your life?

8. All of the committee members have secrets, some worse than others. How big of a difference is there in how we present ourselves to others versus how we are when no one's watching?

9. Suzie runs a radio show in Marlow. Do you still listen to the radio? What do you listen to? Do you prefer radio or podcasts?

10. Did you figure out the murderer before the reveal? Why or why not?

11. The murderer is angry about the unfortunate circumstances with his mother's grave. How would you feel if you were in his situation?

12. Despite the proclamation at the end that "none of the three friends were ever likely to change," do you believe Becks, Suzie, and Judith evolved throughout the book? In what ways?

Acknowledgments

I'm writing this in July 2023, when—wonderfully, amazingly—the TV show of the first Marlow Murder Club book is filming just down the road. (It's being broadcast in the USA by PBS/Masterpiece, so do look out for it once it's aired.) As my family and I have lived in Marlow for the last ten years, this is a good chance to thank all of the people we've met along the way who've always gone out of their way to welcome us to their town so warmly. In particular, our Postie, Fred. He's a legend around these parts, and his kindness to all those he meets exemplifies why Marlow is one of the best places in the UK to live.

I have to confess, I was a bit worried about how everyone would take to a TV crew clogging up the streets and generally getting in the way, but my concerns were misplaced. The town couldn't have been more supportive of the whole endeavor, and I really hope we can deliver a TV show that makes Marlow look as wonderful on the screen as it is in reality. (I should also take this chance to apologize for suggesting that there are so many murderers in my hometown. Anyone who knows Marlow well will know there aren't actually black-hearted killers behind every door. Well, not *every* door.)

So thank you, Marlow, and thank you to Susanne Simpson at Masterpiece and all of the team at Monumental TV who've helped me turn the book into a TV series. It's been a dream working with Deb Hayward, Alison Carpenter, Lucy Rawlinson, Katharine Rosser, Tamara Campos, Jane Wallbank, Steve

Barron, and all of the amazing cast and crew. I can't wait for audiences to see how wonderfully all of these amazing people have brought Judith, Suzie, and Becks to life.

I'd also like to thank my American publishers for taking a punt on Judith and her friends all of those years ago. Jessica Thelander, Mandy Chahal, Emily Engwall, and Anna Michels have been brilliant at helping the Marlow novels find an audience, and I was thrilled when their efforts resulted in the first book in the series being nominated for an Edgar Award. It couldn't have happened without them, and I'm eternally grateful.

These books also couldn't have happened without my terrific American literary agent, Ginger Clark. At our first meeting in person following the pandemic, she was sitting at a table in a New York steak restaurant sipping a martini at midday, and you don't really get much cooler than that. But I'm so very grateful for her sound judgment and quick wit (and even quicker responses to emails), and I'm very lucky to have her in my corner.

Finally, as ever, my biggest thanks go to my wonderful wife, Katie, and our two children, Charlie and James—and also to my mother, Penny, to whom this book is dedicated with love.

About the Author

Robert Thorogood is the creator of the hit BBC One TV series *Death in Paradise*, and he has written a series of spin-off novels featuring DI Richard Poole.

He was born in Colchester, Essex. When he was ten years old, he read his first proper novel—Agatha Christie's *Peril at End House*—and he's been in love with the genre ever since.

He now lives in Marlow in Buckinghamshire with his wife, children, and two whippets called Wally and Evie.

Follow him on Twitter @robthor.